Corpocracy

Cheryl King

This book is dedicated to my husband, Harland. Thank you for believing and giving me the strength and the courage.

A special thanks to Jennifer: your instant focus, your sharp eye and thoughtful criticism made all the difference.

corpocracy

<u>noun</u> cor·poc·ra·cy \ ˈkȯr-pä-krə-sē \

1 a : government by corporations; especially : rule of the stakeholder majority
b : a government in which the supreme power is vested in corporations and exercised by them directly or indirectly through a system of representation usually involving periodically held free elections typically influenced and controlled by corporate lobbyists
2 : a political unit that has a corpocratic government
3 : capitalized: the principles and policies of the Corpocratic party in the U.S
4 : the corporate body especially when constituting the source of political authority

corpocratic

<u>adjective</u> corp·o·crat·ic \ kȯr--pä-ˈkra-tik \

1 : of, relating to, or favoring corpocracy (see <u>corpocracy</u>)
2 : often capitalized : of or relating to the major corporate political party in the U.S. evolving in the early 21st century from the control corporate lobbyists wielded in government and associated in modern times with policies of major social restructuring and globalism
3 : relating to, appealing to, or available to the broad influence of the corporation as a citizen
4 : favoring social control : serve the many

corpocratically \-ti-k(ə-)lē\ <u>adverb</u>

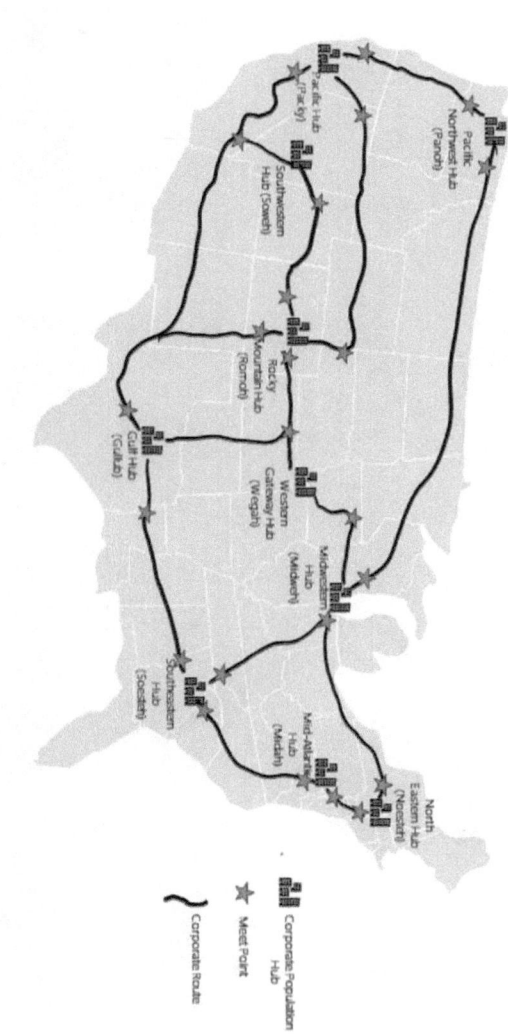

United States of America, Incorporated

Pacific Hub
(Pacify)

Northwest Hub
(Panoff)

Pacific
(Panoff)

Southwestern
Hub (Soweb)

Rocky
Mountain Hub
(Romah)

Gulf Hub
(Gulub)

Western
Gateway Hub
(Wegah)

Midwestern
Hub
(Midwey)

Southeastern
Hub
(Soeshy)

Mid-Atlantic
Hub
(Midahy)

North
Eastern Hub
(Noreast)

Corporate Population
Hub

Meet Point

Corporate Route

.

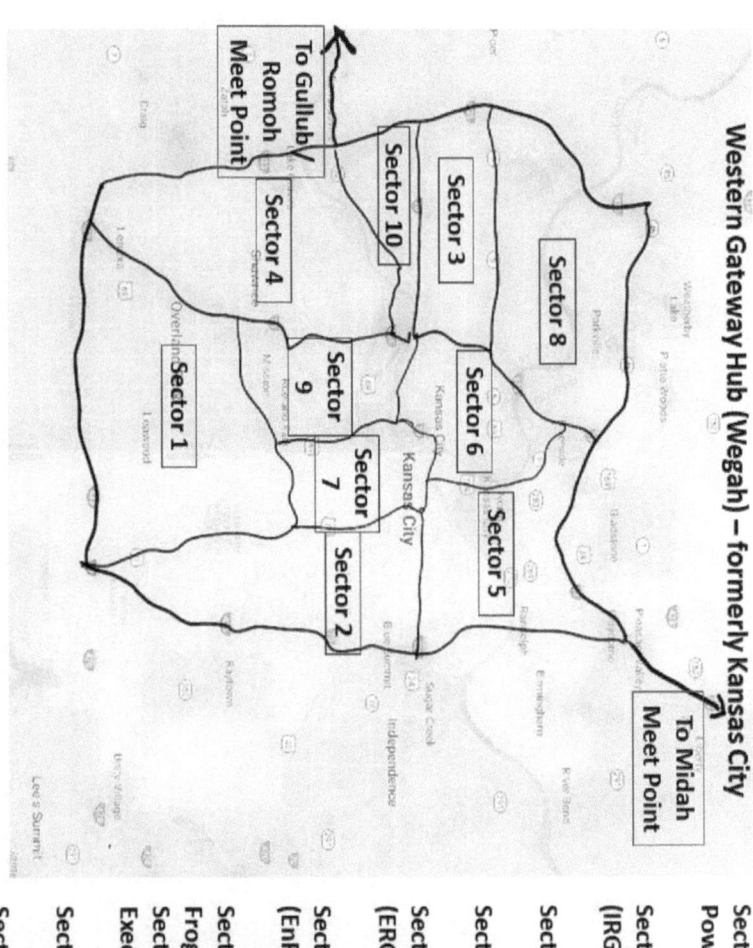

Western Gateway Hub (Wegah) – formerly Kansas City

Sector 1 – Public Works Group (PWRG / Power)

Sector 2 – Infrastructure Resource Group (IRG)

Sector 3 – Media Resource Group (MRG)

Sector 4 – Human Resource Group (HRG)

Sector 5 – Education Resource Group (ERG)

Sector 6 – Environmental Resource Group (EnRG / Energy)

Sector 7 – Facilities Resource Group (FRG / Frogs)

Sector 8 – Financial Operations Group – Executive Branch (FinOps)

Sector 9 – Supply Chain Group (SCG)

Sector 10 – Security Resource Group (SRG)

CHERYL KING

Saint Peter don't you call me 'cause I can't go
I owe my soul to the company store...

          —Tennessee Ernie Ford

PROLOGUE

Jordie Miller's hand was shaking as he reached for the knob to open the tank of propane. *How had it come to this?* He shook his head bitterly and carefully twisted the metal collar just a little towards the open arrow…not a lot, not enough to be obvious. Then he levered the tank into the small space reserved for a spare under the cabinet in the small travel trailer leaving the cabinet door just slightly ajar. Nothing to do now but wait.

It all seemed so implausible…that it should come to this. Why, the last five years he'd been flying high and seemed to have the Midas touch…

"Jordie!" Megan squealed as Jordie grabbed her and pulled her into a tight hug.

He grinned and squeezed her even tighter, lowering his mouth to plant a sweet and tender kiss at the base of her neck--right where he knew it tickled her and drove her crazy. She squealed and struggled to pull away. "Stop, Jordie!" Fighting the giggles. "What's up with you?"

He pulled back and smoothed a tendril of hair back from her temple. "Well, Mrs. Jordan Miller, you are now talking to the newest Regional Manager for the Southwest Region."

"Oh, Jordie! You got the promotion? Oh, good for you! Tell me all about it." She grabbed his hand and pulled him down to sit next to her on the sofa.

"I was on the phone with that engineer in network ops and he was, as usual, giving me a hard time. He's not going to make the date…again! Well, maybe he'll listen to me now and stop slipping these dates. Anyway, I was on with him getting an update when I got a ping from Roger. He wanted to know if I could step into his office for a minute. Well, you don't put off your Director, so I told Charlie I had to go but I expected him to improve on those dates he'd just given me, and I hung up. I pinged Roger back and said I was on my way."

Jordie had just taken a breath to tell Megan about the all-important meeting with Roger when the front door came banging open and their twelve-year-old son came charging in with his friend Mike right on his heels. Seeing Jordie and Megan on the couch, Adam pulled up and Mike ran right into him, resulting in a short but fierce shoving match. "Watch out, dude!" "Man, don't stop like that!" Words spilling over each other.

Finally, facing his parents, Adam gushed, "Mom! Dad! Hiya! Hey, would you mind if I stayed over with Mike tonight? We've got a pick-up game pulled together and everyone's gonna meet out at the Drummond farm at seven. Mike's mom offered to grill up some dogs and take a load of us out. It'll be kinda late prob'ly before we finish so I figured…" All of this except for the

1

last sentence came pouring out at near light speed with Mike nodding vigorously alongside. The word "figured", however, came out like it had twice as many syllables and just sort of faded into a sudden silence.

Jordie cleared his throat and glanced at Megan while Megan dove right in, "And so you just figured…what exactly?" Her eyes pinning Adam like one of his science class insect specimens in a laser focus.

"Um, you know, it being late and all…easier if I just hang out for the night over there." And quickly, before either Jordie or Megan could respond, "If it's okay with you, guys, you know." Mike again nodding his reinforcement.

Jordie took a deep breath and sighed, "It's okay with me if it's okay with your mom."

Megan shot him that look that said *Gee, thanks*. Then back to Adam. "I guess so. You still haven't mowed the lawn and I want that room picked up. I was in there getting your dirty clothes today and it's in terrible shape."

Jordie decided he better back Megan or at least make the appearance. "You be sure you're home early tomorrow morning. Use the bag to pick up the trimmings. I know your mother wouldn't appreciate dragging grass clippings all through the house. Wash your feet off when you're done, too. Your grandparents will be here this weekend and I want this place looking nice. Who'd you get the pick-up game with?"

Mike jumped in, excitedly, giving a quick nod to Megan first. "Hiya, Mrs. Miller." Turning back to Jordie he gushed, "Asher Brown's cousin knows a bunch of boys from Allen and they got to talking and saying how they can beat anyone and the Drummond farm is about halfway to Allen and Paul Drummond's dad just got done roughing out a playing field for them in his south field that he's not using so we all agreed to meet and see who's best!"

Megan just sat and shook her head as this river of words came tumbling out. "I've got to check something in the kitchen. I'll be right back. Want a beer?" she asked Jordie, standing up and smoothing out her tan capris.

"Yeah, sounds good. I need to finish what we were talking about anyway. Hurry back."

"Hey, Mike," Adam called as he headed down the stairs to his room, "C'mon, I want to grab a few things. You think Donnie's gonna have that new bat tonight? Man, it hits a killer ball." Voices and the stamping feet of teenage boys faded down the stairs as Megan pulled two beers from the fridge, popping the caps and flipping them in the garbage. She gave the spaghetti sauce simmering on the burner a quick stir and headed back to the living room where Jordie was leaning back in the corner of the couch. He patted the cushion next to him, reached for his beer, and said, "Where was I?"

"Okay," she said, as she snuggled back next to him. "You were about to meet with Roger."

Vicky smiled broadly at Jordie as he approached her desk. "I've been expecting you, Jordie. How've you been?"

"Just wonderful, Vicky. And you?"

"Keeping busy but that's a good thing, isn't it?" She smiled and nodded towards Roger's door, "He's expecting you. Go on in."

As he reached for the handle, Jordie glanced back at Vicky and was that a wink she just shot him? He quickly wiped his hands on his slacks, suddenly nervous they'd be damp, and just thinking about it made him suddenly feel like he was going to break into a sweat. *Get a grip. Don't let him see your nerves!* With another deep breath, Jordie opened the door with confidence and walked in with a bright smile. "Hi, Roger! You wanted to see me?"

"Jordan Miller! Come in! Have a seat." Roger rose from behind his impressive cherry wood desk and came around it, gesturing towards two side chairs placed in front of a floor to ceiling bookcase filled with volumes bound in leather. The office itself was impressive. The floors were hardwood, a dark gleaming wood that shone like a mirror, reflecting bright sparks of color from the central stained-glass pendant chandelier. The cherry wood furniture gleamed richly in contrast to the dark floors and a massive, lightly colored Oriental rug covered the central area in front of the massive desk.

Roger must have noticed Jordie's appreciation of the tastefully appointed room, bright in the afternoon light streaming in from the window wall beyond the desk. He leaned back in his chair and said, "Pretty impressive, isn't it?"

Jordie cocked an eyebrow and smiled. "It is, indeed, sir."

"It's a bit overstated for my own tastes," Roger demurred, "but I'm expected to entertain and meet with our clients here and it's the image we want them to see. Executives are more comfortable, it seems, in surroundings like these. And…" here he paused for a minute, leaning forward with his elbows on his knees, hands clasped between, and met Jordie's gaze steadily, "this is also the reward for working hard. This is what you have to look forward to if you continue on the path you're on." He smiled again and settled back once more into the comfort of the wingback.

"Thank you, sir. It's always my goal to do the best job I possibly can."

Roger nodded. He pulled a blue folder into his lap from the table next to his chair and held it across to Jordie. "I know and that's why it's my pleasure to present this official offer for the position of Regional Manager that you applied for. We are very impressed with your performance and I believe you are the right candidate for the position."

Jordie accepted the folder and flipped open the top cover. There, indeed, was an official letter offering him the position. He quickly scanned it, looked at the figures and swallowed a small lump in his throat. It was so much more than he had expected. A ten percent salary bump, a nice annual incentive target, stock option grants. He looked at Roger. "I won't let you down, sir."

"I take it that means you accept the offer?" Roger asked.

"Absolutely!" Jordie didn't hesitate and broke into a huge grin.

"Welcome to the team, then! Now, we'll want to work things out with Sharon, your current manager, as far as the official release and start date. In the meantime, I also want you to get some time in with Ken Hopkins. You know Ken?"

Jordie nodded. "Yes. He's the Regional Manager for the Northeast."

"That's him." Roger agreed. "He'll be your peer now. He's been very successful, and his metrics are always ahead of target. I want you to get some time with him, learn his process and what he does—and we need to be doing the same in the Southwest."

"Yes, sir. Do you want me to talk to Sharon?"

"No. I'll handle that. She'll let you know when we've worked out the transition." Roger rose and held his hand out to Jordie, signaling an end to the meeting. "Again, welcome to the team. Vicky will be adding you to email lists and sending meeting invites. Try to attend as many as you can."

"I'll do that." Jordie rose, shook Roger's hand and managed to leave the office without any major incidents. The first thing he saw was the huge grin on Vicky's face and he let out his breath, not realizing he'd even been holding it. "Wow!" was all he could manage.

"I'm so happy for you, Jordie. Congratulations!"

Jordie recalled the memory now with bitterness. He had glimpsed the road to riches, even walked briefly along its path, and that, perhaps, made the subsequent fall that much harder to bear.

He had indeed risen swiftly in the next five years, eventually securing a position as a Senior Manager reporting directly to a Vice President, the equivalent of a Director with the actual title tantalizingly just within reach. Not that the years had all been rosy and there were times Jordie's personal values were plagued with unease regarding the actions performed in his role. So much of the work that had formerly been handled by well-paid middle-class Americans were now supported by entry level, low wage resources located in the Philippines and India. Jordie had been a major player in moving that work. He had become all too skilled in delivering the layoff message, or Activity, as Human Resources preferred to call it. The very word Activity had formed ominous overtones in Jordie's vocabulary.

Megan and Jordie were beginning to enjoy the real fruits of success and he ignored the low murmur of unease that crept at times into his awareness. They bought a vacation home on the shores of Beaver Lake near Eureka Springs in Northwest Arkansas and enjoyed every opportunity of going there that they could manage. The invigorating and breath-taking outdoor environment with the sprawling Ozark mountains, numerous limestone caves, and crystal-clear waters were balm to shattered nerves. Adam also enjoyed the new lake home and energetically pursued the outdoor activities that abounded in the region.

Finally, in 2015, Jordie assumed a position that enabled him to work virtually anywhere and he secured permission from his department President to move permanently.

Then, in 2016 the great American slide into the abyss began. That year, for the first time, by the end of the second quarter the upper level executive team nervously realized the company was going to miss its stated targets by a large margin. Jordie had it from a good source that the board of Directors had already started talking about a severe cut in the annual bonus. Since bonus payout wasn't until the following spring Jordie knew financial outlooks must be bad indeed for them to already be discussing it. At the start of the fourth quarter there was a ten percent reduction across the board and that was just the beginning.

The years of 2017 and 2018 continued the downward spiral and morale in the company spiraled right along, keeping pace with the companies declining revenues. More work was shifted offshore, greater stores of talented employees were cut loose to manage in a worsening employment environment as other companies felt the same financial pressures and contributed to the ever-increasing unemployment statistics.

Jordie and Megan had long talks over coffee in the early morning on the deck before he sequestered himself for another grueling day on the phone in his office.

Jordie kept a close watch on their personal finances, knowing the hammer could, and eventually would, drop. They had invested the sale of the home near Dallas into the home in Arkansas and had a modest mortgage remaining, but the reality was the couple had little in the way of liquid assets to fall back on. True, they had paid off two massive college loans, but the result was they had little cash in the savings account to carry them should Jordie suddenly lose his job.

Late in 2018 the company bounced back for a bit when the R&D team came out with a new gadget that became the had-to-have item of the year. A new organization was formed to handle the launch and while Jordie tried to leverage himself onto the team he was left out in the cold, handling quality and metrics for the traditional core business—a none too favored role as neither the quality of the new offshore resources nor the metrics had very encouraging prospects. None of which mattered when the worst tragedy in American history occurred early in 2019.

One of the reasons the company struggled so much during the years between 2016 and 2019 was directly related to the President of the country at that time, Timothy D. Portillos. The ultimate businessman, he brought all the questionable ethics and shady practices of corporate boardrooms right into the oval office of our nation. Worse, he used the same bullying tactics Jordie had grown wearily accustomed to in his own company into his dealings with foreign diplomats.

Initially his election was viewed favorably in most boardrooms as most corporations thought they would finally have the control they had long desired with a peer in the oval office and restrictive regulations would finally be overthrown. Wall Street also viewed the change favorably and for the same reason. What no one ever dreamed was that he would pick a fight with the unstable and insecure leader of North Korea. It was late in 2017 that the two began slinging threats at each other.

Hostilities flared, and news hounds barely released one story before another one came along to trump it. All the beasts of war began to be mobilized while America built up heavy defenses in the South Korea peninsula and staged naval fleets in the Pacific Ocean. Rather than back down to the blatant intimidation displayed by the United States, North Korea aggressively pushed forward developing its own nuclear arsenal while the continual launching of newer missiles with greater range brought yet more pressure to bear on President Portillos to act. And act he did. On February 28, 2019 President Portillos relayed the launch command to two Ohio class submarines at undisclosed locations in the Pacific Northwest, launching two one-hundred kiloton nuclear warheads and virtually annihilating North Korea.

The last four months had been of nightmarish aspect for Jordie. The world response to this atrocious act plunged America into the final spiral of despair. Trade partnerships ceased and massive sanctions cut off the economy from the world stage. Corporations floundered as economic platforms failed, and major banks struggled to keep their doors open. Jordie knew what was coming but was powerless to stop it. He tried to keep a positive appearance for Megan's benefit, but he was grimly aware of what lay in store for him and his family. There would be no wealth building years for Jordie. The only chance that offered any security for Megan and Adam during his critical senior year in high school and college years would be if an accident happened to Jordie. In one more week his work through date would arrive and his life insurance benefits would cease immediately. He could not bear to watch the lives of the ones he loved most fall into a ruinous disaster that may well leave them homeless. The 401K they had been relying on had crashed to almost nothing along with the rest of Wall Street on March third. There was a chance the insurance would hold up long enough and be sufficient to care for Megan and see Adam through a good college. Hell, the kid already had offers from some of the biggest schools in the nation. It would be hard on them, but they'd recover.

Jordie shook a cigarette from the pack laying on the table before him. He could feel a headache starting and thought it must be from the propane fumes building in the camper. Speculatively he sniffed but could detect no odor. He raised the cigarette to his lips and was proud of himself for having only a slight tremor in his hand. He raised the cheap plastic lighter and his thumb flicked the wheel, striking a spark from the flint, and everything went white.

At the same time a small camper was exploding in a remote campsite in the Ozarks, in a plush conference room, at the top of one of the tallest high rises in Seattle, nine of the most powerful men in the nation sat together in conference. A silver haired, handsome man in his early sixties, his expensive suit and finely manicured persona exuding power, was speaking. "The American people will unite in one thing only and that is change. If nothing else has been proven, their united resistance to change is the one constant we can rely on in our recent past. If you go out blathering that we must change this, and we must change that, you can be assured of failure."

He paused and allowed the silence to extend. A glance around the table and he saw several heads nodding in agreement. He rose and walked to the bank of windows looking out over the metropolis and grimaced at various signs of fire burning throughout the city. An all too frequent sight in these troubled times. He turned his back on the view and strode back to his seat at the head. He did not sit as he continued.

"It is unfortunate that less than direct approaches must be considered but sadly subterfuge has all too often proven to be the most effective way of achieving the desired result. Our latest President, that has enmired us in these issues, is merely a symptom of the fear and anger in the heart of this nation. The people *want* change but lack the fortitude to make it happen. Change is hard work. Change does not come easy. It is far easier to continue to bicker and fight over the same petty issues and we never make progress." Another pause; brief this time. "And we never will."

Looking around the table he saw more heads nodding and knew they were in the palm of his hand. He sighed deeply. "It's hard to assume the mantle of responsibility but we in this room must now do so."

Before him, on the glossy surface of the burled wood table, was a tall stack of folders. Each folder had a colored side tab with a name written in bold black strokes. He counted the men in the room and inquired, "Lawrence is not here. Does anyone know where Lawrence Johnson is?"

A thin waspish man sitting three from the speaker's left spoke up, "Flight delays in Houston. Some weather related, more related to the current chaos in the FAA."

"Do we have any ETA at all?" The speaker's voice was dangerously soft, almost too low to hear. The waspish man swallowed and pulled out his cell phone. While he began fingering the screen with a rapid blur of fingers the speaker shook his head once, glanced to his right to the man seated in the middle seat who made some notations on the pad in front of him while the speaker moved on.

He steepled his left hand on the stack of folders before him and then swept the room with his right hand, indicating the men seated before him, as he continued. "Alone, each of you is responsible for a budget and gross income that exceeds that of many small nations. You employ the people that are peers to the many people that are currently panicking, while we watch our government, and our nation, enter the slow and deadly process of shutting down. Our government cannot recover from this. Oh, it will for a while. Make no mistake this won't happen overnight. No. It will be slow. It will be painful." A long pause as he engaged the eyes of each man one by one. "Who knows what our future will look like." Another long pause. Then, very quietly, "If we allow it to happen."

He resumed his seat and looked again around the table. "Together we control the largest corporations in this country and between us we cover most of the major service industries." He ticked off on his fingers, "Communications, construction, the largest media company in the northeast," a nod here to James Nocitra, a man in his mid-fifties with hair unnaturally dark and deeply tanned skin, who nodded back solemnly, intent on the speech. "We've got food service, transportation and housing. One of you manages the largest financial conglomeration operating anywhere in the world. I don't know of a more qualified team to manage affairs than I see sitting here at this table. But to succeed will take commitment from each one of you. Every part of this plan must work, or the entire thing will fail." More nodding accompanied this flatly delivered statement. "Now, I have prepared a prospectus here in great detail..." he broke off and silence fell as the latch turned and the door quietly opened.

All heads pivoted to see who dared to intrude on this most private of meetings. As one, the group relaxed when a familiar face appeared.

"Lawrence." The leader said, with a slight nod to the man entering the conference. This man was impressive. He was easily the youngest of the group as well as the largest. But not large in a fat way. He carried presence and had a winning smile to match the suntanned handsome face with sandy hair in a stylish cut.

"William." Lawrence returned the nod and flashed a toothy smile before scanning the room and nodding at the others, looking for an open seat. Spotting it at the far side he made his way around the table and seated himself before speaking to the room at large. "The airports are a mess. Things are falling apart fast. Sorry I'm late but there were only two controllers in the tower. It was chaos trying to clear runways for landings and takeoffs."

Others nodded sympathetically having experienced the same thing themselves. Ever since the stock market had crashed, and the subsequent government shut down, the economy and infrastructure were crumbling rapidly.

"It might have made more sense to have this meeting in Chicago. More central." John Andorf grumbled in general and to no one in particular. He paused, and then with a grudging tone added, "Or Dallas or Kansas City. Not like Seattle isn't the end of nowhere." He nodded briefly at Ken Goepferd of Dallas, a man with close cropped white hair, muddy brown eyes and a perpetual frown, and Patrick Repka of Kansas City, a short and stocky man with reddish blonde hair.

William smiled warmly and, ignoring Andorf, nodded at Lawrence as he continued, "You're timing, as usual, Lawrence, is superb. I was about to get down to business." He took a breath and looked around the table, ensuring he had their collective attention. "As I was saying, gentleman, the American public is united in one thing only and that is its resistance to change. They can, however, be led like sheep to it if you don't *tell* them what you're doing." He paused and took a sip of his water.

James Nocitra spoke up in a thick New York accent, "I'd be careful sayin' that 'round my city, if I were you." His voice carried just a hint of a threat.

William smiled tolerantly. "Naturally, James. I, nor anyone else in this room, is an idiot." William's voice was soft, quiet but firm as steel, and his smile was a bit too manufactured, it didn't match the gleam in his eyes as he pinned James in his gaze. James Nocitra squirmed a little uneasily and a red flush crept into the tanned, lined cheeks. He dropped his gaze to his hands, largish for a man of such medium height.

William continued. "Our society is collapsing. The Federal Government has been shut down now for four months and States are struggling to maintain law and order. Food shortages in rural areas have become prevalent as major shipping has shut down. Utilities are beginning to fail as workers remain unpaid. Riots are breaking out in metropolitan areas over simple basics. It is no coincidence that each of you at this table comes from a different major city."

He began with the man seated on his right. Sorting through the stack of folders, he located the one he wanted and handed it to the stocky, overweight man sitting beside him. The man was carrying a good fifty pounds more than he should have been and his complexion was red. The room was a comfortable seventy-two degrees, but he had sweat beading on his forehead. He uncrossed the beefy arms folded across his broad chest and accepted the thick folder William extended to him.

"John Andorf, you cover Chicago." He continued around the table: "James Nocitra, New York; Diego Vizachero, Atlanta; Tony Bahadur, Denver; Patrick Repka, Kansas City; Lawrence Johnson, Washington DC; Frank Baba, Las Vegas; Ken Goepferd, Dallas and Stuart Greenig, San Francisco. I, obviously, cover Seattle."

Each man accepted his folder, and some began to leaf through theirs curiously. "Please, gentleman. We will go through the material in due order. If you could give me your attention." There was the quiet shush of paper as folders were closed and the men shifted in their seats, turning towards William.

"It is also no coincidence that each of you is head of a different industry. Healthcare, construction, education, mining, leisure and hospitality, finance, retail, communications, security and the media." William paused again and took another sip of his water. He strolled back to the window and looked out over the Seattle skyline, the Needle piercing the clouds up near Lake Union. He looked at the large Ferris wheel etched against the Sound and distant Bainbridge Island. Wincing, he noticed more plumes of smoke even from there.

"Collectively we have the knowledge, the brain power, and the financial resources to save this country." He spoke firmly, his voice barely quavering with the passion he felt. He turned and the men at the table had collectively twisted to watch him. His eyes blazed as he punctuated his next words by lightly pummeling his right fist into his left palm. "We don't allow a single man to have sole power of a publicly traded corporation so *why* do we allow one man to have this ultimate power over our *country*?"

Shaking his head in disgust, he returned to the head of the table and placed his hands on its surface, leaning towards the center and pulling them in with him. "I care about this country and I believe that each of you do as well." His gaze swept the table and met eager nods.

Leaning back, he swept his hand at the distributed folders. "Inside those folders is a carefully thought out plan. I have been working on this for a long while and I believe this is the team to implement it. As I said, our society is collapsing. Our government is in a stalemate and our President is not capable of coping with the present emergency. I believe the flaw in our democratic government is the role of the Presidency itself. It has served its purpose and the Office should be abandoned." He stopped speaking and let this revolutionary thought settle into the astonished faces he saw before him. This was the make or break moment. He would either win them to his view or they would laugh in his face and leave the room, chuckling amongst themselves and calling him a quack. His heart seemed to hang in suspense for the briefest of moments before he plunged on, hoping he was at his most charismatic.

"We don't allow one man to have ultimate control of any corporation. We can all agree on that and that's where I'd like to start. In order to maintain the best interests of a company and its finances we have a Board of Directors. This is an elected group...the heart of the democratic process." Again, a pause, a moment to notice a few nods among the group.

"That Board selects a *qualified* person to manage the entire operation, to be The President, Chief Operating Officer...whatever you wish to call it. And that is the role to which each of you has been elected." Another glance, catching the self-satisfied smiles among this hugely egotistical group.

He smiled humorously, "Imagine if the employees of your company elected the corporate President or various Vice Presidents." There were several outright laughs among the group.

William allowed his smile to fade and his face became somber. "Yet that is precisely what we do when it comes to the most critical position in this nation. We allow the uneducated, the *people*, to make a decision, without even requiring that this chosen candidate have the *necessary* credentials to do the job!" He shook his head again in disgust. "Which is what has led us to our current situation. The role of the office of President in this nation has been changing since the advent of television." He gave a nod towards James Nocitra, head of the largest media conglomeration in America. "No offense to the media, James, but in large part your industry has driven quite a lot of the change we've seen politically. The American public has fallen in love with the sensational, and they want to be entertained. Candidates for office have long been a joke and a spectator sport. We all know how career politicians get elected. Offices are bought, not won!" He looked savagely around the table, daring anyone to contradict him. "And that is why we are where we are!" Vehemently he brought his right fist down on the table before him, causing Patrick Repka on his left to roll back from the table.

"At the barest minimum the office that holds the most power of any job in the country ought to at the very least come with some minimum requirements. We know that's not feasible and we'd be in gridlock for the next fifty years figuring out what those requirements would be making sure we are ever so careful to not exclude some out flung group no one has ever heard of or offend some other group that is always getting offended." He stopped, his voice dripping sarcasm.

"No," he spoke softly again. "No, the best way is to abolish the position. Besides, it's antiquated!" His tone became vibrant once more. "It's old school thinking and outdated. Before you is a detailed prospectus of a proposal to replace the office of President with a Council of Ten." He paused and heard a few snickers. He glared around the table. "I am *serious*, gentleman, and I ask that you be the same. This is possible *if* you will hear me out and read through the proposal. You think a Council of Ten is a *funny* idea? The ancient Greeks did not when they invested power in their Senate. Today's Millennials will *love* the idea! The key, as I said before, is to do this slowly. The first step is to stabilize our economy and get control of what resources remain. That is step one of our plan. The switch to a Council form of government is a couple of years down the road. We plant the seed in the interim." He waved his hand at the folders, "Go ahead and take a look."

The room was silent except for the susurration of paper as the men scanned rapidly through the content of the folders. Ken Goepferd closed his with a grunt and said, "It will take years."

"Yes, Ken, it will. Do you know of any other five-year plans that make you one of the most powerful men in the world?"

Ken Goepferd laughed expansively, "You aren't offering me anything I don't already possess, pal!"

William smiled tolerantly and gave a minute nod of assent. "Yes. Perhaps..." He let the word trail off and gave a small shrug. "I beg to differ a bit as not even I, the King of online retail, has the power to match our President."

There were a few chuckles of appreciation around the table and general relaxing.

"The idea has merit," John Andorf stated quietly. He nodded at William and held up his folder, "Good work here, William. You've been quite thorough. I noticed my folder is specific to Chicago. Am I to assume each of my peers has a location specific plan as well?"

William nodded, trying to subdue any indication that the answer should have been obvious. It was critical that he win these men over. He truly believed the future of their country depended on this change. If he applied a bit to their less than altruistic natures, should he be blamed if it resulted in the transformation necessary for their nation's continued survival?

Frank Baba spoke up, his voice reflecting sarcasm, "And I suppose you see yourself leading this Council, eh, William?"

William smiled, "Actually, no, Frank. I thought that position should be assigned by consensus of the group. The Council should jointly make decisions like that." His tone was educational, as if he were patiently explaining to a slightly slow student. "It's also incredibly premature to even be thinking about that just yet."

He looked around the room and straightened to stand tall before them. "I will not take more of your valuable time. I know your companies are handling many crises and you need to get back. Who knows how much longer we will even be able to fly if the FAA cannot function? Take the material with you and please read it in detail. I have set up a group email which you can use to communicate safely with the other members in this room. That email is on page two of the information and I ask that each of you set up a secure computer that will receive the emails sent to that group name. We will use this to communicate. It *must* be as secure as possible and should be the *only* thing the computer is used for. It is my hope you will agree that establishing ten population hubs with employment and housing for everyone is a future that benefits both the corporations we represent and the citizens of this nation. We have the means to offer them housing, manage the media they consume, the food needed to feed them, the security, *everything* a city needs to function—and we can do it better. We can do it more efficiently and *no one* in this nation need be homeless or hungry. We do not use the resources available and we have suffered for it. We can rectify the problem—and offer a brighter future for our Nation. Please, refreshments have been set up in the next room." He walked to the conference room door, swung it open, and waved expansively to the hall outside.

CHAPTER ONE

November 2035

Adam Miller scanned the duty roster and grimaced. He'd pulled William Magee for the day's run. That meant three hours confined, each way, on the journey to meet the convoy outside of what used to be Des Moines, Iowa. He'd been looking forward to getting out of the hub and while many complained of the cold weather and ugly scenery of winter, Adam found beauty in the stark forms of the bare trees, thrusting against the soft underbelly of snow heavy clouds. Now, he knew, that peace and enjoyment of nature would be shattered with Magee's incessant chatter.

Trying to think in a more positive manner, he considered the eerie drive through the many small towns he had to pass by and the deserted outskirts of Des Moines, in equal states of neglect, before reaching the former Love's Travel Stop at the junction of old route six, Hickman Road, and Interstate 35/80. He knew the Corporate Population Hubs had saved America, but it was painful to see reminders of the past.

Adam glanced at his watch as he logged into his work terminal at the Security Resource Group Building Three, Floor Nine, cubicle E1129, where he spent very little of his time. A hot cup of coffee sat steaming before him as he pulled up the cargo manifest for today's convoy. It was just past seven-thirty and he wasn't scheduled to meet the convoy until noon. They'd need to be on the road in another hour which meant he could expect to see Magee stroll in the door in another forty-five.

Adam printed the manifest, relieved to see that the load would be a light one. They had some media material from the North-Eastern Hub passing through to them from Midwestern and Midwestern was adding two freights of dairy products. That was good. Adam had overheard some of the Supply Chain Group grumbling that cheese stocks were getting low. He wondered what the media material might be. It seemed like something that could have been flown by drone or maybe even sent electronically. It was pretty cost prohibitive to ship items from New York to Kansas City. Adam smiled at his tendency to revert to the old names. The manifest was vague and merely listed one freight load of sealed, thirty-six by forty-eight-inch box cartons. Contents insured and seals to remain unbroken. Adam raised his eyebrows. First time he'd seen a restriction like that.

He passed down the remainder of the list, hoped there would be no road issues as they'd not want unnecessary delays with those reefers hauling dairy. He pulled up the GPS information on his terminal and was pleased to see a recent update from the Infrastructure team that the route was clear and road in good repair.

Adam allowed himself to smile again at an old memory of his dad complaining about lines of traffic when they took their annual summer vacation road trip and inevitably passed through some backwater construction reducing the highway to one lane. One advantage to the hubs was the complete elimination of that problem. Infrastructure Resource Group was responsible for maintaining the key interstate segments connecting each of the ten Corporate Population Hubs. Each hub took responsibility for the segments their hub relied on...meeting their sister hubs at a midway point. They didn't maintain all lanes, just one direction with a minimum of two lanes, which kept the maintenance at a supportable cost ratio.

Adam saw no reasons to be concerned about undue delays and tucking the manifest into his work portfolio headed for the lower levels to pick up the keys for today's assigned vehicle.

Fleet was part of the Facilities Resource Group but had personnel and facilities partnered with each of the resource groups that needed transportation on a regular basis. They maintained a parking garage in the bottom two levels of sub-basement below Adam's building and he took the elevator down to the check-in desk. He smiled cheerfully when he saw Roxy behind the counter. "Good morning, Roxy! How are you today?"

Roxy was an attractive twenty-something with a spectacular figure, perfect smile and the friendliest, warmest brown eyes Adam had ever encountered. She flashed that perfect smile now, dimples appearing in her cheeks. "Adam!" She crooned and the smile became even more fulsome. "It's a much finer morning now, I would agree." She batted her eye lashes at him coquettishly and then picking up a pen with her well-manicured fingers asked, "What can I do you for this morning?"

Adam felt some heat in his cheeks and hoped she couldn't see it. Her relentless pursuit had continued unabated now for the five or so years he'd known her. At first, Adam had been as equally flirtatious, but the fun had dissipated for him over time. He was never going to seriously consider dating her. She just wasn't his type and endless flirting became a mere frustration. She was friendly and attractive, but there was no chemistry, no spark. At least, not for him. He wasn't sure how much of her come-on was real, and how much was play. "You should have a vehicle assigned to me."

Roxy sat at a counter immediately to the right of the bank of elevators Adam had just exited. Straight ahead was a cavernous, dimly lit space with the gleam of light on painted metal. Rank after rank of cars and trucks sat. Adam felt another twinge of memory. Cars filling shopping mall parking lots, reflecting the sun. Lost in thought, Adam missed the momentary tender smile that touched Roxy's lips as she saw the profoundly sad look that had crossed his face. "Hey," she called, softly.

Adam jolted out of his picture of the past. "Yeah?"

Roxy smiled and looked back down at her list. She scrolled a long, painted nail and came to a stop about a fourth of the way from the top. "Yep. Here you are." She ran the nail across the line, frowned, picked up her pen and crossed something out, making a notation.

"Something wrong?" Adam asked.

She looked up and smiled. "Nope. In fact, you've got a real sweet set of wheels for today." Humming, she swiveled to her computer terminal and began tapping quickly on her keyboard, eyes intent on the screen before her. Adam waited patiently while Roxy did whatever she had to do. A few moments later she opened a panel behind her and retrieved a set of keys, sliding them across the counter to him. He reached for them and wasn't surprised to find her hand lingering over the keys just briefly enough to make contact.

He smiled, picked up the keys, and said, "Appreciate it. Which one is it?"

"The Tesla Roadster."

Adam whistled. "Wow. Really?" He couldn't believe his good fortune. The Tesla Roadster had been the last luxury sports car manufactured before the automotive industry collapsed and was never revived when the hubs were formed. With the population centralized into ten hubs, and housing provided near employment, the need for personal vehicles had been eliminated. The phase out had happened quicker than anyone could have anticipated. Adam was in his final years of college and lusting over the Roadster, and three short years later it was practically unheard of to know anyone that owned their own car. All that old rolling metal had been requisitioned by the Facilities Resource Group and the better vehicles were now managed through the Fleet program.

"Car's in spot one nineteen, row twenty-three, section J. Who's riding shotgun?" Roxy asked.

"Magee. William Magee." Adam glanced at his watch. Five to eight. "Ought to be here in about fifteen or twenty minutes would be my guess. I'm going to run back up to the Supply Pantry and grab a coffee for the road. Be right back."

"Hurry now," Roxy purred at her sultriest best, giving him a suggestive wink.

Adam ducked into the elevator as quickly as the opening doors would permit.

He met Magee at the elevator as he headed back with the freshened cup of coffee. So much for good luck holding, Adam thought wryly, I don't even get the elevator ride to myself.

Roxy was ready with another exaggerated wink and made hand motions to indicate dialing a phone as Adam and Magee left the elevator. Magee veered toward the counter and fell behind as Adam strode purposefully towards Section J, third bank of cars on the left-hand, middle portion, of the huge underground parking bay. A large letter J was bolted to the corner pillar and Adam didn't need to look at row numbers or slots as his eye caught the cherry red Roadster sitting on the end of the fourth row. That had to be it.

Adam raised the key and clicked the door lock and was rewarded by a flash of lights and blast from the horn. He heard Magee call out from behind him, but Adam was already sliding behind the wheel, the door pneumatically sealing behind him, shutting off all exterior sound. He was turning over the powerful electric motor when Magee slid into the passenger seat, the door whisking shut quietly.

"What's your hurry?" Magee asked breathlessly. He was a bit out of shape and the short jog trying to catch up to Adam had winded him. Adam wondered how the man passed the annual physical requirement the Security Resource Group was supposed to adhere to. "We've got plenty of time to get there."

Adam nodded complacently, "Yeah, but a few minutes extra never hurt anyone, and I'd rather have a few on the positive side if it's all the same with you." He glanced at his watch, eight twenty, ten minutes earlier than he'd hoped. They would have time to spare.

Pulling out of the slot, Adam slowly cruised past Roxy and the counter, never taking his eyes from the lane in front as it curved up out of the subterranean parking area. The dark underground gave suddenly to the brighter daylight, though overcast, and Adam was relieved when the Tesla's windshield auto adjusted. So far, the rain mixed with snow falling north of Wegah was missing the hub.

As Adam took the car through the graceful turn Magee chuckled, "Froggie wants a little bit of your action, Adam." He leered at Adam and waggled his thick eyebrows.

Adam felt vaguely disgusted and looked back at the road, executing the turn out of the SRG building and heading for the access ramp to I70. "Got your badge handy?" he asked Magee tersely.

"What? Hunh? Oh! My badge? Yes. Got it right here." He fumbled around, leaning over on his left hip and pulled a plastic card out.

"Mine's in my portfolio," Adam explained.

"Oh, sure." Magee placed his badge in the slot mounted in the center of the windshield so the automated attendant system on I70 and the other streets would allow them to pass without raising alarms. One perk of working Security, Adam often considered, was easy access to any place in the hub and the ability to get out of the hub. Regular civvies weren't given much opportunity to do anything outside of the hub. It was commonly understood it was unsafe anyway, and for the most part there was no real desire to leave the hubs. Everything and anything a person could want was available without ever leaving a sector, much less the hub. Everyone knew there were crazies and mutants roaming outside the hub just waiting for a chance to get hold of you. The fact that in his nine years with Security Adam had never once seen one of these purported crazies or mutants did not in the least convince him they were not there. He had seen Newscasts featuring incidents with them. He'd seen the riots after the Collapse at the end of the old Democracy.

If he had hoped to distract Magee with the badge, he was disappointed as Magee again prodded him, "Why don't you make little Froggie back there a happy person, hunh?"

Typical of Magee to not let a topic go, Adam thought and scowled. "Leave it alone, would ya? And don't call her Froggie. I don't like it."

"Why?" Magee asked, honestly mystified. "She works in Facilities. Everyone calls them Frogs. What's the big deal?"

"I don't know." Adam shrugged, irritated. "It just doesn't sound nice. I don't like it. She has a name. We all do."

"Ok. Chill." Magee turned towards the window and Adam knew he was pouting. He'd hurt his feelings and Magee would now sit in injured silence until Adam made amends. Well, he'd be damned if he would. Besides, a bit of silence wasn't such a bad thing.

The day was gray with a wet snow falling, melting as soon as it hit the pavement, as they passed into the rolling hills northeast of the hub. The wheels of the Tesla sung as they slushed over the wet highway. Within half an hour of leaving Wegah behind them, all trace of the hub vanished; the car moving through low, undulating hills and broad stretches of flat prairie with fence line trees. Adam knew that at one time this land had been rich farming country and the countryside was dotted with farm holds. It had all gone back to nature. Here and there groups of trees hid dilapidated structures nature was rapidly consuming.

The fertile field running next to the road at this stretch of I35 showed signs of feral hogs and he kept a close watch on the scrub along the side of the road. One of them charging in front of the Tesla could do some real damage.

He held his tongue and thus learned that Magee could hold his for an astounding forty-five minutes. Adam must have underestimated how badly he'd stung him. Regrettable, really, since it had not been his intention.

"I heard Erick Scharfe got RIF'd." Magee ventured as they left what had been Cameron, Missouri behind them.

Adam was momentarily stunned. He knew Erick, of course. He had joined SRG two years after Adam and they'd been on the same squad for a short while back when Adam was working internal security beat in sector six, Environmental Resource Group's sector—or Energy as they'd been more commonly nicknamed. He'd been likeable, and Adam had even started having regular racquetball matches with him, before Adam got reassigned and moved up to a cross-sector initiative partnering with the Infrastructure Group setting up security surveillance along the Wegah convoy routes. It was

Adam's success completing this five-year project two year's ahead of schedule that had landed him his current position running convoy escort. Only it was a bit more than just escorting, though the work amounted to much the same thing.

"I hadn't heard that," he responded flatly.

"Yeah. I heard he complained to his supe about some mandatory OT the team was doing and next thing you know—bam! He's gone! RIF'd." Magee punctuated the bam with a slam of his right fist into his left palm.

Adam winced at the overly dramatic gesture. "When did this happen?" he asked stonily.

Magee was insensitive to Adam's mood shift and continued blithely. "Let's see, today's Thursday. I heard it at Café Yunhui…which is in the Frog…" He paused, realized his word choice, and then smoothly continued, "Excuse me. The Facilities pod. You know, sector seven." He glanced at Adam to see if he would react. The clubs in sector seven were known to allow things to progress a bit further than the other sector clubs, with the exception perhaps of sector two, infrastructure. Adam ignored him and with a small shrug Magee resumed. "I was there Monday night so it would have happened Saturday."

Adam nodded and didn't say anything further. He hated gossip and chose not to participate in it whenever possible. This was largely impossible with Magee as that seemed to be all the man did but Adam was able to tune out much of the remainder of what he said. Listening, but only on the surface, mind busy at work underneath.

Where had Erick been assigned? Last Adam had heard he'd been working some project in partnership with the Communications Group. It was a little-known fact that the telecommunications, internet, computer services and other critical electronic functions and networks fell under the purview of Public Works Resource Group. Adam had never understood why this critical function had not been part of Training or even Security. Apparently, at one time, the telephone was something like a utility. The small sector-within-a-sector was isolated deep in the heart of sector one, the largest sector in Wegah. Personnel assigned to Communications were not allowed to leave their sector, and mingling was discouraged.

Adam was not familiar with the project Erick had been assigned to and didn't have access to that level of information with his current position and security clearance. He had heard rumors though; they were part of the information network operating in every sector in the hub. Some project Security was working with Communications was tanking, working long hours with bad results. Adam remembered the pressure cooker days getting the convoy surveillance network up and running and could empathize with Erick if he'd cracked under that sort of pressure.

Adam had been fortunate. Well, he reflected modestly, it had been a bit more than luck. He'd worked hard, and he'd worked long days to bring that project in early. He'd spent countless hours of his personal time agonizing over timelines and schedules, GANTT charts and graphs, until he saw them even in his dreams.

Erick had been a light-hearted guy. Easy-going, always ready with a funny anecdote, usually using himself as the butt of the humor. Adam just couldn't see Erick under the pressures of a difficult project. Not that he wasn't capable. He just didn't have the temperament for it. Adam would try to do a little snooping when they got back this evening.

They pulled into the old Love's Travel Stop at a quarter to noon relieved to find that the convoy was not running ahead of schedule. Adam parked the Tesla next to the charging bay and went and entered his secure access code to fire up the generator. The power would supply three of the gasoline islands so the convoy trucks could top off their tanks while also providing juice to recharge the Tesla. Then there was nothing to do but wait.

The vast empty parking lot of the old shopping mall was always especially unsettling, it seemed, this time of year. The landscaping trees planted ages ago in a vastly different culture had grown wild. Some had died and their twisted hulks lurked grotesquely in the overcast light. Others had spread beyond their original boundaries, small groves determined to defeat the slab of concrete which was crumbling before the relentless onslaught. The pavement was buckled, and warped, and wild vines and runners ran across the surface, further breaking it down. Out of this jungle of ugly, weedy vegetation the husk of the mall itself rose, largely undamaged. That was what was so unnerving, Adam decided. The building looked like it should have people moving in and out of the entrances, mainly hidden from Adam's view where he stood at the far corner of the Love's parking lot.

Adam's eye roved across the landscape, not expecting to see anything different and rewarded accordingly. The old mall entrance sign had long since had any reusable plastic, glass or metal removed. Only the frame of the sign remained anchored firmly into its concrete base and footer. Adam looked again towards the building, finding the one entrance on this side, a black hole in the façade. His eye began to move on when suddenly he froze, his eye turning quickly back. Had he just seen movement? But that wasn't possible.

For one thing there was nothing in the building, beyond shelter itself, that anyone—or thing—might want. Adam knew that for a certainty. Shortly after he'd gotten the assignment with convoy escort, he'd made this run with his first team lead, Mary Beth O'Connor. She had instructed him to meet her at Fleet an hour early that morning. It had given her time to take him through the dark empty shell. It had been extremely unsettling walking through the cavernous structure with suspended walkways over darkened corridors, store fronts and their pitch-black havens beyond seemed to yawn ominously, waiting to snatch the unwary.

Mary Beth had been a great introduction to convoy escort, and she ran a tight crew. She had been in her late forties and part of the Security Resource Group at Wegah since its inception. Adam had learned early on to respect her leadership and he had learned a lot from her before she was promoted elsewhere, and he lost track of her. She had recommended him as the best candidate to step into the vacant team lead position and he'd moved up three years after joining the team. She had taken the job of convoy escort seriously and as part of her dedication had made it her responsibility to periodically run a security sweep of the buildings immediately surrounding the convoy meet points in both old Des Moines and Salina, Kansas, the Dallas and Denver meet point. Adam had picked that practice up and it occurred to him now that he'd been lax lately. It had been since at least late spring since he'd done a security sweep and he made a mental note to rectify that the next time he made a run.

Now, he peered intently at that black entrance in the side of the distant building. For a second, he thought he had seen a flash of lighter color, the white oval of a face—but then it had been gone so quickly that it may have been his imagination.

Just then his ears caught the sound of distant motors and he knew the convoy was growing near. He turned back to the Tesla, where Magee was lounging next to the car, leaning his overweight frame against the front fender while his fingers were busy on the screen of his personal comm device. Adam sighed resignedly and walked across the cracked pavement to him. "Convoy's almost here. Put that thing up." He made another mental note to have a discussion in his next team meeting about the use of comm devices while working. It was one thing to check them occasionally and quite another to spend undue amounts of time on them. Suppose there were someone across the street in that mall? Some crazy or mutant the Media Group was always warning them about. Magee would be easy prey for them in his current distracted state.

Magee straightened and shoved the unit into the front breast pocket of his heavily padded winter coat. Hunching his shoulders, he shivered and said, "Bloody cold out here. I hope these boys make it quick." He went to stand attendance at the first fuel pump while Adam went to the second and made sure all lights were on and the system functioning. Everything was ready as the three semis with the lead security car pulled up to the bay of pumps.

Adam grinned when he saw the lean frame of Chip Carlsen unfold from the capacious front seat of the black Cadillac ATS. He stretched and returned Adam's grin. "How's life treatin' ya?" He extended his right hand and exchanged a firm handshake with Adam.

"Good!" Adam replied. "How's things in Midweh?" Chicago had been renamed the Midwestern Hub and that had been reduced to Midweh a long time ago.

21

"Brutal! We've had a lot of snow this winter and the wind coming off the lake could cut right through you. The only good thing is the cold keeps the peas in their pods, if you know what I mean."

Adam smiled commiseratively. It was true that in inclement weather people tended to stay home rather than venture out and it reduced the minor incidents that always occurred anytime people gathered together. "Hope the drive wasn't too bad."

"Nah. As usual, by the time we got to old Davenport the roads were clear. Those Infrastructure and Power teams in Midweh know how to handle the worst winter can send us and they do a good job staying on top of it."

Adam nodded and then got down to business. He laid his portfolio on the Cadillac's long gleaming hood and pulled out the manifest. Chip handed over his copy and Adam did a quick stare and compare. The lists matched and he saw Chip's signature at the bottom of his copy confirming all items had been accounted for. "Well, let's do this."

The two men strolled over to the first of the three semis and they began the process of verifying the cargo. It was only later, as Adam was steering the Tesla back out onto old Route 6 and he passed the deserted mall, that it occurred to him he'd forgotten to ask Chip if he'd noticed anything unusual in his last couple of runs. Adam again glanced at that entrance in the side, but everything was still. With the convoy on his heels he couldn't stop and do a security check now and Chip had left while Adam was still running through his lock up procedure.

The return drive with the convoy in tow was uneventful and they were safely back inside the hub walls before dusk settled. Adam was grateful as he wouldn't want to find himself on the wrong side of those gates after lock-up. Once darkness settled it was a hub rule, inviolable, that all egress points to the hub were locked until the following morning and the advent of dawn. There were emergency shelters placed in strategic locations that Security was familiar with and had access to, but on the few occasions he'd had to use them, Adam had always found it to be extremely unsettling and he never slept well outside the hub walls. He entered his personal unit on the eleventh floor of his building and the vid screen welcomed him.

"Welcome home, Adam! How was your day?" The voice was a pleasantly modulated husky female but not at all sensuous, like some of his co-workers appeared to prefer from the infrequent visits he had made to their personal units.

"Good evening, Siri. My day was busy and I'm tired."

"A hot shower should help." Siri offered suggestively.

"That does sound good. Please prep the shower, Siri."

"Yes, sir."

Adam proceeded into his sleeping area where Siri followed him. "Would you like to consume your daily news feed now?" she inquired politely.

"No. Let's wait until I've had my shower." The daily news feed was a requirement of life in the hub. The Media Resource Group issued news feeds keeping hub inhabitants informed on news across the nation as well as internationally and all people living in the hub were required to listen to at least the first hour of a news feed once daily. Their attendance was tracked by the individual computers provided in each personal unit. Adam knew that there was a mainframe computer deep in the upper levels of the SRG that diligently tracked every person's participation. He wasn't sure what punishment attended those that disobeyed but he did not want to find out. An infraction that serious could result in RIF treatment and that was enough to ensure his compliance.

"Very well," Siri replied silkily. "Alexa has asked me to remind you that you have twenty-eight hours and forty-four minutes in which to enter your monthly voting choices."

Adam sighed in irritation. He knew it was a critical component of their democratic society, but he grew weary of the constant issues that required citizen votes for resolution. "Please print the list for my review, Siri."

He heard the printer in its hidden alcove above his workstation whir to life and retrieved the pages, giving them a quick scan. Only five items this month and, as usual, nothing that Adam was interested in. He laid the pages down beside his terminal keyboard for review later and headed off to the shower.

CHAPTER TWO

"We've got to increase production of those microchips or we'll miss the delivery deadline and the incentive bonus that comes with it!" Yolanda Webster, President of Supply Chain, spoke in angry frustration, burying her hand in her hair at her right temple, a gesture she always subconsciously engaged in when aggravated.

Ben Larocque, President of Security, located in the Rocky Mountain Hub, or Romoh, leaned back more comfortably into his padded seat. This discussion would take a while and he wouldn't be called on or didn't expect to be.

Ben had been President of Security for the past eight years and was the second to hold the title, having been promoted when the original President, Tony Bahadur, had retired. He was approaching fifty-five, but most thought him much younger. He kept himself fit with a discipline for the fitness facility that shamed a few of the younger men in his peer group. He didn't allow himself to overindulge in any of the classic sins: food, alcohol, or women. Much of his demeanor was a carryover from his former military career. He watched idly, not really invested in the discussion, as Phil Gradic, President of Energy in the Midwestern Hub, Midweh, responded.

"I've been trying to get an update on that very topic myself." His tone was dry, and he arched his eyebrows at the video image on his monitor, an image they all saw in their separate offices across the nation. Ben's was a wall wide monitor with nine individual sections in a grid, oddly reminiscent of that old game show based on tic tac toe, allowing him to see all the participants. "Perhaps, Kate, you have an answer for me today?"

Kate Luca, President of Training in the Pacific Hub, gave a nasty smirk vaguely disguised as a smile and replied, "I've been pressing your subordinate to give me those details, but he's been unresponsive."

Phil smiled, no warmth in the smile at all, and replied coolly, "That's not what he's been telling me. He has been begging you to assign some resources to assist and you've been unavailable to him."

"That is not the truth, Phil." Kate's face, not quite pretty but more interesting than could be termed actually homely, was twisted into an ugly expression, her wispy blond hair framing the pallid face which light blue eyes blazed from. Leaning into her video camera Kate, typically, revealed more of her freckled bosom than Ben cared to view. Why didn't the woman dress appropriately for her age and position?

Ben hoped Phil had plans for this subordinate because any future the man had in Packy had just ended.

Judy Rice spoke up silkily, "Kate, I could send a team over to lend support if that would help. What's the shortage, Yolanda?"

"We're down five hundred thousand units with total shipment delivery of a million seven hundred and fifty thousand units due in eight months. If we don't make this deadline, Japan gets a ten percent price reduction and we lose the five million bonus. It also places our future contract at risk."

"Kate, send me a list of what skillsets you need. I'll have my folks send you a team before the day's over."

"Copy me, Kate. I think I can do the same." Janet Byron, better known as JB, spoke up.

"I appreciate you lending a hand and, Yolanda, I'll trust you to keep the Japanese delegate happy in the meantime. Phil, I'll expect updates from you on this daily until production is caught up." Frank Baba, President of FinOps, interjected smoothly. As current Speaker for the Council of Ten, he was also their de facto leader. Ben admired him tremendously. He had never known the man to raise his voice in anger, yet you did not want to be the unlucky individual that did invoke his ire. Ben knew, all too well, having had to execute some of the more unsavory commands sent through the channels from that office. His stepping in now was his signal that the discussion was ended. Yolanda inclined her head gracefully in compliance and sat back in her padded executive chair, the Needle gleaming in the background over her shoulder in the Pacific Northwest Hub, Panoh.

Frank then proceeded through his weekly list of active major projects, making note of progress and delays. It took about forty-five minutes to run through the current list and Ben was restless before Frank asked, "That's a wrap from me. We'll have a round table now. Ben, you've been quiet. Any updates or things we need to discuss?"

Ben looked at the list in front of him, noting no items that were suitable for general discussion, and shook his head. "Quiet is as quiet does. We're good."

Frank smiled, a genuine warm smile, and asked, "Can you stay for a few minutes after the meeting? There're a few things I'd like to go over with you, not for general discussion." He ended a bit aimlessly, uncustomary given his typical well-organized control.

Ben glanced at his watch and surreptitiously noted the body language among some of his peers, making small seat adjustments. It had not been lost on them that the Speaker of the Council was requesting a private meeting with the President of Security. That was sure to have a few of them wondering and he smiled, imagining the texts being exchanged. He had no doubt the three vipers were already communicating with each other. He really needed to keep an eye on JB, Judy and Kate. Ever since they'd joined the Council of Ten, JB the first with Judy and then Kate not far behind, they had formed a cadre and seemed to delight in sowing discontent and wreaking havoc. Ben believed JB wanted to make a power play for Frank's position. While he would like to believe that was an impossibility, with the looming retirements of Lawrence Johnson and James Nocitra, the current balance of power on the Council could make a major shift. He did not want to consider what the nation would look like if JB were to secure the seat of Speaker.

"Ben?" Frank interjected politely, startling Ben back to the present.

"Oh, yes, excuse me, Frank. Was just thinking through today's schedule and I've got time to spare."

"Great. I'll call you direct on SecComm."

Ben nodded and smiled while Frank moved on, asking each President if they had anything to add or needed to discuss. Each was as eager for the meeting to end as the other and it wrapped up quickly.

Ben's Secure Communications device lit up within moments of the meeting terminating and as Ben turned off the large monitor, he pressed the connect and returned Frank's smile as the image came through. "Three Vipers to the rescue, again. As if I wouldn't notice that a rescue wouldn't be necessary if…" Frank cut himself off and sighed. "How are things in Romoh, Ben?"

Ben returned the tired smile and hoped his offered encouragement. He respected Frank and knew how much the man was trying to deal with. Having the three subversives on Council was making a difficult job damned near impossible.

Frank waved a hand dismissively now. "Not what I wanted to talk to you about. Have you made any progress on finding the non-hub locations? I mean—they have to have centers of operations—don't you think?"

Ben frowned. Of all his charters this was his most challenging. "They've become incredibly careful, Frank. We rarely even catch a whiff of them anymore. I suspected a couple of places but when we sent in the teams, we didn't find even a hair that shouldn't have been there."

Frank's frown deepened. "I heard through channels that there was activity captured on satellite."

Ben nodded, "I heard the same, but our ground crews turned up nothing."

Frank turned away from the camera to look out the window at the view of the fabled Las Vegas Strip stretching out below him. "The Western Gateway Hub had a project a few years' back. Some kid with a Computer Science degree set them up with a convoy surveillance system. If I recall correctly, the team lead, Mary Beth O'Connor, thought there might be something going on at the meet point in Des Moines on the Midwestern route. She was Old School—believed in regular security sweeps, that sort of thing. I think she might have had Army background prior to the hubs. Anyway, she had this suspicion and you guys, Security, came up with this guy."

While Frank had been talking, Ben had quickly run a check on Mary Beth O'Connor and recalled immediately what Frank was remembering. "Yes," he said. "Adam Miller. Double major out of University of Missouri in Criminal Justice and Computer Science. He got the system installed in record time. Mary Beth requested we move him to convoy escort when the job was done and after a couple of months we did. He's Team Lead over the group now."

"Yes." Frank replied softly, nodding, turning back to the camera. "How'd that work out?"

Ben shrugged. "The system works. It went in early and has operated without a hitch ever since. They find it useful, eyes in the sky, so to say. They can visually monitor the meet point from Security pod in Wegah."

Frank nodded again. "Do you monitor when there is no convoy?"

Ben frowned. "Yes. I must tell you Mary Beth's suspicions never did pan out. We never saw or found anything near that meet point."

"We had an occurrence here, at Soweh." Frank got to the point. "It happened about two hours ago so I doubt you've had word of it yet."

Ben switched applications on his screen and noticed a flashing alert. He looked back at Frank. "What are the details? What have you been told so far?"

"Convoy escort arrived at Romoh meet point in Mesquite, Nevada forty-five minutes ahead of schedule. After unlocking the generator and priming the gas pumps, the two men were attacked by fifteen well-armed assailants who then proceeded to fill cannisters in the beds of trucks with fuel. They left the two men handcuffed to one of the island poles with the keys a bay away. By the time the convoy pulled in the attackers had disappeared."

Ben sat in shock. "The men...?"

"There were no injuries sustained. Frankly, Ben, I'm more worried about what's happening outside of the hubs than I am by what I know is going on inside—and that's worrisome enough."

Ben's mind was spinning. "Yes, yes." He went back to Adam Miller's file. "I've got some ideas, Frank. First, I'm going to get my best men deployed to Soweh. Second, I'm going to give Mr. Miller a promotion and we'll get his network deployed at every meet point in the nation. Finally, I'll get a crack team to locate and eliminate these outsiders."

Frank held up a restraining hand. "Let's think about elimination before we go there. We've got some work centers that could use some able bodies and I don't want to have another forced RIF if I can help it. It destroys morale. RIF's should be reserved for punishment, if possible. I'd honestly like to avoid them all together."

Ben knew Frank spoke from the heart. As a President, even he realized he no longer thought of the lower ranks of his group as he once had. He could remember his first across the board cut, when he'd had to tell his Vice Presidents that five percent of their workforce would be mandatorily RIF'd. It had been personal that first time. The thought of good employees reduced to work camps in remote locations in squalid conditions under harsh labor when they had done nothing to deserve such treatment was almost unbearable.

Frank, after all these years, still felt that way about people. He still believed in the good the Corporations could do for the citizens of America. Ben wished there were more like him that thought that way in the Council of Ten. Several of them had no qualms at threatening their hubs on a regular basis with RIFs, believing fear was the best way to control the populace. Ben always found those hubs to have a grimmer feeling than the one's that reduced, or at least minimized, exposure to the RIFs they did have.

"I think that's wise, Mr. Speaker," Ben said now, respectfully.

"I like your plan," Frank said with satisfaction. "Why don't you plan to come to Soweh for a few days? We've still got the finest entertainment in the nation and it'd be great to sit down together over a few. What do you say?"

Ben thought about the glamor of Las Vegas, now Soweh, and smiled quickly. "I like the sound of that. I'll have my assistant get with yours and block it on our calendars. Meanwhile, look for some updates on that situation within a couple of hours."

"Thanks, Ben." Frank said as he closed the connection.

Erick shrugged into the heavy, down-filled jacket. "Time to check the fuel level in the generator."

Jerry Goes nodded, never taking his eyes off his computer screen.

Erick sighed, wondering how long before the resentful chill he felt from the man might begin to thaw. He didn't know what had led to Jerry's assignment to the remote outpost, but he knew no one drew this sort of duty favorably. In the past week since Erick had arrived, Jerry's demeanor was laconic, and he had restricted conversation to only essential discourse. It was going to be a very grim work assignment indeed if the man's humor did not improve.

Erick closed the main door behind himself, briefly sheltered by the facilities entrance cubby, and pulled on the warm arctic gloves to protect his hands before opening the outer door. The frigid blast of northerly wind stole his breath and his lungs protested from the freezing oxygen he pulled in. There had been fresh snowfall the previous night and while he was no expert at assessing accumulation Erick guessed there was an additional six inches. It had been a dry and powdery fall and it made it difficult to walk across the uneven ground to the building that housed the main generator, smoke pluming in great white clouds from the ventilation pipes in the roof. Erick's tall frame sank into the new buildup of snow as he trudged the quarter mile distance up a steep path hugging close to the shoulder of the sheer mountain, his boots growing heavier with each step he took. By the time he had reached the corrugated metal building he was exhausted and thankfully pulled the heavy door on its track closed behind him. The building was not heated other than the heat the working generator engine threw off, but it was a relief to be out of that bitter wind.

Erick quickly checked the fuel tanks, topping them off before continuing with the next morning task, the one he dreaded the most. Another half mile up the winding track was the relay tower they were here to monitor and maintain. With the fresh snowfall Erick knew he would have to make the hike and ensure snow and ice had not foiled or blocked any of the communication equipment on the tower. That would mean a grueling hike and then to climb the tower itself, nothing protecting him from the relentless wind that never seemed to abate this far up in the frozen reaches of the Rockies.

It took Erick the entire morning and it was close to one in the afternoon as he made it back to the main shelter and housing facility nestled in a natural valley between two massive granite bluffs. Jerry looked up from his computer screen when Erick came through the main door and Erick wondered bitterly if he'd moved at all while Erick had been out doing the morning routine. Now, he grunted and nodded his head at the kitchen stove in the corner of the single main room they shared as work and living space. Four sleeping alcoves along with bath and shower facilities were accessed through a door that led to a hallway running the length of the structure at the back.

"Got some hot soup waiting for you. Hope you like chili."

Erick glanced in surprise and saw the pan with steam rising above it. "I love chili!" Erick exclaimed; his enthusiasm genuine. "Thanks! It's brutal out there this morning and I need a warmup."

Jerry nodded and went back to his computer while Erick gratefully crossed to fill a bowl with the thick, meaty soup. He returned and took the seat across from Jerry, taking a spoonful and savoring the richly spiced concoction full of beans, pepper and onions. He could see slices of garlic along with the thick chunks of tender beef. "This is really good," he said appreciatively, glancing at Jerry.

Jerry returned his look and said, "Rowena made it. She was a good cook, a good partner to have up here." He dropped his eyes back to his screen.

So that was it, Erick thought. Jerry hadn't wanted Rowena Himelright to leave. Erick had only met her briefly the first day he arrived as she was heading out with the team that brought him in. She'd been a husky woman. Not fat but thick, of a medium height and while not attractive she had appealing features with large, expressive blue eyes. Perhaps there had been more than just a working relationship between Rowena and Jerry.

"Any idea where she was reassigned?" Erick asked, keeping his eyes on his bowl as he spooned up more chili.

"No. They just told her to be ready to go, new assignment and she'd get the details at HQ."

Erick nodded in response, "They don't like to tell more than they need to, do they?" His voice filled with acrimony. He was staring into his bowl and didn't see the way Jerry looked up at him, eyes squinting minutely in assessment, as he studied the younger man across from him.

Erick, lost in his own thoughts, recalled how his manager had called him to a meeting in the main Security office in sector eight of Wegah. Sector eight was where FinOps and Executive Management were quartered and where all managers worked unless you managed front line activity in a pod and then you were more likely quartered there. Erick had not had many occasions to go to sector eight, and as he had been the few other times he'd been there, was always surprised at how different it was. The buildings were spread out further and there was a lot of greenery and landscaping, beautifully manicured flower beds brightening the open spaces while trees lent graceful elegance alongside the modernistic offices. Erick knew management living pods were further out along the edges of the sector and their opulence was fabled elsewhere in the hub.

Daniel Sprouls, Erick's manager, had been on the phone when Erick walked into his office. When he'd looked up and seen Erick an ugly scowl had crossed his face, he'd gestured brusquely at the chair across his desk, and then swiveled so Erick could only see the back of his executive seat and hear the growling voice, "My next meetings here and I've got to go now. I'd like an update within the next three hours. I'll expect you're call." Turning back around he drilled Erick with an angry look, brows lowered into an angry frown. Erick felt a leaden ball in his stomach. "You're being reassigned," Dan snarled. He looked up at the round clock on the wall to his left and continued, "You got a flight to Romoh that leaves in two hours. Should give you time to get your clothes and personal items packed." He folded his hands on his desk and sat in stony silence glaring at Erick.

Erick felt a bead of sweat pop out along his hairline and swallowed convulsively. "I don't understand, sir. I…"

Dan's frown deepened and he waved a hand in an angry gesture for Erick to be quiet. "You've been on this project in CommPod for six months now, Erick. Where are the results? Why are we so far behind?" With each question,

Dan's voice rose, and Erick slumped deeper into his chair, lead in his stomach turning now into hot lava burning him from the inside.

"Sir, we're doing our best. As you know, we've been working seven-day weeks, ten-hour days. It's Development, sir. There are critical problems with the code, and we keep telling them—but each time they deliver a fix it still doesn't work the way it needs to."

Again, Dan waved him off, "Don't want to hear it, Erick. That's bullshit and we need this program up and running! We don't have all year to do it! I'm moving someone in that I know can get the job done. There's nothing else to discuss. As I said, your flight leaves in two hours. Be on it."

Erick sat, stunned, disbelieving what was happening. "Where am I being assigned?" He asked bleakly.

Dan shrugged. "Don't know, not my problem. You go to Romoh and you'll report to…" He dug through some paper on the disheveled desk and finally found the one he wanted. Peering at it closely he continued, "Report to Darlene Meador at Security. She's your new boss." Then he waved a hand dismissively and picked up his phone. The meeting was over.

The memory still rankled Erick. He had not even received a fair hearing on the issue, in his opinion, and the failure of the project to make its deadlines had not been the fault of either his project management or the team of professionals he'd been leading to test the new software.

Erick was so lost in thought that he missed what Jerry said. The sound of his voice registered, but not the words. Startled that the man had said something he looked up quickly, "Hunh?" he asked, swallowing the mouthful of chili he had just spooned up.

"I said, do you wanna talk about it?" Jerry had leaned back in his chair and folded his arms comfortably across his narrow chest.

It was the first time Jerry had shown any interest in Erick and Erick didn't hesitate. "Sure. Mind if I fix us a cup of cocoa first?" Not waiting for an answer, he carried his empty bowl to the sink and washed it, setting it in the drainer while water heated. Carrying the two cups back he resumed his seat across from Jerry.

Jerry accepted the frothy beverage, nodding his thanks. He sat silently as Erick told his tale. When Erick stopped speaking, Jerry acknowledged severely, "Getting assigned to Darlene Meador is a form of punishment. She's one of Baba's hatchet men. You make the grade on her team or you're headed for a work center."

Erick studied Jerry, wondering what his story was and how he'd come to be assigned to this remote corner high in the Rockies where spring came late, summer was fleeting, and autumn had come and gone before you noticed. Winter predominated here eight months out of the year. "How long have you been here?" Erick inquired.

Jerry smiled; his expression ineffably sorrowful. "Let's see now, it will be seven years this January. Next month." He looked up at Erick and Erick saw the depths of pain in those eyes. He smiled wryly again, "We'll save my story for another day."

CHAPTER THREE

Aubree Holten armed the sweat out of her eyes and put her hand back on the handle of the hydraulic weight resistance machine. She was thirty years old and in the prime of her life. A beautiful woman, she had striking green eyes with silky long brown hair. Dressed in an old exercise outfit, damp now with the sweat of her exertions, her exposed muscles gleamed in the harsh fluorescent lighting. Just five more, she thought. Five more reps and you can cool down on the elliptical. Come on—you can do it! She strained and pulled the weight up for one more rep. Four more!

"You set a great example, as always, Aubree."

The voice intruded on her fierce concentration and the heavy weight almost slipped out of her grasp. Tightening her hold and gritting her teeth, Aubree made herself slowly return the weight to its stationary position and not allow it to slam into place. Even though no actual metal weights were involved the machine simulated the sound to discourage improper weight release. "Good morning, Drew," she said, as coolly as possible, not wanting to give any sign of encouragement.

Andrew Shipley, known as Drew by all who knew him, was standing almost out of her peripheral vision on her right side, watching while she worked the machine. Aubree decided the additional four reps could be skipped for today and stood up, wiping her hands and forehead with her sweat towel as she turned to head for the elliptical at the opposite end of the large exercise facility. Drew fell into step beside her. Aubree quickened her pace.

It wasn't that Drew wasn't attractive. In fact, he was very handsome. He had dark hair, almost black it was so dark, that was thick and curly, falling across his forehead in a careless wave. He had hazel eyes that Aubree admitted were the most arresting she had ever seen. The look in them, however, often made her think of the raptors she had watched in wildlife films—there was no warmth, no empathy. The eyes of a predator. The face the eyes were set in was well sculpted and very pleasing to look at with near perfect skin complexion and tone. And yet, something about him made her uneasy and wary. Some instinct warned her that this was a dangerous man.

At thirty, Drew was fit and deeply muscled. Aubree knew he was part of the Security Group. He exuded a sense of physical power that was overwhelming, and he had a habit of standing too close, stepping within what she considered the limits of her personal space. She was tall at five seven, but he towered over her at six three.

She slung her towel over the center console of an elliptical machine, disheartened that the large facility was mostly empty this early in the morning, no one else using any of the large bank of ellipticals, treadmills and stair climbers. Rank after rank of exercise bikes stretched out behind them. Aubree swung into position on the elliptical and keyed in her program, smoothly launching into stride. Drew laid his hand on her shoulder and she suppressed a shudder, not quite succeeding, earning a low laugh from Drew.

"Cold?" He asked, his lips forming a sneer. "Or is that just animal lust responding?" He ran his finger down her arm and then lightly gripped her wrist.

Aubree kept her eyes straight ahead, fixed on the far window wall and it's view of the cherry trees, stark now in mid-December.

With another low laugh, he removed his hand, and a moment later Aubree heard the bicycle behind her fire up. She tried not to think of him, there behind her, watching her as she worked through the cool down routine but by the time the program ended twenty minutes later her entire body felt grimy, and not solely from the workout. Careful to avoid looking at him, she headed for the sanctuary of the women's locker.

He was waiting for her as she came out. Freshly showered and changed, Aubree was busy tucking items into her shoulder bag as she came out of the locker and looked up just in time to avoid a collision with Drew. Even though she came to a complete stop two feet from him he still used the opportunity to grasp both of her upper arms, his strong hands exerting just enough pressure to let her know who had the upper hand. She froze. "The last game of the season is this Sunday. I'll pick you up at one." Statement, not request; directive, not inquiry.

Aubree tried to curb her anger. The audacity! Squelching her rage down, knowing she could not afford to make an enemy of this man, she smiled apologetically. "No, Drew, I'm sorry. I've already agreed to attend the game with some girls from work." This happened to be the truth and Aubree smiled sweetly in the confidence she had spoiled his plans.

A scowl crossed his face and his eyes narrowed. She could see frustrated anger as a flush crept into his cheeks. "Isn't that too bad," he drawled. "Well, some other time!" He turned sharply on his heel and strode off towards the men's locker. Aubree watched until he'd disappeared through the wooden door, before she proceeded out of the facility to cross the campus to the opposite side where her small living space was located.

Aubree had a Specialist title and was only allotted a small space with a total of three rooms. Having a separate bedroom was a luxury. Lower level titles had just the one room and a small separate bathroom with shower stall. While she had never actually been in one, Aubree had heard that living quarters in the Facility, Supply and Power groups had large dormitories with rank after rank of bunks and everyone shared a large common bathroom.

She closed the door behind her, thumbing the deadbolt into place, as Siri greeted her. "Good morning, Aubree! Did you enjoy your morning workout?"

Aubree headed for her bathroom, replying, "Yes. Very enjoyable until the nuisance appeared again."

"What nuisance?" Siri asked politely.

"Drew Shipley!" Aubree replied, exasperation evident as she flung the sweat towel into the clothes hamper and turned to her closet. Sunday breakfast at her parents. She could dress casually. She began to sort through the slacks hanging in the neat space.

"Andrew Shipley, Security Resource Group, rank Detective. He is assigned to Sector Four, Human Resources. His service record is exemplary. Why do you use the term 'nuisance'?" Siri inquired, still polite, but Aubree detected a slight change and wondered again just how much of her conversation with Siri was private and how much was monitored. "Never mind, Siri. Disregard. Any messages while I was out?"

"Yes, Aubree. No. No messages."

Aubree nodded absently as she began to change into the blue jeans and sweatshirt that she had selected. "Siri, arrange transport to my father's house in ten minutes."

"Yes, Aubree."

Aubree strode into her main living space with the tiny cooking facility along one wall. She had a single sink, small refrigerator and microwave. A hot plate served as a stove. Cooking was uncommon as most people preferred to eat in the common dining areas. Aubree didn't use the space much herself, but she did enjoy a cup of coffee when she wanted it, and it was inconvenient to have to go to a food dispensary just for a cup of coffee.

She brewed one now and had it ready to go when Siri announced, "Your transport drone has arrived."

"Thanks." Aubree locked the door behind her and hurried down to the hovering drone. Strapping herself into the passenger seat in the front, relieved to find it empty of other passengers, she sat back and enjoyed the short flight to her father's spacious residence on the outskirts of sector eight.

Aubree's father was Mike Holten, the Vice President of Human Resource

Group and a direct report to founding Council of Ten member, Lawrence Johnson, who still presided as President of the Mid-Atlantic Hub. In the beginning, he had been the first Speaker and held that position for six years before stating someone else should take the role, it was unseemly for anyone to persist too long in the office.

A rumor had begun circulating that Lawrence planned to retire soon, but Aubree didn't join in the office gossip. She knew for a certainty that he was indeed planning to retire, very soon. He was identifying likely candidates for replacement throughout his vast corporation as well as the available pool of other corporate candidates, both from within the hub and those offered by his peers. Aubree knew it was likely to be a lengthy process. The replacement would be critical to the balance of power on the Council.

The drone landed smoothly on the large expanse of lawn, gold in the early light of winter, that stretched from the impressive front of the three-storied house. Very few residences of this sort endured, and their occupancy was reserved for the upper echelon of the corporate executive positions. Few married couples remained as more and more of the post-Centennial Crash generation began to come into the higher levels of office. Aubree's parents were more the exception than the norm.

She entered the spacious marbled foyer, catching the sounds of muffled voices coming from the dining room to the left of the main entrance. A maid hurried out, a covered dish held in her hands and an offended look on her face, until she spied Aubree in the foyer and then a bland mask descended. "Good morning," she mumbled, and quickly looking away hurried off towards the back of the large home where the kitchen was located.

Aubree took a deep breath and strode to the dining room doorway. Her mother, Sheri Holten, stood near the center of the large dining table that had seating space for eight, though only four ever used the room on a regular basis. The light from the brightly glowing chandelier reflected in Sheri's silky rich brown tresses and it was easy to see where Aubree got her looks. She was a mirror image of her mother physically. There the resemblance ended.

Sheri inspected her daughter now, her gaze sweeping her from top to bottom and she frowned as she fussily moved a bowl of strawberries to a different spot on the perfectly laid table. "I'm glad to see you didn't go to any trouble on our behalf this morning," she said waspishly.

Aubree shrugged, "Are we expecting State company? No one told me."

Her mother shot her an angry look. "No. We do not have State company joining us but it would be nice to think we ranked a little more than a sweatshirt and some jeans." She smoothed the flowing sheer material that draped artfully around her slender figure as she spoke.

Aubree rolled her eyes and went to pour some coffee from the urn on the sideboard. "Where's TJ?" She asked as she added sugar and then cream.

"Terry is getting dressed in appropriate attire for breakfast." She said primly, stressing her son's name, refusing to recognize the common nickname, a name he preferred everyone to use. "He and your father had an early game of tennis."

Aubree wandered to the double French doors overlooking the wide back terrace. The morning sunlight reflected brightly off the ice encrusted flagstones.

"There's my angel! How are you this morning, sweetheart?" The richly toned voice filled the room. Aubree turned to her father with a genuine smile and met him as he came around the table, planting a kiss on her forehead and giving her a hug.

She may not agree with all her father stood for, but she loved him deeply. She gave him a tight squeeze, inhaling the familiar scent of him before releasing her hold. "I am great, Dad. How are you? Did you beat TJ this morning?"

Mike Holten stood five feet ten inches tall and was athletically fit in his mid-fifties. Dressed in navy blue slacks and a striped blue sweater that Aubree recognized as an old favorite, the blue making his blue eyes even more prominent in the handsome face, Mike was the image of casualness, tattered old slippers peeking out from under the crisp edge of the slacks. "Three sets out of five." His smile was playful. "The old man's still got it."

"Show me an old man," Aubree sneered.

"It's not normal," TJ volunteered as he came into the room. "Just not normal that he should still beat me at tennis. My coach says I'm good enough to play real competitions—yet, he beats me every time!" He thrust a hand in frustration through the thick dark brown hair that resembled his father's. If Aubree had gotten her looks from her mother, TJ had received his from his father.

Mike grinned at his son and tapped his temple, "Psychological. I've told you and I can't stress how important it is. Know your competition. Half the game, half the win, is psychological."

"Psycho-whatever." Sheri interrupted in a chilly voice. "Can we save the psychobabble until we've been seated. Before breakfast gets cold?"

Aubree and TJ exchanged glances and took their accustomed seats across from one another while Mike sat at the head and Sheri took the seat beside TJ. "Terry, you just need to practice harder and you'll beat your father one of these days," she said with complete assurance as she began to dole out portions of scrambled eggs laced with melted chunks of cheddar cheese, sprinkled with fried onions, peppers and mushrooms.

Aubree took a deep breath and turned to her father, "I'm still having problems with Drew Shipley. He was at the gym again this morning."

Mike frowned and looked down at the piece of toast he was buttering. "Did he say anything in particular to be concerned about?"

"No." She hesitated, flushing a bit at the nasty remark he'd made when she'd shuddered at his touch. She didn't want to repeat that. Not in front of her mother and her brother.

"I don't see why it's a problem, Aubree," Sheri offered now.

Aubree sighed in resignation, shoulders slumping a bit as she sensed her mother was just warming up. "It's high time you did your civic duty, dear." Sheri added primly, spooning a portion of the eggs onto Aubree's plate.

Aubree cocked an eyebrow, "Civic duty, Mother? And what civic duty might it be that I'm remiss in performing?" Her tone was icy.

Sheri was unconcerned with Aubree's rising temper. She looked steadily across the table at her, raised a manicured right hand and rose her index finger, holding it up. "One, you are now thirty, soon to be thirty-one in less than six months. Two, you have a superior family line between your father and I," the left-hand index now rested on the raised middle finger and as she raised the ring finger, moving the index finger to it, she continued, "Third, you have not yet had a child to benefit society as you ought to have done." She took a deep breath and sat back in the finely crafted chair. "I, for one, find Drew Shipley to be an excellent candidate!" She turned her flashing green eyes on her husband who squirmed and kept his gaze firmly fixed on his toast.

TJ cleared his throat and Sheri snapped her frigid glare on him. "This is not a discussion you need to participate in, Terry!" She said sternly and then looked back at Aubree.

Aubree struggled to control her anger, keeping her voice tightly under control as she replied, "Yes, Mother, I am thirty. No, I have not had a child." She smiled in an angry sneer as she asked, "Is that what TJ and I are? Your contribution to society, what with your fine lineage and all?"

Sheri gasped in shock and anger flashed, "That is uncalled for! I'll not be talked to this way. I am merely reminding you that you are running out of time. Drew comes from a fine family. He's intelligent and good looking. I don't understand your objection."

"My objection is that I do not care for the man!" Aubree exploded. "Do you have some delusion that just because you're the niece of Lawrence Johnson that you're going to be allowed to keep and raise the child as your grandchild?" Aubree's voice was heavy with sarcasm. "You are aware they begin testing children at two and place them in appropriate learning pods within the Training Resource sector. Parents and grandparents are allowed partial visitation through the year and holiday sojourns." Aubree turned her eyes to her father, "She does understand that, right, Dad?"

Mike shrugged and said in a tired, resigned voice, having heard the argument many times, "Sheri, Aubree, can we set this aside and enjoy a family breakfast? A breakfast free from family squabbles? Please?"

"You got my vote," TJ mumbled around a forkful of eggs.

Sheri pinned one last furious glance on her daughter, exhaled a loud aggrieved sigh, and picked up her glass of orange juice.

Aubree turned her eyes back to her father, raising her eyebrows questioningly.

"I'll see if I can have a word with security. Maybe if I can get him reassigned…" He drifted off aimlessly.

Aubree sighed in frustration and pushed disconsolately at her plate of eggs, appetite vanished after the quarrel.

"It looks like the 'Skins have a shot at winning the division this year!" Mike said enthusiastically and TJ was quick to respond.

Aubree finished the remainder of her breakfast in silence and left as quickly as she could.

Monday at lunch, Aubree met her three friends at one of the round tables in the far corner of the eating pod. Setting down her tray of roasted pork in mushroom gravy with rice and seasoned green beans next to Sacha Benscoter, she got a good whiff of the chicken wings the younger girl was voraciously devouring. Her own meal seemed suddenly boring and unexciting as her mouth flooded from the tangy aroma.

Sacha shot a brown eye at her from under the fringe of short straight jet-black hair that framed her pixyish face, a daub of wing sauce smearing one corner of her finely carved mouth. "Want one?" She asked around a mouthful, waving a half-devoured wing towards Aubree.

Aubree brightened considerably as she snagged a wing from the plate.

Wendy forked more meat and salsa topping onto an already sagging tortilla chip as she asked, "Did you have breakfast with your folks yesterday?"

Aubree nodded, savoring the hot and spicy sauce the wings were slathered with.

"Well?" Wendy asked, exasperation in her voice. The overloaded tortilla failed, and the entire load slid back onto Wendy's plate. Determined, she dug the fork back in for another attempt.

Aubree hid a smile. "Well, what?"

Wendy frowned and managed to get the tortilla and its freight to her mouth which prevented further questioning.

Michelle giggled and picked daintily at the stuffed baked potato she almost religiously chose, occasionally getting a salad or wrap, but always the potato in cold weather. Her blonde hair tended to be lank and oily looking rather than lustrous, and where blue eyes were normally appealing on a blonde, on her they somehow just left her looking washed out and colorless. Her skin was alabaster white and tended to redden in ugly splotches easily. Obsessed with her weight, which for her diminutive five two was perfect at one hundred twenty pounds, she continually insisted she needed to lose weight. "Hi, Aubree," she said quickly while Wendy finished chewing.

"Did he say anything more about candidates?" Wendy whined as soon as she cleared her mouthful of food.

Aubree frowned. "No. I didn't get a chance to ask him. I told him about Drew. He showed up again, you know." She took a bite of the pork, pleased to find that the chef had not over-roasted it and the meat was nice and tender, the outer edge crisp with a nice crusty coating of herbs.

Sacha put down a bone devoid of any fleck of meat and reached for another wing. "And what did your father say about our boy Drew?" She tore into a fresh wing.

Aubree shrugged. "It was what my mother said that really pissed me off. Can you believe she had the audacity to suggest I should maybe consider having a child with Drew? Fulfill my obligation to society, as she put it."

Wendy's jaw had dropped, not a pretty sight, and Sacha froze in the act of biting into a wing. Michelle raised her head and stared at Aubree in wonder as if she had suddenly begun spouting ancient Greek. "She what?" she breathed in shock.

Aubree nodded her head. "You heard me right."

"Wow," Wendy finally expelled. "That's all I've got. Just wow."

Aubree shrugged and said nonchalantly, "Oh, you know, good family, nice bloodline and all that. Good looking. What could be better?" Her attitude ended on a bitter note.

"Can your dad help?" Sacha asked.

Aubree shrugged again. "I don't know. He mentioned something about speaking to security and maybe he could get him reassigned."

"I wonder who his security contact is," Sacha wondered, expression rueful. "That may or may not help the situation. Drew Shipley seems to have some connections. I'm not sure how high. I don't think Larocque but someone close to him."

Aubree nodded miserably, "I tried to access his file, but it's blocked, like most of security is at our level."

Michelle asked timidly, "Was there another incident? You said he showed up again."

Wendy and Sacha glanced quickly at Aubree, Sacha looking contrite that she had overlooked that part of Aubree's original statement.

"Yeah." She told them about the incident in the gym.

"You've got to change your schedule," Sacha said pragmatically.

Aubree nodded. "I've already considered that. There's a facility in the pod building where we work. I can go there after work instead of using the one by my home."

Michelle nodded in agreement. "Out of sight, out of mind. Maybe he'll forget about you if he doesn't see you for a while."

Aubree sighed wistfully, "That would be so nice!"

"Corinne's a little worried about it, you know," Sacha said before picking apart another wing.

"Why is Corinne worried?" Aubree asked alertly.

Sacha raised her eyebrows and cocked her head at Aubree. "Really? Security? That mean anything to you?"

Aubree reddened, a little embarrassed but also understanding that Sacha was right. "I know," she whispered and pushed her tray away, her appetite suddenly gone.

"Hey!" Sacha suddenly cried out, making one of her lightening changes from somber to gay. She wiped her hands on the wet towel provided with the messy finger food, dried them quickly and clapped Aubree on the shoulder. "It's cool. We know it's not your fault and we'll figure it out. We just need to be careful, that's all. Like always, right?" she asked, looking quickly around at the other three, mood briefly serious again.

Aubree nodded along with Michelle and Wendy. "Speaking of Corinne," Michelle spoke quietly, glancing around to be sure there were no obvious eavesdroppers nearby. "She got a new list this morning. Another one from Packy."

Wendy groaned and Aubree felt her own shoulders slump. Sacha sat up straighter, carefully setting aside her last wing and wiping her fingers on the wet towel. "Again?" she asked in surprise, looking at Michelle, brown eyes wide with shock. "Packy just hit ten percent two months ago."

"I know." Michelle responded a little defensively, body language speaking volumes as she shrank away from Sacha.

"I'm sorry," Sacha mumbled. "It just gets to me, you know?" She looked pleadingly at Michelle, hoping for understanding and knowing after long years of experience that her friend would commiserate.

"That explains why she wouldn't come today, then," Wendy said, pushing away her own plate of mostly finished nachos. "I'll bet she's doing the prelim scan and narrow. Let's be ready when she asks us to help, okay?" Wiping her mouth, she quickly collected her things and the rest followed suit.

It wasn't until the end of that afternoon that Aubree heard from Corinne. She had been busy making updates to the database on the last batch of inter-hub transfers when she saw the notification at the bottom of her screen from Corinne. She quickly tapped on the icon and a small window opened. Corinne smiled and asked, "Do you have plans for this evening?"

Aubree shook her head. "Nothing urgent. Catch dinner at the dining center and I was thinking I might watch that new series this evening."

Corinne nodded. "Well, in that case, care to join me for happy hour?"

Aubree returned Corinne's smile and nodded. "You bet. Usual place?"

Corinne nodded again. "Meet you there at five thirty?"

"Works for me!" Aubree said brightly.

Corinne terminated her end of the connection and Aubree got back to work, wrapping up her end of day activities.

She was not surprised to find Sacha and Wendy already seated with

Corinne at a table not far from the over loud speakers flanking the small stage in the club the women frequently met at in Sector Four. The club was called The Sherwood Taverne and was styled like an old English pub. Aubree always found the loudness of the speakers near their table to be annoying but understood that it drowned out the possibility of being overheard or recorded. Corinne was never too careful.

She smiled at Aubree now and nodded as she took the seat next to Sacha. "Michelle coming?" she asked the group.

Wendy nodded. "She got delayed with a system patch update. She should be here soon."

A waitress sauntered up and asked what Aubree was having and did anyone else need a refill? Aubree ordered a spiced cider and looked around the club. This early in the evening it was sparsely populated, patrons sprinkled around the tables in the large, dimly lit room. Stone pillars divided the space and offered privacy.

Michelle arrived along with Aubree's cider and she hurriedly gave her order of white wine to the waitress as she settled into the seat between Corinne and Wendy. "Sorry! I don't know why I never seem to get my system updates until five minutes before I shut down," she sighed with exasperation.

Corinne smiled commiseratively and then took a deep breath before addressing them. "We've got a new list from Packy."

"So we heard," Sacha murmured.

Corinne looked at Sacha, sadness etched in the lines at the corners of her eyes and mouth, her usually glowing mahogany skin a pale ashen color in the weak light, the brown eyes mournful. "I don't know what's going on."

Aubree ventured, "This is the second time in two months. It was ten percent the last time. How many this time?"

Just then the waitress appeared with Michelle's wine and the table was hushed until she left. Corinne reached into her purse and discreetly passed a small chip to each of the other four women. They quickly palmed the tiny devices and they disappeared into the various purses and clutches each carried. "There were, by my guesstimate, another five percent this time. All destined for work centers."

Michelle groaned and shook her head. "So many. And we've had the same thing going on in Gullub and Wegah."

Corinne nodded. "Unfortunately, OUR can only absorb fifty more coming out of Packy right now." OUR was the short name for the Outsider Underground Railroad, named after the original Underground Railroad from the Civil War era and its function was much the same. There was a network of outsiders that had made contact inside the various hubs and helped to transfer work center bound individuals to a new life outside of the hub. Aubree wondered what that life was like without the protection of the hub walls keeping dangerous elements out. She knew conditions had to be better than being in a forced labor work center.

At the sounds of muttered distress passing around the table, Corinne added softly. "It's better than zero, isn't it?"

Aubree had no choice but to agree. If, through their efforts, they could reduce even one person being assigned to one of the secretive work centers then she felt she had done something good.

"Do the usual, please. Each of you has a list of two hundred names. Go through the list and identify the top twenty-five. Get the chips back to me as soon as you can. I'll need to make the final decision and get the information back to my point of contact in Packy. I'll give each of you the list to scrub the database once we've confirmed the transfer."

No one cared to stay long after that, each depressed by the volume of people they wouldn't be able to assist, small comfort in the fact that some would be saved. Aubree collected her heavy coat and pulling on her gloves walked with Sacha to the door.

"Call a lift?" Sacha asked.

Aubree shook her head. "No. I think a walk would do me some good."

Sacha shivered as they went out into the dark winter evening, streetlights brightly illuminating the already dark sidewalk at seven at night. "Not me!" she said "Too darn cold! Where is that drone?"

Just as she spoke the words, a drone dropped soundlessly out of the sky above them, hovering at the curb, while Sacha inserted her identification card in the slot, confirming she had called it, and then payment was automatically deducted from her available credits. She tossed Aubree a wave as the drone shot up and quickly out of sight.

Aubree turned to begin the short walk three blocks away to her housing unit when her arm was suddenly ceased in a strong grip. Heart pounding, Aubree pulled back and looked quickly up to meet the cool hazel eyes of Drew Shipley.

CHAPTER FOUR

"Good day and welcome to the only news that counts, the news you need to know, today's True News broadcast. This is your news anchor, Erica Campbell, along with my co-host, Edward Sanner, coming to you today from the sunny Pacific Hub! The weather is frigid back home in North Eastern Hub with temps rumored to reach a new record low in the coming week while it's a balmy sixty-five here and a rare sunny, if windy, day." The screen was showing a vibrant blonde with perfectly sculpted features deliver this news with her award-winning smile. The screen shifted to her co-anchor, an equally striking male with arresting pale blue eyes.

"That's right, Erica! We'll hear more about the weather later in our broadcast. First in today's news, Frank Baba, Speaker for the Council of Ten, met with the Crown Prince of Saudi Arabia to discuss sanction relief. The United States has been under heavy sanctions from the European Pact and other international countries since the Cataclysm of 2019. Today's talks represent a major breakthrough in America's recovery from her egregious errors of the past and a potentially bright future as we move forward to partner globally once again." The anchor smiled a winning dimpled smirk into the camera.

"Thank you, Edward. Now, in other news, Yvette Musk, the granddaughter of space magnate and genius Elon Musk, announced today that they will be opening the lottery for the new deep space expedition vessel, The Enterprise, which is scheduled to launch in an amazing nine months! Tune in tonight to channel 2419 for a detailed view of the vessel docked now at its space foundry and how you could be a member of this exciting historic event!"

The screen dissolved into a picture of space, galaxies dazzling with gaseous clouds in varied colors. A voice began to speak as the scene slowly revolved, revealing more wonders. "The Enterprise, named for our beloved vessel of television antiquity is fully constructed and is even now being stocked with the necessary supplies to sustain life in deep space." The screen now began to reveal a gleaming vessel, massive in construct, lights glowing across it's surface with portholes gleaming whitely in the vast blackness of the surrounding space. Along both sides was stenciled the name, The Enterprise, in bold script.

The screen switched to a view of the impressive main deck of the vessel where the captain and crew would command the ship as it navigated out into the vast distances of space. Seats were luxuriously appointed in rich leathers and gleamed in the well-lit space. Large screens lined the walls with views of the surrounding space and switches at the captain's seat would allow the views to change to various cameras located throughout the ship.

Then the screen began to show images of other areas of the ship: the common dining area, the exercise facility, the algae farm where fresh air would be produced for the entire ship, the agricultural deck where fields of agrarian crops flourished under artificial lights simulating the sun's necessary spectrum, the health bay with all the advanced equipment to rival the best healthcare facility on the planet, the well-appointed sleeping bays.

"Be sure to watch tonight's broadcast on channel 2419 for a detailed overview of the ship and it's first destination, the Andromeda galaxy. Once a mere concept of science fiction, now a reality."

The screen changed back to the newsroom and a dark-haired man with sparkling brown eyes and a thick mustache smiled into the camera. "Good day. AJ Olivier here with this evening's sports update. The US Figure Skating team competed in Toronto today for next year's Winter Olympic Games to be held in Tallinn, Estonia. Two promising young ladies, both from the North Eastern Hub, look to be staunch defenders of the current US Gold Medal." An image of the two skaters, posing on the ice, appeared over his shoulder along with the logo for the upcoming Olympic Games.

Then he turned, the camera tracking, and the logos for the Gullub Cowboys and the Midah Redskins filled the image behind him. "This Sunday will be the showdown between historic rivals, Gulf Hub Cowboys and the Mid-Atlantic Redskins. The two teams will be competing for the Division Championship and the winner will go on to meet the winner of the match-up between Western Gateway Chiefs and Rocky Mountain Colts scheduled for next Sunday. I don't need to remind you that the winner of that match-up will advance to Super Bowl Seventy!" He grinned and the camera cut back to Erica and Edward.

Erica flashed a toothy smile and Edward shook his head, "That'll be some game, AJ!"

The camera focused in on Erica as she continued smoothly, "Elsewhere in news today, a man was seriously injured by an attacking bear outside the walls of the Pacific Northwest Hub." The screen showed a map of the US with the ten corporate population hubs indicated with stars and then it zoomed in to a detailed view of the far northwest of the country where the Pacific Northwest Hub was located. A red dot was steadily flashing off to the east of the star and the screen zoomed in further and dissolved into a satellite image of the densely forested area to the east of Panoh's walls.

Then the image changed to that of a badly bruised and injured man, one side of his face grotesquely swollen, his body strapped securely into a portable stretcher and being rushed towards a waiting med-drone.

"It's unclear why the man was outside the hub walls and authorities say they were lucky to pick up his homing device beacon. The extent of the man's injuries required immediate sedation and Security has not been able to question him. It is surmised that he must have activated his beacon when the bear attacked. Medical authorities say he is in critical but stable condition and expect him to make a full recovery."

The screen switched back to a now somber image of Erica Campbell. "As a reminder to our valued citizens, the Security Group cannot protect you if you wander outside of a corporate population hub. There are numerous dangers, not the least of which being wild animals. As all of you know, we have had to report all too frequently about crazed Outsiders attacking Hub dwellers."

"Thank you, Erica, for that important reminder." Edward smoothly rejoined. The camera switched to him and he allowed himself to be captured in a serious pose before once again flashing his brilliant smile. "The President of Human Resources, former Speaker, founding father and member of the Council of Ten, Lawrence Johnson, announced today that the Senior Living Coordination team was excited to declare spots for fifty-five lucky seniors in this year's annual Hawaiian Retirement lottery! As a reminder, the lottery will be drawn during the half-time show for Super Bowl Seventy in each hub HR center. All seniors are eligible and will be automatically entered. Good luck!"

The screen changed to an image of a turquoise blue wave crashing on a pristine white sandy beach where senior citizens lolled in relaxed poses on lounge chairs facing the sparkling water with a volcano emitting a cloud of smoke in the far distance. "Senior living has never been so good as it is on the white beaches of Hawaii! Enjoy finely crafted meals prepared by master chefs from the nation's top culinary schools!" The screen changed and a crowned rib roast gleaming with sauce and surrounded by pineapples, cherry tomatoes and oranges filled the screen, a frothy Pina Colada with a slice of pineapple on the sugary glass rim and a jaunty paper parasol in bright colors glistening beside it. "Turn down room service provided daily." A sumptuous suite with an over-sized bed now filled the screen, a white terry robe and slippers invitingly arrayed. "There are tons of activities to keep you on the move!" Images of exercise facilities, Olympic pool, jogging trails through tropical foliage, bicycle paths on the edge of breathtaking cliffs above the crashing surf and underwater scuba diving played across the screen. "As a reminder, extra lottery entries can be purchased through your local Media Resource agent."

The screen changed again, focusing back on Edward Sanner who was not quite prepared, the camera catching him reading the script on his teleprompter built into the desk surface in front of him. Realizing he was back on camera he jerked slightly and automatically smiled at the camera, a long-ingrained habit. "And now we'll cut to Barb Warrenton with tonight's national weather forecast. Barb?"

The camera switched to a chunky woman in a tight-fitting red sweater dress standing in front of a map of the United States showing the latest weather patterns. "Thanks, Edward! Hello, citizens! We've had an exceptionally dry and cold start to the winter season, especially in our southwest region. Pacific Hub reports warmer temperatures than normal but elsewhere temps are on average five degrees colder than normal. A cold front is pushing down out of central Canada and we have a rare snow fall forecasted for the Southeastern Hub the day after tomorrow. Northeastern, Mid-Atlantic, Midwestern and Western Gateway Hubs can all expect to see some potential accumulation from this weather pattern. The system should move out by this weekend and we expect to see warmer temps moving into next week with no other major storm systems on the horizon."

The screen switched back to Erica again and she smiled broadly. "Well, that concludes our global and national portion of today's broadcast. As always, please access the 2000 series of channels to locate various news broadcasts and visit our web site for the most up-to-date information! We will switch our broadcast now to your local service."

The camera zoomed out to capture both smiling faces as Edward and Erica faced the camera with the True News logo shining between them from the screen behind.

This transitioned to the network logo and then faded into the local channel logo for Western Gateway Hub, Wegah. Two news anchors appeared on the screen, a man of clearly Asian descent with high cheekbones in a handsome and strongly framed face with brown eyes and an attractive woman with cat-shaped russet colored eyes, deep brown hair with auburn highlights framing a squarish face.

"Good day!" Henry began. "I'm Henry Jackson. Welcome to today's Western Gateway Hub True News Broadcast coming to you from the Nocitra Building here in Sector Four of Wegah along with my partner, Jean Campo. In today's news, a woman was injured in a mid-air drone collision. Authorities and members of the Facilities Resource Group are investigating the cause of the accident. The collision occurred during lunch hour traffic when drone usage is at its highest. The woman suffered a broken leg and a broken wrist while the other drone passenger suffered no injuries."

The screen cut to a frantic looking dark-skinned man with thick unruly dark hair, of apparent Hispanic descent, dressed in a Supply Chain delivery uniform. "I was on lunch break," he stammered nervously into the microphone thrust in front of him while the camera shifted to show the wreckage of the two drones. "I don't know what happened! One minute I'm heading to the commissary in Sector Nine…" He looked around nervously, licking his lips, "I work here in Sector Five, you know…" Another pleading glance around. "I don't know what happened!" He wailed.

The camera cut back to Henry, a placid smile on his face. "The woman injured was a teacher in the Training Resource Group and was rushed to a nearby medical facility. Human Resources advises that she is fine and after a period of recuperation will be back in the classroom."

"Wow! I'll bet that was frightening," Jean exclaimed, and the camera shifted to focus on her. "What's going on in sports today, David?"

David Coley, sun-streaked tannish-blonde hair swept carelessly back, smiled seductively, blue eyes twinkling. He had a habit of pausing ever so briefly with a picture-perfect pose before launching into the daily sports news. "There's lots going on, Jean! Next weekend our own Wegah Chiefs will be contending for the title against the Romoh Colts! Our rookie quarterback has been challenging records in all categories and they're on a hot streak!" The screen filled with the statistics for the professional football team. "The Colts have a few injuries on their offensive line which means our Chiefs defensive line has an opportunity to inflict some damage! The game is scheduled for next Sunday and will be hosted here at the Wegah Repka Stadium in Sector Three. Local channels will carry contests for tickets and tickets can be purchased through a Media Resource Concierge. This weekend will be the faceoff between division rivals, Midah Redskins and Gullub Cowboys. This is going to be another barn shaker, Henry and Jean! You won't want to miss it! It will be aired on channel 1120 and in every major sports bar! Don't miss the excitement of watching the game with fellow fans!"

A young, buxom brunette, hair cut in a short and sassy style, curling in a cute cap across her head, wearing a low-cut peach colored blouse that revealed quite a bit of cleavage, beamed into the camera, balancing a tray laden with a foaming pitcher of amber beer, frosted mugs and a four-person hookah.

"Come on down to O'Neill's Sports Bar in Sector Two! We'll have the game on four big screens, bottomless buckets of hot wings and refreshing pitchers of cold beer to wash them down!"

The camera zoomed back from the waitress, framing her posed seductively in the center with pool tables, dart boards and a shuffleboard game arrayed behind her, a bar stretching off and out of the image to one side while a jukebox gleamed opposite.

The screen shifted back and was again focused on Jean. "A community Christmas dinner will be held at the Sector Six community dining center on Christmas Day from eleven in the morning until one in the afternoon. It's hard to believe, Henry, that we're talking about Christmas but it's only a couple of weeks away!"

The screen pulled back and included Henry, looking at Jean and nodding his head agreeably. "It sure is, Jean. It just snuck up on us this year!"

"What's in store for us with weather, Dana?" Jean asked and the camera turned to center on a young woman in her early twenties with long wavy brown hair and a pretty smile, wearing blue blouse and black slacks superimposed over a map of the Western Gateway area.

"It may not seem like Christmas, Jean, but it feels like Christmas! Today is relatively mild as we registered forty-one this afternoon, but temps are going to plummet tonight as a cold front moves in. The warmer air we've had coming out of the Gulf will push back and will leave behind plenty of moisture…so, unfortunately, this means we're going to see some ice! If you don't have to be out tomorrow…don't! Isn't it a blessing so many of us can work where we live and not have to worry about the weather, Jean? I wish I could say this system would be moving out in the near future, but it looks like it's here to stay for the next five days. It's going to be a cold and icy start to December!"

"Thank you, Dana!" Henry took over. The camera centered on him, "A reminder from Alexa: next year, 2036, being an even numbered year, citizens will be expected to vote on national and local issues on the fifteenth of even numbered months. That means the next mandatory ballot is slated for February fifteenth. Issues on the table for vote are outlined in detail at the Wegah Voting Administration website. Failure to comply can result in severe disciplinary action.

"And we'll end this evening's story on a lighter note! Morgan Davis, a chef from Supply Chain Group assigned to the O'Neill's Sports Bar kitchen in Sector Two, received a surprise visit from Supply Chain Western Gateway Vice President, Brook Crawford."

The screen showed a beaming man with chubby cheeks, thick eyebrows over widened brown eyes, mouth gaping in surprise, clasping the hand of an ebony-skinned woman with luxurious black wavy hair cascading to her shoulders, dressed in a gray two piece skirt suit and white blouse, matching gray pumps on her feet.

"Davis was recognized for excellence in service and received a significant credit award in addition to a commemorative plaque. Great job, Morgan! And that will end tonight's broadcast. Have a wonderful day!"

CHAPTER FIVE

"Good morning, Adam," Siri cheerfully greeted Adam as he switched on the light over his bathroom sink and peered at the stubble that had appeared overnight. "Today is Monday, December seventeenth. There are no urgent items on your Alexa To Do List. Your Director, Alan Vince, wishes to see you at eight-thirty in his office in Sector Eight. Do you know the location, Adam?" Siri asked politely.

He was frowning at his reflection. Why would Alan Vince want to see him? "Yes, Siri," he said absently. "Siri, notify my manager and update my schedule so everyone can see that I'll be in a meeting."

"Already done, Adam."

He smiled, appreciating the niceties of a feature like Siri. It kept life organized. "Coffee ready?" he asked.

"Of course."

He quickly shaved before heading to the tiny kitchen alcove where a hot pot of coffee sat waiting. "Today's weather, Siri?" he asked. Usually she volunteered this information and he wondered, amused, if she had been piqued that he might assume the coffee was unprepared.

"Today will be mostly cloudy," Siri announced cheerfully, and he chuckled at his own foolishness. Siri was a machine, artificially intelligent, not capable of emotions. "It is not a laughing matter," Siri continued smoothly, "There will be a wind out of the north between six and nine miles per hour with a temperature predicted to be no higher than thirty-six with a low of possibly thirty-two. That means ice is possible."

He glanced at the clock. It was seven thirty, his usual time, which normally allowed him to fit a workout into his morning schedule. Today he'd need to travel from his pod in the south-central portion of Sector Ten, across Sector Three, to the main security executive pod on the northeast side of Sector Eight. It was only about ten and a half miles, a ten-minute drone flight, but

50

it was much too cold to consider drone flying.

"Siri arrange for a vehicle with fleet. I'll need to pick it up in fifteen minutes." That would give him about thirty minutes, after he'd checked out the vehicle, for the drive which shouldn't take more than twenty. He didn't want to be late for this meeting. He wracked his brain again, wondering why his director would want to see him, but there had been no recent event, that he could think of, that would result in this summons.

"They have already been alerted, Adam, and a vehicle has been delivered for your use. It is parked in front of the housing pod."

He was impressed with this foresight. "Thank you, Siri."

Nervously, he carried his cup of coffee back into his tiny bathroom cubby and peered at his reflection in the mirror. Cool grayish colored eyes returned his gaze, appearing calmer than he felt inside. His brown hair was combed neatly in a side part, the thick waves falling neatly into place. The face was strong, shaped squarely, with eyes well-spaced above a classically sculpted nose. His lips were thin but nicely formed. The gray of his Security uniform enhanced his eyes. Glancing at the digital time display in the bottom corner of the smart mirror, he decided there was no reason to delay.

Grabbing his warm winter coat from the hook near the door, he went out into the dim hall of the housing pod. His unit was in the far northeast corner of the building, and the hallway extended past seven identical doors to a facing window at the opposite end. The elevator was located midway down the hall and he rode it to the lobby. He nodded at Angela Fujisawa at the service desk. Angela was in her mid-forties and always had a cheerful disposition. She smiled at Adam now and nodding at the front door said, "Your ride's here. Nice wheels. Be careful out there. Could be slick."

"So Siri says," he grinned and opened the outer door, the cold air making him catch his breath.

A black Hummer sat idling at the curb, plumes of white smoke exhausting into the frigid air. Hunching into the coat, Adam ran for the idling vehicle. As he slid behind the steering wheel, he was pleased to note it was one of the upgraded self-driving versions. He was grateful. He trusted the computer instincts onboard far more than his own with the potential for black ice on the bridges when they got near the Kansas and Missouri Rivers. The Hummer was well equipped to deal with these conditions and Adam could just sit back and let it do the work. He verified the destination on the navigation system and then sat back to watch the scenery as the vehicle took him to the Security Western Gateway Hub Headquarters building.

The drive was mostly gray with little to be seen other than pod buildings, alight in the overcast day. Few people were out that did not need to be. A Power group was working on a utility pole at the intersection of sectors ten and three and he was thankful his job allowed him the comfort of being indoors in the warmth. It hadn't always. Back when he'd been on beat with

Erick, they'd been outside. Of course, they'd usually been in a cruiser—but not always. Thinking of Erick now reminded him that he'd wanted to check up on Erick, see if he could trace where he'd been reassigned.

It took eighteen minutes for the Hummer to deliver him to the white marble, four-story structure squatting amidst beautiful landscaped groups, barren now in the cold of winter, a glint of the Missouri River sparkling in the distance behind and to the east of the somehow ominous structure.

For all its beauty, he had always felt uneasy and had never liked the hushed feeling in the echoing corridors. No one ever spoke in loud tones. The lobby soared the three of the four flights with a massive bank of glass windows. The main lobby was formed in a half circle facing the main entrance, wings extending to left and right behind secured access glass doors. Three people in the gray SRG uniform stood behind the desk alertly watching everyone entering.

He advanced to the desk where a small line had formed in front of two of the three attendees. While two assisted people who had forgotten badges, or, like himself, were there for early meetings or a day of substitute work, the third kept a steady eye on the entrance and flow of traffic through the controlled access doors, making sure no one slipped in behind someone else's access, each person being required to swipe.

It was finally his turn and he laid his employee badge on the counter. A man that appeared to be in his twenties with dark brown hair, dark eyes and a mustache looked Adam over quickly and then looked at the badge. His name tag declared him as Jim Seidenberg.

"Good morning, Jim," Adam said as smoothly as possible. "Adam Miller. I've got a meeting with Director Vince at eight thirty."

Jim looked at him for a minute and then with no change in expression and with no response dropped his eyes to a clipboard on the desk in front of him, only the edge visible from Adam's line of vision. Apparently satisfied that Adam was indeed on the list, without further preamble, he picked up a phone receiver from a base Adam had not been able to see and Adam heard him say, "Director's eight thirty is here." He was silent, listening. He nodded. Adam wondered if it was habit or was it a vid-phone? "Thank you." He returned the receiver to the hidden base and looked back at Adam. "They'll be down to escort you up shortly. You can have a seat over there." He indicated an upholstered bench that was anchored to the curving wall that flanked the central lobby area.

Adam retrieved his badge and went to sit close to the middle of the curve where he could watch all entrances. A glance at his watch and he saw he was still twenty minutes early. It was only ten minutes after eight. The flow of people through the lobby was steady until about fifteen after the hour and then it trickled to a few that were obviously frantic at being so late.

He had just begun to wonder if they intended on leaving him here until eight thirty when a man of moderate height with ginger hair and sparkling brown eyes, in his early thirties came through the glass door to his right and approached Adam with his hand extended. "Adam? I'm Hank. Hank Flaherty. Welcome! Apologies for the delay. It seems the elevator was busy with its morning freight delivery." He smiled apologetically and pumped Adam's hand in a firm handshake. "Please follow me."

Adam followed him through the glass door and down a narrow corridor, windows lining the walls on both sides with views of the front and a private inner courtyard. Adam saw two squirrels in hot pursuit in the private courtyard before they exited that corridor and arrived at an elevator bank. Here they stopped and waited with a handful of other late arrivals.

They exited on the third floor and Hank led Adam down a hallway that led off in both directions from the elevator. As they cleared the elevator bank another glass door appeared on the right and Hank motioned Adam to follow him through. They were in a lushly carpeted seating area, chrome chairs with bright orange stuffed fabric bringing brightness to contrast with the gray day on the other side of the large plate glass windows looking over the front of the building. Adam thought he saw the Hummer parked at the front of the large parking area, not far from flagpole. Four doors led off the seating area. Hank indicated an orange chair, and said, "Mr. Vince will just be another moment or so. Would you like some coffee?"

"Yes, please. Two sugars, one cream."

Hank nodded and disappeared behind the door on the left hand in the wall facing the windows. Adam glanced around. There were tables with magazines scattered, a silent television monitor played in an upper corner of the room with a European Stock Market ticker tape running at the bottom, some talking head with some news channel talking to some other talking head, an image of Frank Baba's office in the background.

Within moments, Hank reappeared with the coffee in a ceramic cup, in security gray with the SRG logo in orange, and then disappeared back behind the closed door, leaving him to wait. He sat on the edge of one of the seats, being careful not to spill the hot coffee.

He had time to watch one set of talking anchors be replaced by a new set, this time two women, before the door opened again and Hank motioned for him to follow. "Mr. Vince will see you now."

He followed through the door, finding a small office that was apparently Hank's, filled mostly with a three-sided desk that had a pot of coffee perched on one end. A door to the left of the one he had come through was standing open and Hank waved him through it now.

Alan Vince was not what he was expecting. He was a slight man, almost effeminate in build. He stood about five seven and was extremely thin. He had receding light brown hair thinning into deep pockets at his temples with reedy, almost non-existent, eyebrows above wire frame glasses from which a pair of intelligent brown eyes peered above a blade of a nose. He stood behind an impressive walnut desk which stood before an expansive view of a large rolling lawn that ran down to the shores of the Missouri River in the distance, dark on this overcast day.

Adam strode across the short distance with what he hoped appeared to be confidence and shook the proffered hand before taking a seat in one of the two chairs facing the desk. Alan Vince resumed his seat and sat for a moment looking pensively at a folder. Deliberately, he opened the folder while stating, "You've done very well in Security."

Adam wasn't sure what to say. "Thank you," seemed appropriate.

More silence while Alan read the page and flipped to the next one. "A double major in Criminal Justice and Computer Science?"

Adam nodded, proudly, "Yes, sir. Missouri State."

Alan nodded and kept reading. Adam fought the urge to fidget. Finally, he closed the folder and looked back at Adam. "Tell me about the project to install the surveillance system." He had a soft voice. Adam suspected it might be deceptive.

"We installed camera systems to provide surveillance at the meet point locations. Located in the Love's Truck Stop in Des Moines, Iowa and at the Pilot Travel Center in Salina, Kansas. There are three cameras at each location. One provides a view of the generator, another of the fuel island and the third of the entry point at each location."

Alan nodded. "I am familiar with the specifics. What would you do different?"

Adam thought for a moment. Considering how well the project had gone he hadn't spent a lot of time thinking of doing things differently. He'd been pleased with the results. All of the postmortems he had conducted said the same thing. There was one thing, though. "I'd have installed twice as many, maybe even three times as many, cameras."

Alan's eyebrows shot up and he leaned back in his seat, resting his hands on the armrests of his chair. "Explain."

"What we installed is sufficient. We can monitor the fuel islands remotely, we can keep an eye on the generator, and in the case of Des Moines, we can watch the only entrance." He shrugged negligently as he added, "Salina isn't much of a problem. There's more than one entrance but we can really see all we need to with the one camera we have. No one is entering from any entrance without us knowing about it."

"So why more?"

Adam shrugged, struggling with how to explain instinct. "I just think we should have greater surveillance of the road itself for a distance leading up to the meet point. Once your fifty yards from the meet point, we're blind. If we see something suspicious, we can get air support, but Des Moines is a couple of hours away by car. Less by drone but still too long."

Alan nodded and Adam grew quiet. "What, in your opinion, is it that you did right?"

Adam smiled. This was something he had spent a lot of time thinking about. "Planning. I'm a big believer in planning and this project proved it to me. I spent hours planning. Not just on how things needed to go and when, but on contingencies. The what ifs. I know a lot of that was wasted effort because I never needed to implement those contingencies. But a couple of times I did, and I was glad I'd done the planning in advance. It took a lot of the stress out of it, too."

Alan smiled in response to that, chuckling softly. "I'm sure it did. By the way, I happen to agree with you."

"Sir?"

"More cameras. I agree that we need more cameras. Unfortunately, that project is going to have to wait for a bit. Unless, perhaps, you could spec if out and hand it off to someone else to implement. I have something else in mind for you. Can you do it again?"

"Sir?" Adam hated to sound like an idiot, repeating himself.

"I have a request from no less than Ben Larocque, President of Security, to install surveillance measures at every Corporate Population Hub." He stopped speaking, folded his hands on the folder on his desk, and leaned over them towards Alan, eyes watching intently from behind the thick lenses.

Adam waited a moment and then answered the original question. "I believe I could do it, sir. Yes. That's a huge scale though…" The true scale struck him for the first time. This was something big. He met Alan's gaze squarely and sat a little straighter in his chair.

"I'd like to offer you a promotion, Adam," Alan said, voice still silky soft. He extracted a slim blue binder from the folder and held it out to Adam. "You'll find in there an offer for a Global Technical Manager of Security reporting to Brent Gear. Brent reports to me. You'll work out of this building, in fact. If you accept the offer, that is. If you accept the offer, you'll be expected to coordinate the installation of a surveillance network at every meet point for every hub. All ten of them. One is done."

Adam sat stunned. A promotion to management. Relocation to Sector Eight. The demands and satisfaction of working a large project again. "Yes! I'll take it!"

Alan chuckled softly, "Wouldn't you care to look at the offer first?"

Adam grinned and opened the blue binder Alan had handed him. The annual credit increase was significant. Adam briefly scanned through the offer, noting he'd change residence to the management housing pod in Sector Eight, and work in this very building in something called the A-wing on the first floor. Adam looked back up at Alan and nodded sincerely. "I do accept this offer. When do I start?"

Alan smiled and sat back. "Immediately." He waved a hand expansively.

"You need to meet with HR, of course. They'll take you through the onboard orientation. There will be a whole regimen of classes you'll need to attend making the step up to management. Glad to have you on the team."

Adam sat unsurely, gripping the folder, and Alan smiled back at him silently. Then Alan pressed a button on his phone, "Can you step in, Hank?"

"On my way," Hank's cheerful response replied. Almost instantly the connecting door opened, and Hank appeared on the threshold.

Alan nodded for him to come in and then indicated Adam with his right hand. "Adam has just accepted an offer to join our Internal Security management team. He'll need to be processed through HR next. Can you set him up?"

Hank grinned at Adam. "Congratulations! Let me give Susan a buzz. Susan Neuville is our assigned Human Resource Specialist. She'll take care of you." Turning smoothly back to Alan he asked, "Was there anything else?"

Alan smiled at Adam and said, "No. Not unless Adam has any questions…?"

"No!" Adam rose to his feet, said, "Thanks," one more time and followed Hank out the door.

Adam paused and looked up at the grim façade of the ugly squat building in Sector Four, near the junction with Sectors Nine and One, called the Shawnee Elderly Living Pod. He tried not to think of it as a nursing center but that was all too clearly what it was. He had tried to fight his mother's transfer to the pod, unsuccessfully. It was mandatory that all unemployed hub personnel accept quarters in an assisted elderly living pod no later than the first day following their sixty-first birthday where the cost of their care could be vastly reduced, and efficiencies gained by centralization. Only the extremely wealthy had other options available to them and Megan Miller, Adam's mother, was not extremely wealthy.

Megan had gotten a job as a bank teller not far from her home in Eureka Springs when her husband, Jordan, died tragically in an accident when Adam was seventeen. She chose to stay there until Adam was a junior in college and it was clear that she would need to be in or near a corporate population center if she wished to live comfortably. She also wanted to be closer to Adam.

She had no problem getting a job as a bank teller in the new hub and was happy to see Adam about once a week until six years ago when the bank automation network went live. With the launch of the new financial network based on employment credits, bonuses, awards and other means of gaining credits the traditional concept of banking was entirely changed, eliminating the former teller position. Megan found herself laid off at the age of fifty-four and no one wanted to hire her. She had enough money built, saved from the original life insurance policy from Jordie as well as a modest amount she added herself, and she chose to retire, staying near Adam. Then, last April, she'd been forced to move here.

He gathered together the large bag he'd packed for the occasion and hurried through the single glass door into the small lobby. There was no attendant at the dark desk, but he didn't expect there to be one today. It didn't matter, anyway. His Security level gave him clearance, and he was on the permitted visitor list. Scanning his identification at the reader on the wall over the elevator button, he inspected his appearance in the overhead security mirror giving the security desk behind him a three-hundred-and-sixty-degree view.

Not that there was much to see. The light bulb was low wattage and flickered occasionally. The red light in the reader panel turned green and he pressed the only available button, up. He could hear the mechanics of the car as it set in motion.

He exited on the seventh floor and turned to the left, stopping at room seven twenty-seven. Combing his free hand through his hair, patting it into place, he shifted the bag and opened the door.

Megan was waiting for him. Her blue eyes, mirrors of his own, glimmered behind a sheen of unshed tears as she rushed to meet him, clasping him tightly, the tears spilling over.

He edged through the door, tenderly guiding her back, while closing the door with his other hand. "Merry Christmas, Ma!" He fiercely returned her hug.

"Oh, Adam. It is so good to see you!" she exclaimed and quickly composed herself, giving him one final squeeze before gently pushing him away. "I made us some hot cocoa. You just lay your coat on the bed and have a seat here." She indicated the small round table under the only window in the tiny room that was dominated by the hospital style bed. A hot plate and microwave sat side-by-side on a little table beside the door that led into the bathroom. A teapot sat simmering on the hot plate, two cups neatly arranged on the table beside it.

He smiled as he set the bag on the floor next to his chair and laid his coat, as instructed, across the foot of the neatly made bed. The ever-present vid-screen played soundlessly in the corner; volume muted. His mother set his cup of cocoa in front of him and took the seat opposite, stirring the hot beverage, a froth forming on the surface. "Reminds me of the old days, a little bit." She smiled wistfully. "Remember how we always had cocoa first thing on Christmas morning?"

He smiled at the memory. His parents had made the holidays special for him when he was growing up. He remembered the traditional tree, pulled lovingly out of storage every Thanksgiving, and how his mother transformed their home in one week into a magical place of lights and Christmas greenery. For as long as he could remember, his parents would be up and waiting for him in the living room, mugs of hot cocoa sitting on coasters on the glass topped coffee table, reflecting the gaily twinkling lights of the tree. His mother would have a plate of kolaches, pastries and donuts sitting in the center of the table to munch on while they opened presents.

He looked at her now, and while the years had aged her, she was every bit as beautiful as she had been when he was a young boy. He had thought she was breathtaking then, and she still was. Her grayish-blue eyes were distant now, lost in memories, and he knew she was thinking of his father. He glanced around the small room. She had turned the dismal area into a cheerful and cozy space. He saw treasured knick-knacks scattered around on shelves and table surfaces that she had had since he was a small child. On the shelf under the vid-screen was the silly pair of seashell turtles, snuggling on a rock, one wearing wireframe glasses and the other a tiny wig and lipstick, that he'd gotten her at the gift shop when his fifth-grade class had a school trip to the aquarium.

"You shouldn't have, you know," she said, calling him back to the present. She was nodding at the bag at his feet. "I couldn't afford much in the way of Christmas." She got up and went over to the small closet behind the entrance door and pulled two packages off the top shelf. They were neatly wrapped in colorful paper, polar bear cubs with bright green scarves cavorting on a red background. She handed them to him while she resumed her seat.

"Thanks, Mom." He carefully set the packages in his lap and pulled three out of the bag which he then scooted out of the way. He handed the three packages to his mother and said, "You first."

She smiled and picked the middle-sized package. "Oh, Adam!" she exclaimed delightedly, pulling an emerald green sweater out of the box and holding it up in front of herself. "It's so soft!"

"Alpaca wool," he said. "It's from Argentina."

"You don't say!" she sighed, snuggling the soft sweater against her cheek and smiling. "Thank you! Now you!"

He opened the smaller of his two packages and found a pair of fur-lined leather gloves that fit his hands perfectly. "Nice! I can really use these with the type of weather we're having this winter! Thanks, Mom!" He knew the gloves had cost her dearly and she had probably saved for them for most of the year and might still be paying for them.

"I'm so glad you like them," she murmured, sipping her cocoa and opening her smallest package next. "Oh, my!" Her eyes sparkled as she opened the small jewelry box, and she turned them to him in surprise. He grinned, happy to see her so astounded. She carefully lifted the emerald pendant, stone set cunningly so it floated in a gold filigreed heart and held it so the weak light filtering through the window caught flashes on the cut surface of the deep green stone. She looked at him with widened eyes and he saw her hand tremble slightly as she lowered the gem back into the box.

"No, Mom. Here, put it on." He jumped up and went around the table, taking the necklace from her hand and carefully working the clasp, settling the pendant on her chest. "Now, go look." He stood back so she could go to the room's mirror hanging on the wall as you entered the room.

She admired the precious stone and then turned back to him, face assuming a stern expression. "Adam, how could you possibly afford such a thing? It's absolutely beautiful. Stunning. Really."

He leaned back and with great satisfaction told her, "I got a promotion."

"What! When did this happen? Tell me!" She rushed back to the table; the necklace momentarily forgotten.

He laughed. "Let's finish with our presents and then I'll tell you all about it."

Her final present to him was a pair of tan slacks and lovingly layered within their folds was a family picture from when he was fifteen and a new sophomore in high school. He studied the image of his father for a long time, thinking as he so often did how much he resembled him. He had good memories of his dad and wished he'd known him as a man.

Megan had the last gift, a large box about two feet by three feet. It was very light, and she shook it experimentally, looking at him with raised eyebrows. "I can't imagine what it might be."

She chuckled as she found the long business-sized envelope nestled in layers of wadded tissue paper. "You are such a trickster!" She grinned as she pulled the paper from the envelope and read the contents. "One hundred extra entries! Oh, Adam! Wouldn't that be so wonderful! And I get a whole month to dream about it!"

He grinned, "You always said you wanted to win the Hawaiian Retirement and I was able to get you some extra lottery entries for it. Good luck!"

She clasped the paper to her breast, "Oh, wouldn't it be grand? White beaches, hot sun. Ah!" She sipped her cocoa and sat back contentedly, hand fingering the emerald, eyes watching him lovingly as he carefully folded the slacks around the portrait and put them, along with the gloves, in the bag. "Thanks, Mom. And merry Christmas." He toasted her with his mug of cocoa.

"You too, son. You, too. Now, tell me about your promotion."

He told her about that and about his move into a new apartment on the western side of Sector Eight. "The apartment is amazing, Mom. I wish you could see it. It's a real apartment. I've got a small dining loft next to a gallery type kitchen nook, a good-sized living area and a sleeping room separate! It's got a full bath with a full-sized tub in it and a separate shower enclosure."

"Wow!" She was impressed. "I'm so happy for you, Adam. Your father would have been so proud of you." Tears filled her eyes and spilled over, splashing down her cheeks and onto her hands, clasped tightly in her lap. "Oh, he would have been proud."

He rose and went to her, hugging her tightly as she cried on his shoulder.

CHAPTER SIX

"Frank, I'm telling you something is up with Kate. It doesn't make any sense. We're behind in production on those chips and yet I heard through my grapevine that she's RIF'd another five percent. If you needed labor, and both JB and Judy have sent extra teams to Packy to lend a hand, why on earth would you RIF people?" Yolanda Webster, President of Supply Chain, asked angrily, burying her hand in her hair at her right temple, a frown creasing her pleasant features.

Frank shook his head and said, honestly perplexed, "Yolanda, I will try to get to the bottom of it. This is the first I'm hearing about any RIFs. If they've been having them, they're keeping it quiet from me. Of course, I'm not President of Training or Facilities. They aren't under any obligations to tell me how they run their business. Unless it impacts my hub here in Soweh. You know that, Yolanda."

"I know, Frank. I just hate to think of more people being sent to work centers. We've got to find a better way. I fear that's what they're doing. There's a kickback on every head sent to a center, isn't there?"

Frank grimaced, "As long as there's an incentive, someone is going to abuse it. All right, Yolanda. I'll do some digging. See what I can find out. If there's actual proof against Kate, JB or Judy that they've been lining their pockets at the hardship of citizens, I'll see to it they get exposed."

"I hope you find the proof while you have time, Frank," Yolanda spoke earnestly. "Any more word from Lawrence or James?"

Frank nodded again, "James notified me officially yesterday and plans to announce at the end of this month. I've got his top three candidates to review and interview. Then the hub will get the vote."

Yolanda looked grim. "So that's one. Nothing yet from Lawrence, then?"

"No. I know he's busy doing his own sweep for candidates, though. It's only a matter of time."

"Something we may not have enough of," Yolanda added bitterly.

Frank shrugged it off. "Let's not spill the cart just yet. Tell me about the outsider."

Yolanda sighed, "He won't say much. We haven't been able to get him to tell us anything as far as outsider locations or numbers. I don't think I have any choice but to assign him to one of the work centers. The farthest from Panoh as possible. A very close watch will need to be kept as he'll be a high escape risk."

"Naturally," Frank agreed. "I'll discuss it with Ben."

"Oh, it's in Ben's hands. I turned it over to him immediately. It was his team that arranged for the release of the bear story with Media."

"Good. The sooner we get his team pulled in the quicker we can maybe trace back and locate a group of them. I understand Ben's got someone assigned now to set up surveillance. I'll ask him to place a priority on Panoh. You said an off-schedule perimeter sweep caught this fellow?"

Yolanda nodded, "Yes. You can get details from Ben, he knows his operation better than I do, but I know his SRG team here does periodic perimeter sweeps."

"All right. I'll discuss it with Ben. I'll be talking to him later today, anyway. Anything else we need to discuss?"

"No. I may send my own team down to Packy. I can have my local management arrange for a meeting. Maybe bring in some of my personnel from Wegah and Gullub, too. I'll attend and I'll discreetly set up a team of my own best to keep eyes and ears open, try to find out what might be happening in those hubs, and if there's anything we should know about."

"Can't hurt," Frank agreed, terminating the connection.

It was a meager Christmas for Erick and Jerry. No decorations brightened the bare living space, no lights twinkled, and no tree adorned it. Erick had considered looking for a downed fir limb, a bit of greenery to brighten the place up and give them some holiday feel, but there were no trees this high up in the mountains and it was not worth the hike to the lower altitudes for something so nonessential. Erick and Jerry limited their outer exposure as much as possible while still meeting the demands of the job. It had taken Erick a few weeks to finally settle into the remote way of life. Cabin fever was a very real danger.

There was no exchange of gifts, neither man having access to or the means of acquiring one, but they did agree to only do the required daily tasks and have a nice meal. While Erick made the trudge to fill the generators, Jerry baked a spice cake. He had told Erick he couldn't promise results, but it was a recipe Rowena had left with him. "She said it was simple. Even I could make it." He'd smiled fondly at the memory. Erick contributed some deviled eggs. They'd gotten their supply shipment in just the previous week and someone had thoughtfully included a quart of eggnog.

There had also been some country style pork ribs in with the usual hamburger, pork chops, tenderloin and chicken breast that they got. Erick fixed it in a spicy sauce they had the ingredients on hand to make which he baked slowly in the oven while Jerry made some mashed potatoes and heated up a can of green beans. It was a huge meal for the two men and a feast compared to their normal rations.

Afterwards, they sat down to play some backgammon and enjoy the eggnog and spice cake. "The ribs were excellent, Erick. Fall apart and saucy. Loved them." He rubbed his stomach in appreciation while sipping at his glass of eggnog.

"It was a good meal. I enjoyed it. Thanks for your portion. The cake looks great." He nodded at the square of cake, topped with a spiced sugar glaze, sitting at his elbow. "I've got to make some room for that. No way can I fit it in right now."

Jerry grinned in response. "Yeah. I'm with you there."

The two men began to position their pucks in their places, and each rolled a dice for the first go. Jerry won the rights and contemplated his first move. While he looked at the board and his options, he asked Erick, "So what do you know about the Outsiders?"

Erick sat silently for a moment, rolling his dice in his hand, studying Jerry. Jerry kept his eyes on the board, not looking up, face expressionless. Erick shrugged. "I don't really know. All I've ever heard is there are people out there that are mental—crazy. They'll attack you." He snorted disdainfully as if he didn't fully believe it, yet at the same time felt compelled to. "And mutants."

The last brought a chuckle from Jerry. He shook his head and moved his two pieces, retrieving his dice.

Erick rolled and it was his turn to figure out a first move. "It does sound kind of silly," he said in the long silence that followed. "I mean, mutants? I've never seen one—not even on vid-screen."

Jerry sat back, body shaking now with his laughter. "Thank you. Ever see one of these mutants?" His voice was filled with sarcasm. Then, soberly and seriously, "No, you haven't. Nor will you. They do not exist. Nor do the crazies. No more than there are crazies in the hubs."

Erick sat back now and returned Jerry's steady gaze. "You sound like you know quite a bit."

Jerry nodded, "I do. In fact, I know one. A few, actually."

Erick stiffened, staring hard now at Jerry. What was he to say? How to respond? It could be a trap, though Erick couldn't get the sense of why. If Jerry was speaking the truth, he was admitting to a serious infraction that could result in severe disciplinary action. Erick suspected there wasn't much farther down he could fall as it was, but he didn't want to find out.

"It's not what they've taught you, Erick." Jerry said softly now. "You're old enough to remember how things used to be. When you were a kid."

Erick looked down at the scuffed laminated surface of the table, game forgotten. He did remember. The whole Corporate Population Center initiative had happened while he was still in High School. He'd been moved to the newly formed Midwestern Hub by his parents. His dad had been a geologist and landed a good position with the Environmental Resource Group, or EnRG – Energy.

Erick had scored well in school and had been placed into the Security Resource Group curriculum and eventually went to the Rocky Mountain Hub for his training before assignment at the Western Gateway Hub.

"Those days are over," he said now in a lifeless tone, studying the board and moving his two pieces.

"Why?" Jerry asked in response.

It startled Erick. He sat up a bit straighter and frowned at Jerry. "Excuse me?"

"I'm serious, Erick. Why? Why did it have to change—and change so much? Who said it was okay? When did we stop having a say?"

Erick was instantly frustrated. "Come on, Jerry. You know the answer to that. This is recent history. People in rural areas were starving. No food was being sent; utilities were failing. If it hadn't been for the corporations stepping in to assist…" He spread his hands out and leaned forward.

"Bullshit!" Jerry exploded. "That's the corporate propaganda bullshit they've taught you!"

Erick was shocked.

Jerry leaned forward now, leaning on his arms on the edge of the table and looking intently, earnestly, at Erick. "Not everyone moved to a hub, Erick. A lot of people chose to make a living on their own. And who represents them? Who speaks for them? When did it become a crime to live your own life when our Constitution tells us we have the right to pursue happiness? Where does it say we are bound to live by and in the corporate structure? Don't you see? They have gone from savior to oppressor and people don't even realize it! They've got everyone snowballed into believing this great myth while they have taken over our country!"

Erick's head was spinning. Of all the things he might have expected from Jerry, this was not it. "That is some serious shit you're talking there, Jerry."

Jerry sat back again, holding himself in control but his eyes revealed his passion. "It isn't right, Erick. Oh, sure—if you live your life in the hub and you do a good job you get treated well and have nothing to complain about. I get it. But that's the ostrich with his head in the sand. I've got it good so everyone else must have it good too. Only it doesn't work out that way. Ever hear of the work centers?"

"Sure," Erick said quickly. "Cotton has to grow somewhere, so do other crops. Mining has to be done. Other things as well. Not all industry is in the hubs. I get that. But being assigned to a work center is a hell of a lot better than the old jails we used to have. You can't possibly try to claim that our old justice system worked?"

Jerry shrugged, "It wasn't perfect. But neither are people. We're prone to error. Only now the corporations prevent you from making errors. Corporations prevent you from making decisions," Jerry stressed. "Why do you have to live in a hub? Just answer that one basic question. Why are you not allowed to venture out and strike a living on your own?"

Erick was speechless. He honestly didn't have an answer. Had never considered the idea. He shrugged, "I don't know."

"There is no reason, Erick. This is a free nation—or we were. We were a Democratic Nation with a government that supposedly represented its people. Now, it's true. Many people agree today that we strayed very far from the original vision, but we also grew in ways that vision couldn't even have believed possible or anticipated. What I want to know is when we all agreed to swap our Democracy for a Corpocracy."

Again, Erick sighed in frustration, "We all voted on it, Jerry. I was what? Maybe mid-twenties? There were seven of the hubs up at that time and we put it to a vote to abolish the role of President and replace it with a Council of Ten. And you can't say we aren't democratic. What about your voting requirements?"

Jerry snorted. "You call that democracy? I call that slamming the people with an overload so that the sheer volume makes the activity meaningless and something to be dreaded. Do you really spend a lot of time researching the things you vote on?" Jerry challenged.

Erick reddened and looked back down at his hands, clasped before him in his lap now. "Not like I should."

"Right," Jerry nodded. "And you aren't alone. Now, add to that all the so-called Outsiders. Outsiders to what? They're still citizens of this nation and that is not a crime."

Erick had no rebuttal for that.

"Work centers, on the other hand, are a crime."

Erick looked back up at Jerry now. "They're brutal places," Jerry continued. "Forced labor. Until they wear you out. Then something less manual but just as menial until you're completely used up. Then—disposed. No one comes out of a center. Well," and Jerry chuckled, "It used to be no one got out." His eyes met Erick's directly. "I've spent enough time with you now, Erick, to think you're a pretty smart man. A little misled perhaps, but that's the corporate brainwash everyone's been subjected to. Don't miss your daily news consumption," he winked at Erick and Erick couldn't help but laugh in response.

"I've got to admit, a lot of what you're saying makes sense to me. It's just things I've never considered. I mean, hell, it was treasonous to consider them, you know?"

Jerry nodded, "Of course. Again, it's what you've been taught and why shouldn't you believe it? All they've ever done is good. Right?" And Jerry raised an eyebrow inquisitively, "Until you talk to someone who was sent to a work center. Are you open minded enough for that?"

Erick was intrigued. He'd heard rumors. He knew work centers were vile places. So much of what Jerry had said was resonating with him. He met Jerry's eyes now and said, "Sure. In fact, I'd like that very much."

Jerry nodded once, firmly. "Done. I was hoping you would consider the idea. There's going to be a visitor here tomorrow. Today is a good day for OUR to operate." At Erick's questioning glance he added, "Outside Underground Railroad. It's a network the Outsiders use to move around and not get noticed on satellites or other surveillance."

"Oh," Erick replied, repeating, "OUR." He nodded. "I like it. OUR."

Jerry grinned, "Anyway, there's someone on the move today, they'll arrive here tomorrow. I want you to meet them."

"I'm glad you could make it back to Soweh for a couple of days. I trust the trip was good?" Frank asked Ben as they met at the bank of elevators in the main lobby of Frank's office building.

"Not bad," Ben Larocque replied. His blue eyes scanned the other people passing through the lobby, several, like themselves, waiting for the next elevator. "I caught an early morning mail flight that was heading over."

The elevator arrived and the others waiting deferred to Frank. The two men entered the small car and moved to the back. Frank turned to gaze out the glass walls at the immense lobby as the elevator proceeded upward while Ben remained facing forward, watchful as the other passengers exited on their floors, some joining for shorter trips further up. Finally, it was just the two men as the elevator made its way to the top floor.

Frank's office had an expansive view of the Las Vegas strip. The location of the financial headquarters for the new Corporate Population Hubs, the Southwestern Hub had quickly usurped the Mid-Atlantic Hub, as the new seat of government. Financial Operations was the primary enterprise in the hub with the typical presence of the other corporate entities necessary to keep a large city functioning. Unlike the other hubs it was a primary vacation destination and was the only hub with extensive International traffic. All the big-name casinos on the Strip still operated under the auspices of the Media Resource Group as a form of entertainment.

Frank crossed to a cozy seating arrangement near a large gas fireplace and settled into a chair, indicating for Ben to join him. "So, how's our project coming along?"

Ben settled into the chair next to Frank's and told him, "Good. Adam's been promoted. I understand he's going through management orientation right now." He laughed and cracked open the cold can of soda Frank handed him from the small refrigeration unit built into the base of the table between them. "You know how Human Resources is. This is his bump to management, and they've got to put him through their training regimen. I've already made it clear Southwestern Hub is his priority."

"I've seen some new faces and there seems to be an increase in your personnel," Frank stated.

Ben nodded, "Yes. I told you I'd bring my best men in and I've started that process. I've got to balance it," he shrugged and spread his hands. "I can't leave us exposed elsewhere though I haven't heard of any other incidents. Not attacks, anyway."

"Pacific Northwest?"

Ben quirked an eyebrow and studied Frank. "Your grapevine doesn't miss much, does it?"

Frank laughed. "I've been in close contact lately with Yolanda. She's up in arms about our three gals."

Ben nodded sympathetically, "I can imagine. Well, the eastern meet point for Panoh is in Snoqualmie. We've got a small Infrastructure and Power outpost group that stay there to keep the hydroelectric plant running and it's a good meet point for traffic coming in."

Frank nodded. "I'm familiar with it. Been there once. Falls were amazing."

"Yes. Well, the Panoh security team conducts regular sweeps of the area nearby, driving through a couple of former communities near the meet point and the highway. On this sweep, they went through a small town, Klahanie, and spotted this guy. They'd gone down to the lake there, Lake Sammamish, and one of the men noticed his tent. He was camping beside the lake. He'd done a good job camouflaging the site and it was fortunate we even saw him."

"Any idea what he was doing there? I take it he was alone?"

"Right. Alone and no sign there'd been anyone else with him. It was a small site and he just had a few provisions. My guess is he was passing through, possibly using the highway, and stopped there to hole up for whatever reason. We can't get him to talk."

Frank sighed. "That's too bad. You know, Ben, sometimes I wonder."

"About?"

"Are we doing this wrong? Making a big mistake? I mean, they're Americans. I don't know, but maybe it would be better to work with them." He sighed deeply and tossed his empty can in a nearby trash bin.

"I don't disagree with you, Frank, but I'm not so sure the rest of the Council see's it the same as us."

Frank laughed bitterly, "Don't I know it. You know, I think Kate Luca is making a profit sending people from her hub to work centers. I'm not hearing the labor shortage complaints from them so much. Of course, in the winter things do tend to slow down."

"I don't think it's just usual slow down, either," Ben agreed. "I've got some feelers out. It's not just Kate. I think JB is the brain power behind it."

Frank raised his eyebrows and nodded, "I think you're right. OK, so our Panoh Outsider won't talk. Too bad. And we have no idea where he came from or where he might have been headed."

"No. Unfortunately. I've asked every hub to initiate perimeter sweeps a minimum of twenty miles out from their hubs and all structures along the meet point routes are to be regularly checked. Other than that, all we can do is wait for one of them to slip up. I'm still working on creating a team that will function outside. I haven't fully developed the idea yet. Ideally, I'd like to infiltrate. Learn as much as possible rather than a quick hit against a single location. For that to work, I've got to know where at least one of these Outsider conclaves is located."

"I like the idea of insinuating someone—or a team. An ambassador, shall we say?" His eyes twinkled as he pulled two more sodas out of the mini-fridge and tossed Ben a fresh one. "I mean, think about it, Ben. We could possibly eliminate the whole issue of work centers and RIFs. These Outsiders are living, apparently, quite successfully without support from the hubs. Why couldn't we negotiate with them to take over some of the work center production?"

Ben nodded, "I'm certain that's what the attack here in Soweh was about. They needed that fuel."

"There's some things they can't produce for themselves without attracting our attention, and fuel would be one of them, certainly. It would give them a viable means of earning things they need and eliminate a horrible practice that has developed. I knew when we started getting bonuses back from the centers for providing headcount that it would spell trouble. You cannot incent that type of behavior."

"It's a noble idea, Frank, and I don't disagree with you, but don't you need someone to negotiate with first?"

Frank laughed and nodded appreciatively, "Got me there! Indeed, you do. I suppose before I worry about getting the Council to agree we should find someone to work with. Our boy in Panoh doesn't seem to be the one, eh? I really like your idea of a plant. That might net the results we need."

"No. He's not our man. We'll find a way in."

CHAPTER SEVEN

Aubree tried to wrench her arm free, but Drew held it tightly in his grasp.

"Drew!" she exclaimed angrily.

"Going home so soon?" His sneer was ugly, his voice a low growl in her ear.

"As a matter of fact, I am! Now let me go!" She pulled against him and managed to free herself. Angrily pulling her coat tight, she resettled her purse on her shoulder, all too aware of the chip hidden in the inner pocket.

"It's still early, and I just got here. Join me."

"Is that a request, Drew, or a command?"

He laughed lightly.

Corinne chose that moment to come out. She stopped and looked at them.

Drew turned smoothly and dropped his arm across Aubree's shoulder, "Good evening, Miss Houston."

Aubree jerked and started to move away but Drew pulled her closely to his side.

Corinne stiffened and her eyes met Aubree's before she responded to Drew. "Good evening. Everything okay here, Aubree?"

Aubree deliberately stepped away from Drew and nodded at Corinne. "Fine. I was just heading home and bumped into Mr. Shipley as I was leaving. Well, I enjoyed tonight, Corinne. Drew, good night." Quickly taking advantage of Corinne's intervention, Aubree turned and headed towards her apartment three blocks away.

Behind her she heard Corinne reply, "Yes, same here, Aubree. Good night, Mr. Shipley."

Aubree continued homeward and as she turned the corner onto her block, she clearly heard the footsteps following. She paused and peered into the gloom between the streetlights, spotting Drew's tall frame half a block behind her and closing quickly with his long strides.

"Aubree," he called softly, tauntingly. "I wasn't quite through with you," he finished as he came up next to her.

"What is it, Drew?" She could not hide her exasperation. "It's getting late and I'd like to get home. It's very cold out here." She huddled deeper into her coat as evidence.

"I could not agree more. Shall we proceed then?" Drew took her right arm in his left hand and turning, indicated for them to continue.

She tried to resist. "No, Drew. Whatever it is you have to say can be said here. Now."

He paused and looked at her intently. "Aubree, I don't think it's a good idea for you to be out here walking around alone. Allow me to at least extend the courtesy of escorting you." He had released her and now politely extended his hand for her to proceed.

She could think of no way to prevent his following her, so she turned and continued to her apartment, Drew keeping pace at her side. Reaching the main lobby door, she paused, not looking at him. "Thanks for seeing me here safe. Have a good night."

She began to pull the door open to slip through when Drew reached above her and grasped the door firmly in his hand. "I'll see you to your door," he said pointedly.

She hesitated and then ducked quickly into the building, taking the stairs at the left of the entrance as quickly as she could. Her unit was on the third floor and she was winded when she reached the hall but maintained firm control so Drew would not see. Trying to appear calm, hands thrust deep into the pockets of her coat, she turned to face him at her door. "Well, you've seen me here. Again, thanks."

Drew put a hand up against the doorframe and leaned nonchalantly over Aubree. "What? Where's your courtesy? Not even a glass of water in exchange for my gallant service?" His hazel eyes pinned Aubree's and she was again reminded of a raptor.

"It's getting late, Drew, and I brought work home with me to finish up. I really need to get started on it."

"I'm sure five minutes wouldn't set you back all that much."

"No, Drew."

"Then I suppose we have a dilemma." A cruel smile formed on his shapely lips.

"There is no dilemma. You walked me home—so I would be safe. Well, I'm home. I'm safe. Job done. This is where you turn and leave."

"Only I'm not leaving."

She was irritated and finally turned to her door, thrusting her ID card into the electronic reader, hearing the click as the latch released. She had hoped to quickly open the door, slip in, and close it behind her. It had been a foolish plan from the first as Drew crowded behind her and pushed his way into the small unit.

"Good evening, Aubree!" Siri cheerfully chirped.

"Goo…"

Before Aubree could say anything further, Drew had roughly grabbed her from behind, spun her around and slammed her back against the wall, fiercely kissing her while holding her tightly in his grip. His mouth was hard on hers, and she felt her lips bruising, as she struggled to push him away. He raised his head and she gasped in breath but before she could speak his hand covered her mouth and he lowered his mouth next to her ear, whispering, "Not a word, my love."

His body pressed against hers, pinning her to the wall. She felt his passion all too plainly pressed hard against her lower abdomen. She twisted her head to the side, trying to free herself from his hand, beginning to feel panic when she couldn't pull enough oxygen into her partially obstructed nose, bucking against him to try to get more air.

He laughed. A low and ugly sound. "Nice moves. Like it a little rough, do you?"

Just then someone pounded on the door. He stiffened against her.

"Who's that?" he whispered fiercely in her ear; hand still clamped tightly over her mouth.

She rolled her eyes at him and tried to shake her head to indicate she didn't know.

The person pounded again and this time she heard a voice, "Aubree? You home? Siri said you were home. Come on, open up!"

She sagged in relief at the sound of Sacha's voice. Her eyes glared back at Drew and then inspiration struck. Raising her right foot, she slammed it hard into the wall behind her, making a loud sound as glass tinkled elsewhere in the small unit. Sacha, on the other side of the door, also heard.

"Aubree?" Her voice was now filled with concern and the door rattled as she tried to open it.

Unexpectedly Drew released her, and Aubree almost fell forward against him. Turning, he yanked the door open and looked down at Sacha's figure, tiny before him. She glared back defiantly. He looked over his shoulder at Aubree, "I'll see you later." Pushing past Sacha, he disappeared into the stairwell.

Sacha turned to Aubree, concern in her expression. "Are you okay?"

Aubree stepped away from the wall, adrenalin making her hands shake and her muscles tremble, delayed reaction setting in. "Yes," she said hesitantly, groping her way to the small sofa and collapsing on its edge. "How did you…?" She looked at Sacha, confused.

"Siri." Sacha replied quickly. "I was just sitting down at my computer to do a little work when she said you were home and needed me."

70

"Really?" Aubree was surprised. "Siri?" she inquired.

"Yes, Aubree?"

"You called Sacha?"

"Yes, Aubree. It sounded like you may have suffered a collapse or were having some medical trauma. I spoke when you entered but you did not answer. Then it sounded like you might have fallen. I could not be sure. I knew Sacha was closest."

"Wow," Aubree breathed out, relieved. "Thank you. Well done."

"Your thanks are not necessary, Aubree, but you are welcome. Do you require for me to contact the authorities? I was not aware there was an intruder or that you were under attack."

"No. Don't call the authorities." That seemed like a useless idea when Drew was one of those authorities and how could she prove he had assaulted her? It would be his word against hers. Sacha had not witnessed anything other than his presence and Aubree was not injured.

"Okay." Siri replied and then was quiet.

Sacha studied her friend. "You're sure you're okay?" she asked.

Aubree nodded. "Yes. Shook me up. That's all."

Sacha crossed and sat down beside Aubree. She took Aubree's hand in hers and looked earnestly into her eyes. "Aubree, you know he's not going to quit. Right?"

Aubree nodded and suddenly her eyes were awash in large, unshed tears. Sacha squeezed her hand and the tears spilled over.

"Sweetie, you've got to do something. You've got to get your dad to help you. He's the only one with enough power to do it."

Aubree nodded again and angrily dashed the tears from her face. She was suddenly furious. How dare he? Just as quickly as it bubbled up, the anger vanished and she was left feeling weak and exhausted, muscles sore. She sank back against the back of the sofa, leaning her head against the bolster. "I just need a few minutes and I'll be fine," she murmured.

Sacha looked at her for a minute and then nodded, standing up. "Well, I really do need to get back to that work. Can I grab you a water or something before I go?"

Aubree shook her head. "Thanks. Really, I'm fine." She sat up straight, and then stood up, legs a little shaky but strong enough. She smiled at Sacha. "I'll talk to my dad. Okay?"

"You should do it tonight." Sacha strode to the door and looked again at Aubree. "Call if you need me."

"There isn't anything you can do?" Aubree's voice trembled; whether from anger, fatigue or hysteria she wasn't entirely certain. She felt overwhelmed by all three. It was later that same evening, pushing eleven o'clock. She'd collected her wits and done the job Corinne had requested, updating the small chip and securing it so she could return it to Corinne tomorrow in the office. Then she had called her father and asked to come speak with him. They sat in his small home office, in the two wing chairs beside the now cold fireplace. Aubree nervously sipped from the small glass of brandy her father had pressed on her. She did not care for the harsh taste of the alcohol, but it was soothingly warm in her stomach and was helping to calm her frayed nerves.

"I spoke to the senior manager of Security over Sector Four just today, after you mentioned it at breakfast Sunday. I don't know what his connections are, Aubree, but they're high up. I was told he was off limits in so many words." He spread his hands in frustration. "You could maybe come live here for a bit...?"

She laughed and shook her head. "I don't think that would work out so well, Dad. Mom and I don't exactly see eye to eye. And I can't hide here indefinitely. I have a job, a life..." She shook her head again.

He nodded, gazing down at his half empty glass. "You're right. I can't protect you every minute of every day."

They sat for a while; the big house silent around them. "Speaking of Mom, there's no chance she'll be up and about is there? I really don't feel like having that conversation tonight."

He chuckled, "No chance. She took her sleeping pill. She's out until tomorrow morning."

She nodded, "One small blessing."

"You know, I do have an idea," he began hesitantly, studying Aubree. "It would mean a big change for you."

"Oh?" She looked with interest at her father. "What are you thinking?"

"If I can't make him go away—well, nothing prevents you from leaving, now does it?"

She sat stunned, never having contemplated the idea before. "Like where?"

He shrugged. "I haven't thought that far ahead. I'd want to talk to Corinne."

"Corinne?"

He smiled and sipped from his glass. "She's good at this sort of thing."

Aubree was glad her father wasn't looking at her when he made this casual comment or he would have seen her involuntary reaction, body jerking slightly, which she masked by quickly standing up and pacing over to the windows, overlooking the dark expanse of lawn. Why would he say something like that? She turned and contemplated him. His blue eyes were studying her just as intently.

"Why do you say that?" she asked, glad to hear her voice sounding calm, unconcerned.

He shrugged now, and glanced away, "She's done a few things for me..."

The sentence trailed off and she didn't press.

Sighing deeply, Mike pushed himself out of the chair. "Stay here tonight?" he offered.

She nodded gratefully. "I'm too unnerved to go back tonight."

He walked over and planted a kiss on her forehead. "You know which room to use. It should be all made up. I'll talk to Corinne in the morning."

Aubree watched her father as he left the room, and she saw the first intimation of age in the slightly stooped shoulders and back, the less than agile gait he typically used. Her heart filled with love and she hated that she kept so many secrets from him, secrets that she knew could do him so much damage.

"I don't mind telling you, I'm going to miss the hell out of you!" Corinne spoke vehemently, almost glaring across the surface of the large executive desk she stood behind. She strode to her office window in the former executive wing of the White House and turned her glare on the National Monument in the distance. "I wish it were him being reassigned!" she added bitterly.

Aubree sat mutely, not sure what to say.

"I've talked it over with your father. He spoke to the local Director of Security this morning. He seems to think Drew is only a threat to you." Corinne stressed the words angrily. "I don't happen to agree but I can't tell him how to run his shop. Fortunately, your father and I both agree something needs to be done to protect you." She turned back to Aubree. "With Drew's role in Security, we think it would only be a matter of time before he tracked you down. I mean, we can easily get you a spot in any hub." Corinne waved her hand expansively and went back to her desk, sitting down behind its spotless surface, bare except for the single folder open before her. She reviewed it again now.

"As I said, relocating you is only half of the solution. It's a given that you'll have to be placed in another hub. That, we fear, won't be enough. He'd still be able to locate you and we can't assure your safety. Especially if you're in a different hub entirely."

Aubree took a deep breath, "I hate this, Corinne. Especially since I've done nothing wrong!" She paused, taking a trembling breath. "I like my job here..." and she trailed off aimlessly.

Corinne looked at her compassionately. "I know, Aubree. You haven't done anything wrong. But if you stay here, I can't promise he won't continue to press his unwelcome advances on you." Corinne spread her hands helplessly. "He's innocent until a crime has been committed."

That was what rankled Corinne the most. Andrew Shipley's relentless stalking of her was clearly captured in video monitor taping, yet he had, so far, done nothing that he could be charged with.

"There is an opening in the Western Gateway Hub that you are well suited for. It means a promotion for you," Corinne added warmly. "The fact is, this could actually be a very good thing for us. We will change your name and you will travel with convoy from here to Wegah. You'll go through Midwestern. From Midwestern it's straight on to Wegah and your new life as Natalie Deckman." She paused and looked at Aubree to see how she would handle this news.

Aubree sat stunned, absorbing this new information, her mind reeling.

"I know," Corinne said softly. "It's going to be hard, but you'll adapt. The chances of him locating you with all these precautions…" She spread her hands apart, palms up. "The odds are so slim. Eventually, he will forget you and, meanwhile, you have a golden opportunity here. This is a very choice management position and rumor has it that Wegah is about to be Ground Zero for a pet project of the Speaker's. You and I both know that a lot of the time it's being at the right place at the right time that gets us the furthest along."

Aubree smiled a bit uncertainly. "Natalie Deckman." She murmured, meeting Corinne's brown eyes directly. "Yes, I think I like that. Natalie Deckman."

CHAPTER EIGHT

Erick pulled the door shut and stomped the snow off his boots, glad to be in the shelter of the small cubby. He unsnapped the clasp on his left boot and paused, hearing the low rumble of a voice on the other side of the main door into the living space. It sounded like Jerry's voice. Quickly he unsnapped the right boot and stepped out of the heavy hiking boots, crusted thickly with snow. Sam, the Outsider, must have arrived while Erick was filling the generator and checking the towers. Pushing open the inner door, he stepped into the warmth of the main living area.

"Here's Erick now," Jerry announced.

He sat facing towards Erick at the small table they spent a lot of their time at. A small figure sat across from him, hunched into a thickly padded coat, hood pulled up, back to Erick.

"I've got fresh coffee in the pot. Grab a cup and come join us. I want to introduce you to Sam." Jerry nodded at the figure seated before him.

Erick nodded and headed for the coffee pot, eyeing the back of the figure at the table. Sam was smaller than Erick had expected though he really hadn't had much of an expectation to begin with. Jerry had not shared much with Erick, preferring to allow Erick to form his own opinion.

He approached the table now and coming around the side was startled when an attractive young woman was revealed huddled in the depths of the olive-green anorak. Small, delicately formed fingers cradled a steaming cup of coffee. She nodded at Erick as he settled into the chair to her left, warm brown eyes sliding over his face before dropping back to the cup in front of her.

"Sam just got here about five minutes ago," Jerry informed him and then, addressing Sam, asked, "Beginning to thaw out?"

She nodded and sipped from the coffee. "It's always a long haul getting the last mile up here. I may need some fuel to top off the sled."

Jerry nodded, "No problem. See anything on your way here?"

Sam shook her head and then glanced at Erick. Silence fell. Erick fidgeted, uncertain how to proceed. Jerry finally broke the awkward moment by standing up and carrying his empty cup to the sink. Coming back, he paused by Sam, "Want me to hang your coat up?"

She nodded and stood up, shrugging out of the down-filled coat and handing it to Jerry. She wore plain denim pants and a simple pullover top that neither accentuated nor hid her trim, attractive figure. Her hair, now free from the hood of the coat, fell softly to her shoulders in a gentle brown wave, golden highlights catching the overhead light. She rubbed her arms briskly as she resumed her seat. "I don't know how you can live in these conditions." Her voice was low pitched, a little husky. She met Erick's gaze and held out her right hand. "I'm Sam. Sam Glenshaw."

Erick grasped her hand, being careful not to exert too much pressure, her small and graceful fingers engulfed by his larger hand. He swallowed past a sudden lump in his throat, aware that he was embarrassed by his unexpected response to her. "Erick Scharfe."

Another awkward silence descended while Jerry took his seat across from Sam. "So, Sam, Erick here is probably bursting with questions and curiosity. I've not shared anything with him other than your name and the basic fact you live on the outside."

Sam faced Erick; the delicate lines of her eyebrows lifted as she smiled. "What would you like to know?"

Only everything about you, Erick thought. He gave a small shrug and smiled. "I guess you could start with what it's like living on the outside."

Sam laughed softly. "That wouldn't be the right place to start. I haven't always been an Outsider." She paused and her fingers curled around the cup. She raised her eyes to meet Erick's. "I guess I don't consider myself one now. I consider myself an American. Same as you." She spoke the words softly, a challenge in her tone.

Erick felt a little stung by her response. "Fair enough," he replied. "Where did you live?"

"My family was from Atlanta." She brushed a strand of her wavy brown hair back from her face. "Well, we didn't live in Atlanta. We lived in Lawrenceville, off to the northeast. When the hub was formed, we were moved inside the walls same as everyone else. I was in high school then."

Erick tried to quickly calculate her age. He had been a sophomore in high school when the first hub, the Mid-Atlantic, was formed. He couldn't remember when Atlanta had become the Southeastern Hub, or Soesteh, but it must have been several years later. They would be close in age.

Sam finished the coffee and rose to carry the cup to the sink.

Jerry stood up quickly, waving her off. "I've got it." He grabbed the cup from her and carried it while she resumed her seat.

"My dad was a director at a major construction firm in Atlanta when everything changed. He placed well in the Infrastructure Resource Group when the hub was formed. We lived in Sector Eight, in a really nice house."

Jerry returned, putting a glass of ice water in front of Sam. She nodded her thanks, took a sip, and continued. "I did okay in school. Not great but well enough to place into a graduate program in healthcare, part of the Human Resource Group. I graduated four years later with a Bachelor of Science in Nursing degree. From there I was assigned to the major medical center in Soesteh."

Sam took a deep breath and another sip of water. Erick noticed a slight tremor in her hand as she reached for the glass. She set the glass back on the table, wiping her damp hand on her thigh. "The manager of our unit was an older guy. I'm guessing about fifty. Well, not long after I joined the team, he started to make the move on me." Sam blushed a little, shifting uncomfortably in her seat. "I managed to keep away from him, not give him any opportunity. It happened during our annual review. I had to meet with him. One on one."

She paused and Erick respectfully kept his eyes on his hands, clasping his cup.

"He made it very clear to me that our situation would have to have some big changes if I was going to survive another year on the team. He suggested we start with dinner, that evening."

She paused again. Erick glanced over at her and saw her eyes were unfocused, gazing off somewhere over Jerry's shoulder. She sighed and went on, "I left his office and decided I wasn't going to go through with it. I couldn't. So, I went to see my Director."

She looked at Erick, resentment in her expression. "You know, exercise the open-door policy? It was a big mistake." She shook her head and her eyes filled with tears. She blinked rapidly, trying to stem the flow, wiping briskly at her cheeks.

"Before the day was over, I'd been informed that I had been subject to a Reduction in Force. It was no reflection on my abilities but as one of the newest members I was less valuable due to my general lack of experience." Sam's voice was bitter. "I was instructed to pack up all personal items and report to the security office within seventy-two hours for conveyance to the Birmingham Work Center. Failure to appear could result in action against family members."

Erick was stunned. "You were assigned to a work center? Because you refused dinner with your boss? And they threatened your family?"

Sam nodded, adding, "I'm sure it was more than dinner I was declining, but, yes, that was the reason. Not on paper, of course."

There was silence for a few moments. Sam gazed pensively at her glass of water while Erick carefully studied her profile.

"What was the work center like?" he prompted.

She glanced at him and then back at her water, mouth twisting into a grimace. "Unspeakable. Let's just say I'd have been better off accepting the dinner invitation."

She refused to elaborate, and Erick allowed the silence to build. Finally, Sam seemed to collect herself, sitting up a bit straighter before looking at Erick as she continued. "It really was unspeakable. The conditions are beyond harsh. People are housed in horrid group shelters, kept under guard." A shudder passed down her slight frame. "I was there—I don't know—three years?" She shot an inquiring glance at Jerry who shrugged in response. She shook her head again. "Yeah. I guess. Three years. The Birmingham Work Center is mostly agriculture. They work you out in the fields. Weeding, whatever. Food sucks and is barely adequate. Same with clothing and shoes."

Another silence settled and Erick shifted uncomfortably. "What happened?" he finally asked.

"I got lucky. Met the right person. I think if I'd been there another six months to a year, I'd have had some serious health issues. As it was, I was having problems. They'd start us out early in the morning. We'd get a cup of coffee and usually something like a donut or muffin. This would be at about five in the morning. Then it was into the fields to do whatever the job was that day. Work until mid-morning. Then we'd get another short break with another cup of coffee. Lunch was anytime between noon and two. There were days I'd be borderline hypoglycemic before we got lunch. I'd have uncontrollable muscle shakes. It was an awful feeling. I passed out finally."

Silence again as she gazed intently into the water glass in front of her. "I woke up in the infirmary. The doctor was a young guy. Nice. He told me my blood sugar dropped and that's why I passed out. Said I was malnourished." A harsh bark of a laugh followed this statement. "Not much could be done about that under the conditions. He gave me a shot of B vitamins and kept me in the infirmary for a couple of days to rebuild some strength. As it happened this doctor knew someone who knew someone else. Two weeks later they smuggled me out of the center, and I joined the Outsiders."

Erick studied her profile thoughtfully. "How long have you been outside?"

She gave another small shrug. "A couple of years now."

"Where?" Erick prodded.

Sam laughed quietly. "I don't think so, Cowboy," she answered smoothly and smiled, taking another drink from the glass.

Erick felt his face flush in response. "What do you do?"

"Me? I'm a runner. I run messages, packages."

Erick nodded, glancing at Jerry. "Let me guess, this is a regular stop?"

Sam shrugged. "Maybe."

Jerry laughed and spoke up, "You'll forgive us for being extra cautious, Erick, but there's a lot at stake. It wouldn't go well for Sam to turn up."

Erick nodded, "I'm sure."

Jerry leaned forward intently now, "Not only would Sam be in danger but so would we and a lot of other people—all the way back to the Birmingham Work Center and one nice young doctor doing as much good as he can."

Both Sam and Jerry were watching him closely now.

"What's your role?" Erick asked Jerry.

"I know how to run this network." Jerry waved his hand expansively at the array of computer equipment set up in the space. "I know how to mask the signal so no one knows what we're doing. The network we're operating here is very advanced and was a key backbone site for the old telecom companies. It was set up to handle traffic on multiple spectrums. Corporate Big Daddy only uses two and they've gotten lax. No one watching the backdoor. Leaves me lots of bandwidth to operate in. And we control satellite alignment programming."

Erick was nodding, seeing how the remote outpost could be an invaluable tool to a resistance effort.

Jerry leaned back in his seat, crossing his right leg across his left knee, folding his arms across his chest. "From here I can get messages to several outposts and I've got ears on four of the hubs. We handle communications to Panoh, Packy, Soweh and Romoh. We were fortunate to get a compatriot in a sister tower that adds Wegah and Midweh information. Beyond that the eastern seaboard is largely dark to us." Jerry shrugged. "That's where people like Sam are so invaluable."

"Like the old postal service?" Erick chuckled. "Delivery by stagecoach?"

Jerry and Sam both laughed.

"Something like that," Sam agreed.

Erick turned back to Sam. "I know you can't tell me where you live and I'm not asking you to. But I'm curious. Is it near here? How many places are there?"

Sam laughed again and her brown eyes sparkled as she returned Erick's gaze. "Too many to count, Erick. There are a lot of people living on the outside. Most have been isolated. For a very long time. They've continued our democratic process—locally. Most have preferred to remain autonomous, but the fact is we're running low on some critical resources that we simply can't manufacture. Fuel is the biggest."

Erick nodded. "I imagine so. You'd need a refinery. You couldn't hide anything that big from the eyes in the sky."

Jerry nodded. "Exactly. Satellites have every bit of this country covered with some very rare exceptions. Those exceptions aren't suitable anyway. Handy for living off grid but there's a reason for that. Other critical needs are not available or are too distant."

Erick was puzzled. "I guess I don't understand why someone doesn't just ask?"

Sam cocked her head quizzically and studied Erick for a second before responding. "Ask who, Erick? Exactly who are we supposed to ask?"

Erick shrugged. "I don't know. That seems better than what you're doing now. Sneaking around and all. I mean, I know you had a bad experience..."

"Bad experience?" Sam cut him off angrily. "Maybe! Maybe I had a really bad experience but there are several thousand people having a really bad experience today in a work center somewhere. I guess we should just walk up to the front gates and ask for them to be released. How do you think that would go, Erick?"

He had no answer for her, and he was robbed of speech by her anger.

Jerry interceded. "There have been efforts, Erick. Naturally the media doesn't cover it. There've been some unfortunate cases of delegates approaching a hub and the delegate is never heard from again. We suspect they get sent to work centers, but we can't be sure. It hasn't helped that people living on the outside are not organized. They've lived in remote locations with very little traffic or interaction with peers. It's only since we've started the railroad, and runners like Sam have been able to locate these outposts, that we've started communicating. There's an effort to begin organizing."

Sam had gotten her temper under control and she spoke up now. "Yes. As Jerry says we've started working towards organizing some of these outposts. The old adage, strength in numbers." She smiled at Erick and he sensed an apology in the smile and in her eyes for the anger she had reacted with earlier. "There are some hot heads out there that think things are moving too slow. We had a group attack the convoy at Mesquite, Nevada. Well, they didn't attack the convoy. They attacked the advance security detail out of Soweh that was meeting the convoy. Security has a habit of getting their convoy conducts there early to turn on power. Two guys are pretty easy to cover." She shrugged. "They got several drums of fuel but it was stupid. It's drawn attention where we don't need it."

Jerry picked the story up. "I handled the SecComm connection between Soweh and Romoh." He paused significantly.

Erick failed to make the connection and shrugged helplessly.

"Frank Baba, President of FinOps, Speaker of the House? Ben Larocque? Security?"

"You have access at that level?" Erick was stunned.

Jerry laughed. "All of it, Erick. That's why these towers are so important. We're the gateway, the center to pass that traffic across the Rockies. Now, I've gotten word that Lawrence Johnson is sending a secure message via convoy to Frank Baba in Soweh. The message is too important to trust to electronic communications so it's being sent securely. I'm not sure exactly what we're looking for, but I know it's coming on the convoy. It could be written or something tiny like a thumb drive. Word has it Johnson is retiring, and this is the candidate replacement list. We'd really like to get our hands on that information."

Erick studied Jerry. "So, what? You're going to try to take it? Pull another stunt like what happened in Mesquite?"

Jerry smiled. "Precisely. It worked in Mesquite because those guys had the element of surprise. So far, it's been an anomaly and Security hasn't seen fit to change their methods. One problem our Big Brother has is his ability to change. He's slow at it. We've got to take advantage of any weakness while we can."

CHAPTER NINE

Adam unlocked the chained gate securing the generator and primed the fuel before pulling the cable to start it, throwing the master switch to bring on the power at the Love's Travel Stop in old Des Moines. He surveyed the area, the bright sun reflecting harshly from the barren landscape of the mall parking lot. Not seeing anything out of place he strolled over to the gray four-wheel drive pick-up Fleet had assigned him and began filling the tank.

His eyes scanned the side of the mall structure, automatically seeking out the dark recess of the entrance on this side. He wondered if the new team leader had conducted the area security sweep as he had suggested at his exit interview. The nozzle handle clicked under his hand and he pushed the thought away. Not his concern anymore.

He wasn't even sure why he was doing this run today. He'd gotten called into Brent's office at the end of the previous day and told he was needed this morning to conduct an escort from the Des Moines meet point. An individual from Mid-Atlantic was transferring. He was also to expect a package, a letter, which was to be delivered immediately to his former director, the head of convoy escort, upon his return to Wegah.

The entire request was highly unusual. Inbound deliveries were usually only accepted on Tuesday and Thursday, while outbound were scheduled on Monday and Wednesday. Today was Friday and it didn't make sense that someone from convoy escort hadn't been able to cover the off-cycle duty. Brent had mentioned something about department-wide training that couldn't be missed.

Adam couldn't recall a single occasion when convoy had been used to transfer personnel. He returned the gas pump to its cradle and screwed the cap back on the tank, flipping the lid shut. Nothing to do now but wait.

He felt a little uncomfortable in the light jacket he was wearing and shrugged it off, tossing it into the back seat of the crew cab. The weather had turned unseasonably warm two days ago after being bitter cold since the first of the year. It was very unusual to have fifty plus degree weather at the end of January this far north.

The bare skeletons of the trees were dense enough to block his view of the road to the east, the direction the convoy would come from. He glanced at his watch. It was twenty minutes before one. The convoy should have been here ten minutes ago.

He got back behind the wheel of the Ram and turned the engine over. Something didn't feel right. He pulled out his phone and dialed dispatch.

"Central Dispatch, Coleen. How can I help?"

"Hey, Coleen, Adam here. Any word from Midweh?"

"No, all's been quiet. What was the meet time?"

"Twelve thirty."

"Hmmm. Give them a bit more time. Probably a little delayed. If they aren't there in twenty, call me back and I'll radio Midweh Dispatch."

"Roger." He terminated the call and set the device back in the cup holder of the console, restlessly drumming his fingers on the steering wheel.

Normally, he would have had someone along with him, but Brent had told him he'd be running alone, no need for a partner. Now he wished he had one.

It had always been a rule that you did not leave your route or your post, but he felt an urgency to head east on Route 6 and meet the convoy. What harm could it do? It would mean leaving the station unattended and fully powered, generator accessible. He really should shut it down, lock it up. Maybe by then the convoy would arrive.

He drove the truck over next to the generator, parking it nose out towards the single entrance. Leaving the engine running, he quickly went through the shutdown process, throwing off the master switch and then cutting the generator. Silence descended across the plaza as he swung the metal gate closed, locking the heavy chain.

A silence that was suddenly broken by a distant sound. The sound sparked an old memory and he struggled to remember what it was. Then it occurred to him. Fireworks had sounded like that. Only that didn't make any sense. The sound had come from the east and as he strained to listen, it was repeated twice. It clicked that the sound was gunfire and he ran for the truck, jumping in and pulling the door quickly shut as he threw it into gear, leaving rubber as he pulled away from the station.

He navigated onto Route 6 and gunned the engine, the powerful motor throwing him back into the padded seat. As he cleared the overpass where the highway from Kansas City crossed, he sensed more than saw movement on his right. Quickly he glanced in that direction and felt his heart leap when a blue Jeep seemed to jump at him from the cover of the trees on that side of the road. Veering sharply, the two vehicles narrowly avoided a collision as the Jeep swerved up onto the surface of the road a bare half a length behind Adam's truck.

Adam tucked himself tightly into the corner of his seat, instinctively offering the pursuing vehicle as low a profile as possible, glad to have the full-sized crew cab protecting his blind side as the two vehicles raced down the section of highway.

The Ram had the more powerful engine and began to pull away from the smaller Jeep. He watched tensely as it began to slide behind him in his sideview mirror, the occupants hidden in the shade of the interior, his eyes darting between the mirror and his forward view of the road.

The Ram had fully cleared the Jeep now and Adam saw the long shaft of a weapon protrude from the passenger window, the metal gleaming as it swung erratically up and down each time the Jeep bounced on the cracked pavement.

Adam grinned to himself. It was one thing to shoot a weapon at a target and quite another to do so from a moving vehicle. He didn't think his opponent had much experience.

Experienced or not, the passenger began to gain control and Adam veered to the right to reduce the exposure of the tires on that side. In the old action movies, the pursuers always shot out the tires but, hitting a target less than a foot wide, and angling the shot at the ground, was very difficult and only an ace could hope to hit it.

The road was straight here, and it would be another two miles before Adam would need to take a left-hand turn to follow Route 6, where he hoped to encounter the convoy. It occurred to him that the Jeep was merely there to prevent him from doing exactly what he had done. The real force, the real attack, was somewhere up ahead. Adam pressed harder on the gas pedal.

Aubree gazed disconsolately out the window at the passing countryside, the wintry scene reflecting her own inner bleakness. She had left Midah under cover of dark, in a black four door sedan. There had been no badging on the interior, so she wasn't even sure what make the car had been. It had been sitting at the curb in front of his house as her father had bundled her into the back seat.

"Now, remember," he had reminded her, "No direct calls. We'll follow the schedule we agreed to and use Corinne's office."

"I know, Dad. I promise." She threw her bag in the back seat of the sedan, turning to face her father. It became very real all at once that she was leaving, that she might never see her father again. "Oh, Daddy!" She threw her arms around his neck and hugged him tightly. "I am going to miss you so very much!" Tears trembled and spilled down her cheeks.

"I'm going to miss you, too, baby girl." His arms circled tightly around her, pulling her in close, his cheek rested on the top of her head. "We'll just give this some time to blow over and then we'll make arrangements for you to come home. Besides, who knows? You may decide you like it there."

Aubree pulled back and gazed up at him, a twisted smile on her face. "I doubt that very much, Dad." She wiped the tears from her cheeks and stood up straight, bracing herself against the car door.

He had taken her chin in his hand, tilting her head up to meet her eyes, and told her, "You go with all my love. Now, be safe, enjoy the experience. I'll be at Corinne's expecting your call like we agreed. Okay?"

She had smiled and nodded, "Sure. Give Mom and TJ my love. I'll miss TJ."

Her dad had laughed, and she had slid into the back seat while he had exchanged a murmured conversation with the driver. Then he had stepped back and blown her a kiss as the car had pulled away and was lost in the darkness of night. Aubree had watched through the back window until they had turned a corner and he was lost from sight. He had seemed so small and alone standing there under the amber glow of the streetlight.

That had been four in the morning on Thursday and it was now a little past noon on Friday. They had covered seven hundred miles in just under twelve hours.

At first, the rolling hills of Maryland followed by the mountainous terrain of western Pennsylvania had held her enrapt. She had never traveled and was seeing the countryside outside the hub for the first time.

Thursday, as the car emerged from the gloom of a tunnel carved through the mountain terrain, she caught her first glimpse of what had once been Pittsburgh. Her mood turned somber and reflective. More and more buildings began to encroach on the thread of highway, and they seemed to loom threateningly towards the fleeting car. Windows blank and black stared accusingly as they passed. Aubree was glad the highway veered to the east of the city and didn't go through the specter of tall buildings clustered around the downtown region. There would be deep pockets of shade at the base of the tall buildings, even spots that perhaps never saw direct sunlight. Aubree shivered and turned her gaze away from the sparkling steel and few remaining bits of glass.

Shortly after leaving the eerily empty city behind them the driver had pulled into a service station where he had gone through the procedure of unlocking and turning on a generator so he could fill the gas tank on the sedan. He had been mostly silent the entire trip, preferring to listen to the music he fed into the cars audio system, a light mix of oldies pop rock. While the gas was pumping he had leaned through the driver's door and announced, "We'll stop here for a bit and eat some lunch." He'd nodded towards a picnic table set up invitingly under the protective arms of an ancient oak tree. "I've got a pack in the trunk I'll carry over."

She had nodded and gotten out of the car, stretching gratefully to ease muscles grown tight from being in one position too long. Lunch had been a silent affair consisting of a tuna sandwich and a bag of chips, an orange and two chocolate chip cookies. She ate everything but the cookies, saving them to snack on later that afternoon. Then it was back into the car, Aubree choosing the passenger front seat this time, and the long trip across Ohio and on into Chicago, or Midweh for Midwestern Hub, as it was now known.

Once through the gate, she felt a palpable relief having the walls between her and the vastness of the emptiness they had traveled through. She knew the empty streets and silent buildings they had passed would haunt her dreams. She slept that night, in a small, cramped room, windowless except for the tiny window in the shower of the little bathroom which had pebbled glass that you couldn't see through. It was a restless sleep. Each time she awoke, feeling apprehensive and scared in the unfamiliar setting, she was unable to remember her dreams, only the aftermath of dark emotion they were evoking in her. It was almost a relief when the rap came on her door at a little after six.

"Escort heads out at seven-twenty. Breakfast is being served over at the dining hub, if you want some grub. I'll be back in fifteen minutes to show you the way."

Fifteen minutes later a short, slightly over-weight woman that Aubree judged to be in her late thirties appeared at her door and with a curt, "Follow me," turned sharply to lead her across a paved lot to a building that people were streaming in and out of at a steady rate. Inside was a large open area where row after row of long plastic tables with folding chairs were arranged. Serving stations were organized along two of the side walls. She guessed there were a little more than a hundred people seated at the rows of tables, many sitting in groups. She felt conspicuous approaching the first food station as the groups fell silent and she felt their eyes studying her as she passed.

Her unnamed escort sat across from her, engulfing two large pastries while she settled for a small bowl of hot oatmeal that she doctored with a little brown sugar, a sprinkle of cinnamon and splash of cream. She added a small bowl of fruit when she went to get a cup of coffee. No one joined the two women and Aubree's already dark mood began to turn sourer. How would she ever settle if it was going to be like this? She couldn't imagine her reception in Wegah would be any easier and she would have the added burden of constantly remembering and keeping up with the many lies she would be forced to tell as she became Natalie Deckman.

They'd kept her backstory simple so she wouldn't trip herself up on the details. No family. Mother and father both killed in a tragic auto accident when she was a junior in college. Otherwise there were only very minor changes and Aubree could make it up as she chose. It had at first sounded easy but now that she was living the role, she was terrified of slipping up.

Corinne had counselled her to keep conversation to a minimum while she was traveling. That, too, had sounded easy. And it had been easy. It seemed people were reluctant to talk to someone they didn't know. She knew from life in Midah that newcomers were rare, and it took a while for them to be accepted. She was glad she didn't have to worry about it, but it made her uneasy of what lay in store for her in Wegah.

Corinne had only shared the basics with her. There was going to be a new project with Security, and it would require staffing. Wegah would be the first site but it would eventually include all ten of the hubs. Aubree would be joining as the new human resources representative and would handle the onboarding, training and many logistical aspects of setting up a new team. Her new role would be a manager level and her first task would be to hire her own support team. The prospect excited, but scared Aubree just a little. She had been looking forward to the change and wished the journey hadn't cast such a pall on her mood.

She was finishing her cup of coffee at a few minutes before seven when a tall, thin man approached the table. He stopped casually beside them and held out his hand to Aubree. "Chip. Chip Carlsen. You must be Natalie."

Even though she had just been thinking about it, Aubree was at first confused when Chip called her by the new name. She faltered briefly before returning his grip firmly and smiling. "I am indeed. Natalie Deckman."

"I understand you have the dubious pleasure of riding with me today?" His eyes were gray tinged with blueberry blue and he had pleasant dimples when he smiled, as he was doing now.

Aubree's companion who had been silent now grunted and collected her things. Aubree wasn't sure if the grunt was an expression of disgust or amusement and the chubby face was perfectly bland as she rose to her feet. "Nice meetin' ya," she said to Aubree before turning and heading back to the door, dropping her refuse in the large bin placed beside the exit.

Aubree raised her eyebrows and gave her head a little shake before looking back at Chip still standing patiently beside the table. "Well, that was pleasant," she smiled cheerfully and collected her own refuse, rising to follow Chip.

He chuckled in response. "Don't let Helen get to you. She's always like that. Not a morning person. Now, catch her at night down at the tap room with a cold one and she can be quite pleasant."

"I find that very hard to imagine," Aubree replied crisply.

Chip was a pleasant traveling companion, telling her they had a five-hour trip ahead of them to reach the Wegah meet point in old Des Moines, Iowa. "You'll be meeting a good pal of mine. Name's Adam Miller. I was a bit surprised to see his name on this morning's manifest. He's not part of the convoy escort team anymore. Got promoted recently."

"Oh?" Aubree really wasn't all that interested but feigned it for Chip's benefit. It was pleasant listening to him talk in his Midwest accent. He had a low, deep voice that Aubree thought she could listen to for hours.

"Yep. Mark my words, Adam will go far. He's smart. He did some project that went well, and it seems they've gone back to revive that and want him to set it up nationwide. Pretty cool, hunh?"

"Very." This did spark Aubree's interest a bit as it sounded like the project she was being assigned to. "You say this was a recent promotion?"

Chip nodded. "Yeah. I guess I saw Adam last on a convoy run in December. Just before Christmas. Then I started handling the Soesteh meet point. We alternate every month. I should be moving on to the Noestah site next but they pulled me off for this duty today." He shot her a grin. "My lucky day."

Aubree blushed and looked out at the flat landscape they were traveling through. "So, tell me more about Adam," she suggested, wanting to change the topic.

Chip gave another small shrug. "Not quite as tall as me. I'm six two and I'd guess he's either five eleven or a solid six. Probably in his mid-thirties. I didn't know him before he joined convoy escort, so can't tell you much about him before then. I know he ran a solid team out of Wegah the last couple of years. I mean, none of his men ever complained about him or talked about him when he wasn't around. Oh, there were the usual moaners and groaners but they're easy to spot. Every team has one or two of them, it seems."

Aubree laughed, recalling a few she'd worked with herself. "That's a fact!"

The remainder of the morning passed pleasantly, and she enjoyed the changed aspect of the landscape. The land here was flat, and the horizon stretched away from them, fading into a haze in the distance. Fence line trees marked the demarcation between the formerly neat farm fields, now gone over to nature and dotted with first generation scrub pushing through the rich dirt, barren now in the winter morning. It was warm for the end of January. She'd always heard in Midah about the dreadful winters in Midweh and had been surprised to find the temperatures in the low fifties. Chip had told her it was very unusual.

At around twelve, as they passed the exit for Newton, Chip told her, "We'll be there in about thirty minutes, maybe a bit more."

As he spoke, he glanced in the rearview mirror and Aubree saw him frown, glance forward and then again into the rearview. She sensed him tensing, knuckles showing white as he clenched the steering wheel.

"Everything okay?" she asked, glancing over her shoulder at the empty highway stretching back behind them.

"I don't know," Chip murmured. "I thought I saw something when we passed under that overpass at the last exit."

Aubree glanced back again but the overpass was no longer in sight.

"I might be being overly cautious, but my instincts tell me something's up," Chip said, keeping an eye on his side mirror. "There's an old amusement park when we exit to Route 6. I'm going to stop and drop you off there. I want you to stay put. There's a long pavilion at the main entrance, place where you used to pay to get in. You can stay there while I go on ahead and make sure there's no problem. You cool with that?" He shot her a quick glance.

Aubree swallowed a sudden lump of fear and nodded. "Sure. Do you think splitting up like that is wise?"

"I don't know," Chip said, left hand massaging his jawline thoughtfully. "I think it's the safest course. Look, if there is a problem, up ahead, and for some reason I can't get back to you…" he hesitated.

Aubree jumped in quickly, "Don't even think that!"

Chip smiled humorlessly and looked at her, "It's my job to think that, Natalie."

His use of her new name startled her and reminded her of the danger she was in. By now there was a good likelihood Drew knew she was gone. She didn't see how but it was possible he was already looking for her.

"Let's just cover our bases," Chip continued calmly. "In the event I can't make it back to you, Adam will. Remember, he's about six feet tall. He's got brown hair, wears it sorta longish, combed back. Eyes are blue—but you'd have to be too close to see that detail. You see anyone else that doesn't fit that description, you get yourself hidden."

Aubree swallowed and nodded; mouth too dry for words.

As if reading her mind, Chip continued, "There's some bottled water in that bag on the floorboard behind my seat. Grab a couple. I don't think you'll be there long but, again, let's play it safe."

Aubree reached back and retrieved two bottles, clutching them tightly.

"You know how to use a gun?" Chip asked, glancing at her quickly.

Aubree shook her head, "No. I never needed to learn."

Chip kept his eyes on the road ahead, glancing at his side mirror frequently. "Well, now's not the time to learn, then. Just remember, if you don't see me or someone that fits Adam's description, you stay hidden."

Adam sped down the highway, the Jeep falling further behind. He kept up an erratic swerve to make it harder to be a target. He was going to have to slow soon to make the left turn to keep on Route 6.

He glanced at the Jeep and took his foot off the accelerator, letting the big engine slow gradually. The Jeep had turned sideways in the street, stopped some distance behind him now. He slowed the truck; the left hand turn he needed to make only five hundred feet ahead. Why had the Jeep stopped?

He sat undecided and puzzled. Should he turn and give chase to the Jeep? There were at least two people and he had seen one weapon. It was safe to assume they would both be armed. He couldn't be sure there weren't more in the back.

Clearly, he wasn't the target. Either he had been led away from the meet point, rendering it vulnerable, or the convoy was the target. Adam didn't think it was the meet point. He had locked it up. It was as secure as it was when it was left unattended. It didn't make sense to lure him away. Besides, they couldn't have anticipated that he'd head off to meet the convoy. What were the sounds he had heard if not the convoy in trouble?

Decision made, Adam gunned the truck forward and slewed into the left-hand turn that should bring him face-to-face with the convoy. He glanced at his watch. The convoy was now twenty-five minutes late.

A few blocks down, he took the right-hand turn that kept him on Route 6, headed east now towards Midweh. He crossed the Des Moines River, the waters gleaming a muddy brown-tinged blue, bare husks of trees leaning out over the water. Down river he saw the eerie outline of the old railroad bridge, iron trusses reflecting the afternoon sunlight. There was still no sign of the convoy and he began to doubt his decision.

A few minutes later the intersection of the beltway, 235, appeared ahead and Adam saw a white Jeep Grand Cherokee sitting slewed under the west bound bridge, tires flattened. No one else was in sight but he slowed and approached cautiously. The driver's door was hidden from his view, turned with the passenger side facing his approach. He could see the driver's door was open.

He stopped the truck and put it in park, leaving himself enough clearance to make a quick escape if he needed to, and began to step carefully around the hood of the Jeep, gun raised and ready. In the silence he heard a small snick and froze in place, calling out, "Chip? That you, pal?"

He heard a clatter and Chip's voice, "Thank God it's you. I'm hurt."

Adam quickly holstered his gun as he moved around the front end of the vehicle to where Chip was sitting on the ground next to the driver's side. His right side was drenched in blood as was his left leg. There was a rough tourniquet above the wound in the left thigh. He could see blood still pumping weakly from the right shoulder wound. As he noticed it, Chip put a soaked red cloth back against his shoulder with his left hand, wincing as he pressed tight.

"The leg shot's clean," Chip nodded at the leg. "There's an exit hole and no bones broken. It bled like a bitch and hurts like a motherfucker, but I got the tourney on it and it seems okay. I don't know about the shoulder. Can't see it. I know it's still bleeding. Gotta keep pressure."

Chip's voice sounded tired and Adam could see how pale he was. He dropped to his knees and pulled Chip's hand carefully away from the wound. "Can you lean forward?" he asked, offering Chip his hand to help.

Gratefully, Chip grasped the proffered hand and pulled himself forward while Adam looked at the wound. The bullet had entered a little high on the right shoulder appearing to have missed any major bones. Adam could see an exit through Chip's back and thought the wound was too high to have damaged the lung.

"I think it's just muscle damage, but you might have nicked an artery." He looked quickly at the inside of the Jeep but didn't see what he needed. "Here, keep pressure on it. I'll be right back."

He ran back to the Ram and grabbed his jacket from the passenger seat where he'd thrown it earlier. It was a light jersey with a hood for the mild conditions and he didn't have too much trouble tearing the sleeve off once he'd gotten the seam ripped with his knife to start. He packed the material into a tight ball against Chip's shoulder, did the same with the other sleeve and then used the remainder of the jacket to tightly bind the material in place. "I've got to get you to help. You've lost a lot of blood. Do you think you can walk?"

Chip looked at his left leg and shook his head, "I doubt it, but if you let me lean on you, I can probably go a little way."

"Let's get you in the truck and you can tell me what happened."

Adam was glad that Chip was in shape. As it was it took all his strength to help the taller man to the passenger side of the Ram. Both men were too strained to spare breath for talk. Adam helped Chip get his left leg up into the truck and then half pushed while Chip tried to use his left arm to hoist himself up into the seat, a deep groan escaping as his right shoulder was pulled in the effort. Finally, he was settled into the passenger seat and Adam swung the door shut behind him.

"They got the package," Chip announced grimly as Adam got behind the wheel.

"How many were there? Did you see where they went?"

Chip shrugged. "I know there were three cars. One blocked me in front as I came under the overpass. Another one pulled across behind me. The one in front was a gray Ford pickup. Little lighter color than this one. The one behind was a black Dodge. Another Ram. Single cab. Not a crew, like this. I never did see the one on the overpass. I can't be sure, but I think they all went north on 235."

Adam glanced at the area surrounding them, seeing how perfect it was for an ambush. If they'd had cameras out here, dispatch in Wegah could have warned Chip.

Chip continued, "I was suspicious. I thought I saw something at the overpass in Newton. That's why I dropped the girl at the old amusement park there at the corner of Route 6 and Interstate 80."

"I thought you said they got the package."

"They did. I was carrying a folder. I think it came out of Northeastern originally, destined for no less than Frank Baba himself." Chip shook his head. "I've had a perfect record. This really blows. Nothing I could do. I tried to draw down on them, but I took the shot in the shoulder. While I was trying to get some cover to return fire, the truck pulled up behind and I took the hit in my leg. I heard someone get in the passenger side of the truck, but I couldn't get up. I guess that's when they got the folder. Next thing I knew they were leaving and then you showed up. How'd you know?"

"I heard the shots. I couldn't be sure they were shots. Not at that distance. You were late and something just didn't feel right. They anticipated that, too," he added bitterly. "I had just gotten out on Route 6 and was coming out of the overpass for 35 when a Jeep came at me from the right. They gave me a bit of a chase. I saw a gun, but the guy never got a shot off. They stopped chasing just before Route 6 turns to the left. So, we've got a girl hiding in an amusement park? I've got to get you to some help, Chip."

Chip nodded. "I know, but I'll be okay. The leg hurts like hell but it's not bleeding out. I think you're bandage on my shoulder is holding. We can't leave her there."

Adam nodded and pulled the Ram out around the Jeep, heading back east on Route 6.

CHAPTER TEN

Aubree paced nervously between the darkened pavilion and the brick wall topped with a rusted metal fence that stood beyond a narrow path. Beyond the brick wall a grassy slope rose to a rambling structure falling to ruin. A sign hung crookedly in front of bay windows declaring a train had once been boarded at the building. The roof was sunken in at two spots and most of the ginger trim that had once adorned the gracious building was now hanging in rotted segments of wood turned a dirty shade of gray. Gates to her left and right gave access to the park. She couldn't see from where she was, but she assumed that after entering either of the two gates you would emerge behind the train station. Trees blocked her view much further though she could see the looming structures of the old amusement park rides. Off in the distance beyond the building that once served a train the skeleton of a roller coaster dominated the sky while a huge Ferris wheel leaned drunkenly to her left, looking like the next strong wind might blow it over, umbrella covered cars swinging at a crazy angle.

She could almost hear the echoes of the laughter and screams of terror as young and old were hurtled along precarious rails at murderous speeds. She caught a ghost memory of the fragrance of funnel cake and corny dogs. Instead, all she heard was the songs of the numerous birds that were the only inhabitants of the abandoned park. The long drive winding in from the main road was visible from her location and she watched tensely for the white Jeep Grand Cherokee to return. She glanced at her watch. It had been forty-five minutes since Chip dropped her off and the silence was beginning to unnerve her.

Her eye caught movement and she saw sunlight reflecting off a windshield. A gray pickup turned into the road leading to the park. Quickly she ducked to the left-hand entrance and slipped through the gate, leaning crookedly on one broken hinge. The gate led into a long tunnel. Ancient spiderwebs hung from the ceiling above her in ghastly drapes that she ducked to avoid, not wanting the sticky strands to catch in her hair as she passed. She could now hear the crunch of gravel under the tires of the truck as it pulled into the parking area in front of the pavilion.

She paused, about halfway down the tunnel. What if it was Adam? What if it wasn't? She glanced around, deciding this wasn't the best place to hide, wishing the pavilion itself had offered a suitable spot. She had checked and after opening the door quickly ruled out using it as cover. The inside was completely open with a broad counter running the length of three of the walls offering no hiding spot.

She emerged from the tunnel now into a large courtyard made to look like an old village square. A garish carousel sat rusting in the center, the canvas top, once a bright red and white stripe, now hanging in tatters of gray and washed out pink. The horses appeared to scream against the bits in their teeth frozen in their endless roundabout.

She hurried to the first building on her left, a sign declaring this was Lost & Found and beside that another door offering Stroller Rentals. She smiled at the irony of Lost & Found and tried the door. It was unlocked and she swung it open, briefly relieved that she had found a place to hide so easily. Her heart sank as she surveyed the bare room in front of her. Four walls, nothing else. She moved on to the Stroller Rentals, but it was the same.

In the distance she thought she heard a car door and decided she didn't have time to try all the buildings in the square. She suspected she would find they were all the same anyway. It was obvious the place had been stripped when it was abandoned.

She jogged quickly past the carousel, following the curve of the central park to another street leading away from the entrance opposite the courtyard. A sign identified this as Main Street and more shops lined the sides. She didn't waste time checking any of the shops but continued to jog deeper into the park, finally coming out of the shops to a bridge that crossed a small pool, an old Dodge 'em Cars at the opposite end. She paused, paths leading to left and right as well.

Over the years the park had become overgrown as plants found root in any patch or crack. She couldn't see far along either path because of the shrubbery crowding close to the water. If it could be called water, she thought to herself. As she watched, a ripple moved across the surface and she shuddered to think what might live in the murky depths.

Not wanting to cross the bridge she turned to her left and ran along the edge of the lagoon, following the path. It took her around and she now saw the rollercoaster structure straight ahead. Surely, she could find a place to hide among the supports of the massive structure.

Slowing to assess her options a wall to her left caught her eye. It was a long curving concrete wall with massive trees growing close behind it. The

Underground. She was tempted. Slowly she walked a short distance into the yawning opening and then stopped. It was pitch black. No, without a light she couldn't risk it. Turning, she again assessed the roller coaster in front of her. Large pylons jutted up, bracing the rails. She would be able to hide easily and still watch the path from behind one of them.

"Looks like the bird flew the coop," Adam muttered as he looked around the vacant pavilion from the front seat of the pickup.

"I told her to hide unless she saw me or you." He saw the way Adam looked at him and added, "I gave her a description but sadly it no longer applies." He surveyed Adam with a sour look. "Why'd you cut your hair?"

Adam shrugged, "Seemed like I should at the time. Why's my hair an issue?" He rubbed a hand across his now shortened hair, almost short enough to be considered a crew cut, eyeing himself critically in the rearview mirror.

"I told her you wore it longish."

"Hmmm," Adam grunted in reply. "So. What's her name again?"

"Natalie. Natalie Deckman."

Adam nodded and eyed the pavilion. "I doubt she's in there, but I'll check. How you feelin'?"

Chip laughed, "Top of my game, man." The laugh made him cough and the cough ended in a groan of pain. "I'm all right. In a lot of pain."

Adam leaned over and pulled a small travel case out of the glove compartment. "Not as good as morphine but better than nothing. Pop four of these." He shook some ibuprofen tablets into Chip's hand and gave him a bottle of water. "Be right back."

He went to the door in the end of the pavilion where employees had once entered to collect money from eager park goers. Opening the door, he wasn't surprised to find the interior empty. He would have discounted it as a good hiding place, too. He closed the door and looked around the area. Behind the pavilion was a narrow path connecting the two gates that controlled access to the park. A brick wall, topped with a metal fence, stood just beyond. Nothing moved and he could hear nothing other than birds.

Returning to the truck he stood by Chip's window. "I'm guessing she went in. Advise dispatch of the delay. I'll go in after her."

Chip nodded and Adam approached the gated entrance on the right. The tall gate was locked shut with a loop of thick chain and padlock. Shaking his head at Chip he took the narrow path behind the pavilion and went to the second gate. This one was hanging open, one side leaning on a broken hinge. He turned to Chip and motioned that he was going in. Chip nodded back at him and Adam turned to duck through the thick strands of cobweb festooning the short passage.

Emerging into the courtyard beyond, he paused, scanning the plaza surrounded by fake fronted buildings. Everything was still and he called, "Natalie!" Even though his voice had been soft a flock of pigeon's was startled and burst noisily from under the rafters of the building at the opposite side of the quadrangle. He eyed the carousel but quickly discounted it as a hiding place. He heard no response to his call. He turned to face where a street exited opposite the entrance as a single path and he strode to it quickly. "Damn it," he muttered as he walked briskly, "Why'd you have to go in so far?"

He came out the other end of Main Street, faced with the choices of following the path either left or right or crossing a bridge spanning a narrow tongue of water. He tried to think like she might. She'd have been scared. Which way would she go?

The path circled off to left and right, obviously following the edge of the water feature. Tall trees shaded the thick tangle of shrubs and tall grasses growing along the verge of water. The water itself was still and cloudy, a thick scum of leaf mold clogging the edges.

He wished he knew the park better or where the paths might lead. He called again, voice pitched low and soft, trying not to alarm her. "Natalie! It's Adam. It's okay. You can come out!"

He paused, listening hard for any response and sighing in frustration as only the sounds of birds and rustle of small animals in the underbrush came back to him. He strode to the middle of the bridge, the highest point in the area, and again surveyed the area around him. To his left the water stretched away and broadened out at its furthest end while to his right it ended a short distance beyond, the path to the right clearly following it and wrapping around to meet the opposite end of the bridge. Some distance in front of him, beyond an old bumper car game, rose the looming structure of a roller coaster. He studied it speculatively and then looked again at the path winding off to the left, apparently curving around the bumper cars to emerge at the rollercoaster.

He started down the left-hand path and then paused again, trying to think like her. She'd want to be hidden yet able to keep an eye on the path. That would mean she'd want to be either in a building with a window or behind a protective shelter. He ruled out the building as too confining and too easy to be trapped. That left a sheltering structure outside.

He glanced around, eyeing the foliage around the lagoon and deciding it was too thick. The bumper car ride was a possibility. The old husks of the metal cars on magnetic rollers sat in gloom beneath the sagging ceiling of the superstructure around it. Creeper vines had overwhelmed the rear of the roof and it was caved in, pulling the two opposing sides inward. He doubted she'd risk going in there and it would be too easy to be trapped there, as well. No, he felt like the rollercoaster was the best option. Lots of things to hide behind and yet be able to move easily.

Which meant she'd be watching the path as it came out. He turned back to the path that went off the right, seemingly away from the rollercoaster. It was his guess, though, that once he got past the bumper cars and the hulk of an indefinable ride at the far corner, he'd find another path leading back towards where he thought she might have gone. He tried calling her name again, "Natalie! Can you hear me? Please come out."

Again, silence settled as his voice died away in the still air. Shaking his head in disgust, he turned and strode off down the path leading off to the right.

Just as he had expected, the path curved around to the left and approached the rollercoaster at its far southeastern corner. Adam spotted a small building sitting almost under the curve of rail, a bizarre chicken sunk halfway through the rotted roof. He crossed over to the near corner, the backside of the bumper car ride now off to his left, the rollercoaster frame itself looming directly above and behind what must have been a food dispensary when the park was open.

He circled the wooden structure, hugging close to the dark walls, until he found a door on the side wall off another path that led through an ornate arch declaring Country Fair lay just ahead. He contemplated passing through to the next area but then turned his attention back to the overgrown broad expanse sprawling beneath the framework and decided that this was the best spot.

His eyes moved over the little that he could see but nothing out of place caught his attention. He tried again to call her name, "Natalie? Are you in here?"

Aubree had headed for the central pylon facing her as she approached the rollercoaster. Small trees and dense shrubbery had taken over the land under the rails and some of the grasses were almost taller than she was. It offered good cover and she worked her way through the tall clumps until she was beside the large concrete block. It stood almost to her shoulders and she was able to kneel behind it and view the path she had come down.

In the distance she thought she heard a voice but couldn't be sure. She sat uncertainly. What if the truck had been Adam? Which could only mean something had happened to Chip. She had thought she'd heard a popping noise while she was waiting in front of the pavilion but it had been so brief and repeated just a couple of times. She wasn't even sure she'd heard it in the first place.

Now she ran through the possibilities in her head. Perhaps she had heard something, and Chip was injured. Adam wouldn't know what she looked like and she wasn't where Chip had left her. What if Adam left and she was left alone here? The thought sent a real tremor of terror through her. She glanced around furtively, trying to think what she would do. She had no idea how to get Wegah from here and Midweh was a long way behind them. She thought of the many empty miles she had covered with Chip and shivered to think she might be alone in the midst of it.

What if the pickup didn't belong to Adam? She couldn't think who it might be. It surely wasn't feasible that Drew would have someone out here. Could he? She knew that didn't make any logical sense, but she also didn't want to discount any possibility. The truth, she knew, was that other than Chip, no one knew where she was.

She was beginning to feel foolish hiding behind the pylon, yet she was too scared to move. She thought she heard someone moving around over to her far right, well out of her sight. From where she crouched, she thought she saw a wooden structure, two darkened wooden walls devoid of doors or windows. She stared at the structure, alert for any signs of movement, but everything was still.

As she watched, she caught movement to the right of the building, out on the path that led in front of the rollercoaster. Foliage obstructed her view but as she sat tensely holding her breath a man appeared in a gap between the clumps of grass and thick shrubbery that surrounded her. She crouched lower, afraid he might see her.

She couldn't be sure how tall he was, but his hair certainly didn't fit Chip's description of Adam. This man had closely cropped dark brown hair and he was wearing sunglasses that prevented her from seeing his eyes. Moving as slowly and carefully as she could she eased behind the pylon, keeping the concrete support between her and the man. She pressed her back against the concrete, left heel braced against it in case she needed to get a good running start.

She was in about the center at the front of the oblong twisting rail structure. She could see five more of the concrete pylons from where she sat. If she ran in a low crouch, using the foliage as cover, she might be able to make it to one of them. From there she could plan her next move. So, which of the five?

The closest seemed to make the most sense and she chose the one to her right. Taking a deep breath, she carefully leaned out to her right and peeked around the pylon, regretting now that she had let him out of her sight. She didn't see him and felt panic. Pulling back, she was uncertain now if she should break her cover. She held her breath, listening hard. Not hearing anything she allowed herself to relax and then carefully eased herself forward into a runner's starting stance. Taking a deep breath, she drove hard with her left foot against the concrete, launching herself to the right and the nearest pylon.

As she threw her weight forward, she had a moment of disorientation when her left arm was suddenly grabbed and held in a firm grip, her shoulder almost wrenching from the socket as her weight was thrown against it. Crying out in pain she fell to her right knee, swinging about to face the tall figure looming her.

It was the man she had spotted on the trail. He held her left arm in his right hand, left hand resting casually on the butt of a pistol sticking out of a holster on his left hip. "You Natalie?" he growled.

"No!" She cried out, forgetting in her panic but then just as quickly remembering. "I mean, yes! Who are you?" She pulled her left arm, trying to free herself from his grip, and almost fell on her back when he released her suddenly. She cried out again and caught herself from falling. Standing up, she brushed the backside of her jeans and scowled at the man.

"I'm Adam," he replied brusquely, extending his right hand.

Aubree flinched and then took the offered hand in her own, pumping it firmly. "Where's Chip?"

"In the truck. He's been hurt. We need to hurry." He turned away from her and began to move quickly back down the path in the direction he had come from.

Aubree was stunned by his brusqueness and concerned for Chip. "You left him?"

He paused and glanced back at her; expression unreadable behind the dark sunglasses. "Would you have preferred I left you?"

Aubree returned his look flatly, struggling to suppress a flare of anger. "Of course not," she responded crisply.

Without another word Adam turned and headed back towards the entrance, trying to set a pace that she could match. He was surprised by his own gruff response to her. He hadn't expected her to be so attractive, that was all. Even now, he could see those clear green eyes. When he had first met her startled gaze, as she fell on her knee before him, he had been mesmerized by those eyes. His fingers had longed to smooth the richly shaded brown hair falling past her shoulders. He could feel the weight of those eyes on his back as she followed him to the truck.

"Chip's in the front seat. You'll have to take the back."

His tone was apologetic, and Aubree softened towards him a little. "That's all right. Is Chip hurt bad?"

He shrugged. "I don't like the look of his shoulder wound and he's lost a lot of blood. We really need to try to reach Wegah before the gates close, but I don't see how we can." He glanced at his watch and shook his head. "We've lost too much time. It'll be five thirty before we get there, and the gates close at four thirty this time of year. I can't make up a whole hour."

"What'll we do? Won't they open the gates for you?"

Adam laughed harshly, "No. Not even for me."

They had reached the tunnel leading out to the ticket pavilion and they ducked through silently, neither wishing to disturb the denizens of the dark tunnel. Adam held the back door on the driver's side open for Aubree and then slipped into the driver's seat.

"Found her, I see," Chip announced, turning his head to give Aubree a strained smile. She was shocked by how pale he was.

"Maybe you should lie down back here?" She offered.

Adam eyed him critically and nodded. "She's right. Though I think laying back that passenger seat and reclining would be better." He met Aubree's gaze in the rearview mirror. "Maybe you could check that bandage I put on his shoulder. See if it's holding. I'm going to call in to dispatch."

Chip used the adjustment on the side of the seat to lay back while Aubree bent over to see if the bandage was still in place. The material was almost soaked through, but it had slowed, and the patch didn't widen as she watched, testing to be sure the binding strip was still tied tightly. Chip moaned when she moved his shoulder but was otherwise silent. She heard Adam keying the mic.

"Dispatch, this is Alpha Main. Are your ears on, Dispatch?"

There was a slight delay and then a tone followed by a female voice. "That's a roger, Alpha Main. What's your situation?"

"Partial package recovery successful. Midweh escort is wounded pretty badly. I've got him stabilized but he needs help. There's no way I'll make the gates by four thirty. Over."

The pause was longer, and a new voice came back, this time a man, "Alpha Main, what's your location? Over."

Adam glanced at the marquee over the long drive in from the road and replied, "Adventureland Park in old Des Moines. Over."

Another silence ensued and Adam shifted uncomfortably in the seat, feeling the minutes passing. He started the truck, and put it in gear, starting down the drive back to the road before the man finally replied. "You'll need to plan to stay the night at the north side safe house. Over."

Adam shook his head angrily before keying the microphone and replying, "This man needs medical help today. Can't you route a chopper or drone?"

"Sorry, Alpha. I've got none available. I'll send a team out to the safe house with a medic kit. It'll have everything you need. Keep him stable until morning and a medic team will pick him up as soon as the gates open. It's the best I can do, Adam. Sorry."

Adam nodded in resignation, "I know, Al. Thanks."

Grimly he returned the microphone to its holder on the underside of the dash. His eyes rose and met Aubree's briefly in the mirror before returning to the road in front of him. "We've got three hours, three and a half to reach the safe house. Chip, you take those pills I gave you?"

"Sure did, buddy," Chip replied. "Could use another swig of water."

"There's more in that duffel on the floorboard. Should be right under your feet," Adam told Aubree.

The duffel bag was there, and she pulled out a bottle for Chip. "You want one?" she asked Adam.

"Sure. Thanks." He held his hand over his shoulder, and she passed him a bottle, opening one for herself as she sank back into the corner of the seat.

She must have dozed because when she next opened her eyes the sun was much closer to the horizon, casting longer shadows to the east. She tried to stretch muscles weary from inactivity, rubbing her arms and shoulder to bring back circulation.

"Have a good nap?" Adam asked.

Aubree glanced at the mirror, not liking that she couldn't tell where he was looking, the dark sunglasses reflecting blankly, reflections within a reflection. She glanced away, nodding. "Yep. Chip been asleep long?"

"About the same as you, I guess."

She read the next road sign as it appeared on the shoulder on their right. Eagleville ten miles. Wherever Eagleville was. She glanced at her watch. It was already four o'clock. She gazed out the window. The land stretched away in a broad flat expanse, a couple of trees dotting it here and there, vegetation sparse and the dead grass waving golden in the wind of their passage. They soon crossed an overpass, the empty highway it crossed stretching away beneath them, disappearing into the mysterious distance.

A sign, the top half white, the bottom half blue, announced this was Missouri, Welcome Center and Rest Area one mile ahead. Many of the signs she had seen as she crossed the country from Midah were fallen or in states of disrepair. Often only the metal struts that once held them remained; the signs they bore long since ripped away by fierce winds. She had not known when they'd crossed into Pennsylvania.

"So, this is Missouri," she spoke aloud, startling herself as she had not meant to.

"Yep," Adam replied. "Welcome to Missouri. Or Misery as some like to call it," he smiled at her in the mirror.

She liked the look of his smile, the dimples that graced the corner of his mouth, the strong jaw. She wished she could see his eyes. "That's the first sign I've seen that looked that good. I was recalling that I didn't even know when I crossed the Pennsylvania border."

Adam smiled again, "This used to be my route. I was team lead of convoy escort. I kept the sign repaired."

"Why would you do that?" Aubree asked.

He shrugged. "I don't know. Old pride, maybe? It got knocked over in a bad storm a few years back and I just decided we'd fix it one day. Seemed to me like we ought to. So many of the old things and old ways are gone now."

"Yeah," she replied softly. "I was thinking that when I was in the park back there. When I was little, my folks took me to Kings Dominion. I was twelve. I had a blast. They had a bumper car arena too. It was called Lucy's Crabbie Cabbies and I must have drove my mom nuts saying it. I just thought it was the cutest thing. They were for little kids though. I remember I pouted because I was too short to ride the Anaconda. I really wanted to ride it. It did a three sixty."

"You were twelve? Takes guts to ride a loop."

His voice held admiration and she blushed. "Maybe. We'll never know. I never got to ride it. I was thinking it's sad those things are gone. I know we have the virtual reality centers now and you can experience anything you want. Ride any rollercoaster, anywhere. But it's not the same."

Adam could only catch part of her profile in the mirror, but he saw the flush that had crept across her cheeks and how pretty it made her.

"How long before we reach Wegah?" she asked.

"Oh, about another hour and a half. Maybe a little less. We'll be going to the safe house, though, which is a little closer for us. We ought to get there," he paused, glancing down at his watch, "I think we'll get there about quarter after five. We'll still have some daylight. That's good."

She leaned over to check on Chip. His breathing was steady, if shallow. He didn't seem to be in any distress and was resting quietly. Sleep was the best thing for him until they could reach the safe house and whatever the medical team had left. She sighed and leaned back into her corner. "Who did this?" she asked, gesturing towards Chip.

Adam shrugged. "I wish I knew. Outsiders."

"Are you sure?"

Adam swiveled his head to the mirror and even with the sunglasses she knew he was looking at her. "What do you mean? Who else would it be?"

She shrugged in response and shook her head, remembering that she wasn't to mention Drew or that situation to anyone. "Nothing. I don't know. They had vehicles. Weapons. I mean, they shot Chip!"

"Yeah? Outsiders have cars and guns. As many as we do, I suspect. You don't think it's someone from Wegah, do you?" He wasn't sure why the implication angered him or why he felt the need to defend his hub. "No one in Wegah would do this," he added sullenly.

"I didn't mean to imply they had," her tone was sharp, and she turned to watch out the window, body stiff with anger. Why was it he managed to anger her so easily?

Adam cursed himself, seeing the tight muscles along her jaw, the beautifully sculpted lips thinned in anger. He pulled his eyes back to the road, surprised to feel a desire to kiss those lips, imagining how they would feel under his.

Aubree gazed out the window, her brief flare of anger quickly spent, and feeling a little ashamed at how she had reacted. She didn't like to think the Outsiders might be the aggressors, that they had attacked and wounded someone, and yet the evidence was clear. Why they would do it, she wasn't sure.

She had quickly concluded Drew couldn't possibly be behind the attack. He might have eyes and ears to help find her, but he would have no reason to wish her harm. At least, she didn't think he would.

"Look, I'm sorry," Adam spoke softly. "I doubt that anyone from the hub would do this, but I don't know everyone that lives there." He gave a small shrug and continued, "I think it was the work of Outsiders. We've had some troubles at a few of the other hubs. Ours has been quiet. We've had no encounters that I know of." Another small shrug. "I'm really at a loss on this."

She could hear the earnestness in his voice, and she softened. "I'm sorry, too. It really doesn't make sense. I mean, they didn't get anything, did they?"

Adam was quiet for a moment before replying. "Actually, they did."

"Oh!" She was surprised. She hadn't known Chip was transporting anything other than herself. She glanced at the mirror but couldn't tell if Adam was looking at her or the road.

"There was a letter being hand delivered to Frank Baba," Adam finally added. "And the only way they would have known to be here today to intercept it is if they've got someone on the inside."

CHAPTER ELEVEN

Aubree came awake with a start when the truck stopped. For a moment she was disoriented, and her neck was stiff to turn. They sat in pitch blackness. Then, she heard Chip groan, and recalled where she was. "Adam?" Her voice quavered a little and she could hear the fear in it.

"Right here." His voice came back to her reassuringly from the seat in front of her. He opened his door and she braced for the flood of light, prepared to shield her eyes, only none came. "Sit tight just a moment," she heard Adam say. "I'll get us some light."

A moment later a light came on and she saw they were sitting in a two-car garage. A tool bench with neatly arranged tools hanging on a peg board, battery charger sitting on the counter and other assorted power tools arrayed along the back, sat in front of the nose of the truck. A line of gas cans lined the wall on her side.

Chip moaned again and she turned to see his eyes open.

"Hey there," he said, and gave her a weak smile.

"Hey, yourself," she replied, "How you feel?"

"Oh, I've been better." He gave a short laugh, and she saw him wince in pain.

"Don't do that," she cautioned. "Stay still." She turned back and opened her door, stepping out into the garage, glad to stretch her cramped muscles. Adam had disappeared through a door into the interior of the house.

She looked around the neat garage, noting the blackout blinds taped to the drywall to prevent any light from escaping around the two windows set together on the right-side wall. Stacked neatly below the windows were crates of canned items and bottled water.

"Everything's secure." Adam announced, startling her as he came back into the garage. "Can you give me a hand with him?" He gestured towards Chip and looked at her questioningly.

"Sure. Tell me what to do."

"I'm going to help him out and get him around the front. When I get him past the hood, I'll need your help to support him. I'll take his left side, his injured leg. You keep an eye on his shoulder. Try to keep it stable. Just hold him around the waist. We'll come into a utility room and beyond that the kitchen. We'll go right in the kitchen. There's a bedroom he can rest in."

She nodded and went to wait at the end of the bench counter, watching as Adam helped Chip out of the truck. The two men moved awkwardly in the narrow space, maneuvering so Adam could close the door and ease Chip around the front fender, along the hood, supporting his injured left leg, Adam taking Chip's weight easily even though Chip was the taller of the two. When they reached her at the end of the counter, she moved to support Chip on his right.

There was little support needed from her as Adam bore Chip and guided him into the house. Aubree stayed at his right side, making sure he didn't jolt or hit his shoulder as they moved through the door frame. The bedroom off the kitchen was small with a twin sized bed, a small nightstand and dresser. Adam eased Chip down onto the coverlet.

"I'm going to check for what the medic team left. I'm hoping they thought of morphine. Be right back." Chip nodded and Adam turned to Aubree, standing uncertainly in the doorway. "Give me a hand?" he asked her.

She nodded and backed out into the kitchen. They found a kit on the kitchen counter and he unpacked the items. There was bandage material, tape, antiseptic wash, three syringes with instructions which he read carefully. Beneath the items was another sheet of paper with more instructions.

"All right," Adam announced decisively, setting the paper aside and reviewing the items arrayed on the counter. "First, we'll need to take the bandages off both wounds. I did release the tourniquet while he was sleeping in the truck and his leg's not bleeding. So that's good. The shoulder may be a different matter. They've given me a packet of powder that will help stop the bleeding if we need it. We'll need to flush the wound with the antiseptic wash and then I need to give him an antibiotic shot. That's this one." He touched one of the syringes. "These other two are for pain. I'll give him one before we start. It's supposed to last six hours, but this first dose may only be effective for four. I'll give him the other one later, should get him through until morning." He looked up at Aubree and paused. "You okay with this? Get sick at the sight of blood?"

She shook her head and swallowed. "No. No, I should be fine. I mean, I've never…" She gestured helplessly.

He smiled tenderly, "Yeah. Not a normal everyday occurrence. Look, if you start to feel sick, dizzy, anything like that, you let me know—get out of the room. I can handle it."

"No," she said resolutely, "I want to help."

She almost regretted that decision but managed to stay through the process staunchly until the end. The leg had not been so bad. The two wounds were gruesome enough but easy to clean and bandage. The shoulder was a different matter and there was no way to work on it without Chip lying on his side to give Adam access to the front and back.

Aubree knelt at the side of the bed, holding Chip's hands while Adam worked as quickly as he could. Even with the shot of morphine she could see that Chip was in a lot of pain as Adam flushed out the wound, sprinkling it with the powder and packing it tightly with fresh gauze.

By the time Adam had finished dressing the wound, Aubree's hands hurt from the pressure Chip had exerted on them. He was pale and clearly exhausted. Adam eased him into a comfortable position on the narrow bed while Aubree found a thin blanket in the bottom drawer of the small dresser.

"The kitchen's well stocked," Adam offered. "Getting hungry?"

Aubree hadn't considered it but as he asked the question her stomach growled in response. She grinned and replied, "I guess that answers that."

He returned her grin and then told Chip, "I'll get you some hot soup, something easy to get down."

"Thanks. Think I'll just sleep a bit," Chip mumbled, already half asleep.

They quietly left the room, pulling the door almost shut, as they stepped back into the kitchen.

"Thanks for your help," he said to Aubree as he moved to the refrigerator, swinging the door open to review the contents.

She looked over his shoulder and saw the shelves had been stocked with the basics. Moving to the cupboards along the wall she opened doors to find more canned and packaged goods along with a tub of coffee, creamer and sugar.

"Looks like dinner's chicken stir fry and rice. There's even a carton of soup in here we can heat up for Chip," Adam declared as he pulled the items out and placed them on the counter. "You'll find some pans in that cabinet next to the stove. Mind filling one with a cup and a half of water? Measuring cups are in that top cabinet next to the microwave."

He measured out the rice while she set the water on high to bring it to a boil, stepping back and leaning against the island while he turned to heat the oil for the chicken and precut vegetables. She studied his profile, admiring the straight cut of his nose, the gentle yet strong set of his mouth, the smooth jawline. Her eyes roved across his shoulders, noting their breadth and watched the muscles of his back move under the fabric of his shirt as he poured the rice into the now boiling water. Her eyes continued down the taper of his back to his lean waist and hips, perfectly sculpted buttocks under the well-worn denim. The long muscles of his thighs bunched beneath the legs of the jeans and she imagined they would be hard under her fingers.

"You like mushrooms?"

"Hunh?" she was startled by his question and flushed when her eyes rose to meet his, imagining he could read her recent thoughts in her expression.

"I asked if you like mushrooms," he spoke slowly and calmly, as if to a child.

She flushed again, this time in part due to embarrassment and in part from anger that he should speak so condescendingly to her. "Sorry. I was lost in thought and missed it the first time you asked. Yes. I like them."

He nodded and turned back, dumping the chicken into the now hot oil. He'd seen her flush when she'd looked at him. What had she been thinking about? And why had he managed to anger her so easily? She'd clearly been aggravated with him just now when she answered him. He had enjoyed looking at her and wished he could engage her in conversation. Every time he spoke to her, he somehow managed to say the wrong thing. It might be best if he just kept his mouth shut, he thought glumly, stirring the soup he'd set on to warm for Chip.

He imagined he could feel those clear green eyes watching him.

"Two percent." He hadn't meant to say it aloud.

"What's that?" she asked.

"Only two percent of the population has green eyes. You're a two percenter. I learned it in college. Statistics."

She laughed, "I like that. A two percenter, hunh?"

He flashed her a smile and she felt her pulse quicken. He was so handsome when he smiled like that. She could see now that his eyes were indeed gray but as Chip had noted they almost looked blueberry blue in the low light of the hood over the stove, his face in shadow. She wanted to study their color and again flushed at the thought of his nearness. She moved into the dining room beyond the kitchen, lying in shadow.

"Go ahead and explore," Adam said, nodding around. "All of the windows are taped so you can turn on lights. Don't open any exterior doors, of course. There's an alarm that'll sound if you do. There's a large bed and bath through the living area there. That's where you'll sleep tonight."

"Oh," she hadn't considered sleeping arrangements. "And you?"

"There's another room just past Chip. I'll stay there where I can keep an eye on him. I'll be staying up for a while to keep a watch, anyway."

"Oh. Okay." She turned and wandered into the large living area, turning on the overhead light with the wall switch as she entered. She admired the well-furnished room. A plush white sofa with big cushions sat invitingly before a large hearth, two navy blue wingback recliners flanking it on either side. A large white, fake bear skin rug filled the large open area between the sofa and hearth. She could imagine lying there while a fire burned in the fireplace beyond.

A door led off the living area opposite from the kitchen and she discovered the bedroom he had said she would be using. She stood in amazement. The room itself was larger than her apartment in Midah had been. A massive king size bed carved in an intricate pattern dominated the center of the room, matching dresser and armoire lining two walls. Plush carpet covered the floor and she couldn't wait to walk barefoot across it.

A third wall gave access to the bathroom and she gasped. A whirlpool tub stood in one corner with a separate tiled shower stall wrapped in frosted glass beside. A long marbled double vanity extended along the wall opposite with a small enclosure with a toilet on her right as she entered. She ran her fingers along the rim of the gleaming tub. It would be such a pleasure to soak in it later.

She returned to the kitchen, the sound of sizzling stir fry emanating from the stove while a tantalizing aroma rose in the steam. He didn't run the exhaust fan and waved the spatula apologetically over the skillet as she took one of the stools on the other side of the island.

"Can't use the exhaust. It vents out and would give away our presence if anyone was around," he explained.

"Makes sense," she replied. "Chip quiet?"

"Yep. Not a peep. Soups warm. You want to check on him and see if he's ready for some?"

"Sure. Should I wake him if he's sleeping?"

"No. Let him rest. The longer that pain shot lasts, the longer the next one will. We can keep the soup warm. He'll wake in a bit anyway when the shot wears off."

"Okay." She went over to the door and eased it open, allowing a crescent of light to reveal that Chip was resting soundlessly, sprawled on his back. She eased the door closed and returned to the stool. "He's sleeping," she told Adam.

"Good. Best thing for him. Medic team will be here as soon as they open the gate. We'll head on over to Sector Eight. I'll drop you at Human Resources and then I'll need to report to my Director on what happened today."

"There won't be any trouble, will there?" She was suddenly concerned. What if he and Chip were blamed for the loss of whatever the package had been?

He shrugged. "I hope not. If we'd had a wider surveillance network we'd have caught more. As it is, I doubt we've got any video of what happened. If a satellite happened to be looking in the right direction at the right time..." He shrugged again, stirring the skillet and pulling it off the burner, setting it to the side. He checked his watch and turned to face her. "Five more minutes on the rice."

"You cook," she stated with a smile.

He returned the smile. "It's something I've always enjoyed doing. My mom assigned me a night to cook when I turned twelve. Told me I needed to know how to take care of myself." He smiled again, and Aubree knew he was thinking of his mom, his face softened in the light by a tenderness that touched her. "I was to cook dinner on Tuesday. There were a good many evenings Tuesday dinner was from the local Dairy Queen when I began to earn some money doing yard work."

Aubree laughed, "That was inventive."

"Lazy is what it was! No, I actually did enjoy cooking and it was cool that I didn't have to lift a finger for clean up on the nights I cooked. That was the other part of the deal. Got to where I was fixing some pretty nice dinners by the time I graduated high school."

"When was that?" she asked.

"2020. The Class with Vision, or so we claimed as our class motto."

Aubree smiled, "You and a couple thousand others, I'm guessing."

He laughed and she liked the sound. In fact, she was discovering she liked a lot about him. She was becoming keenly aware they were alone in the house. Chip asleep on morphine couldn't really be counted on as a chaperone.

The alarm on Adam's watch went off, breaking the silence that had settled comfortably in the wake of the laughter. "Dinner is served. It's serve yourself, so grab a plate and scoop up." He followed words with action and began to pile rice on his plate.

She moved to stand beside him, intensely aware of his presence. Their hands brushed as she accepted the pan of rice from him and she could feel a flush creep up her face. She silently cursed her inability to hide her reactions.

He was as keenly aware of her as she was of him. He caught the scent of her hair as she moved beside him and he inhaled deeply, savoring the rich scent, wishing he could bury his face in the soft tresses, run the silky strands through his fingers.

He glanced at her as he handed her the rice and was captivated by her natural beauty. Long lashes framed the clear green eyes that so enchanted him. Her hair was a rich brown, reflecting red highlights from the overhead dome lights. Her skin was creamy and looked soft, he longed to stroke his hand across her cheek, feel the soft texture beneath his fingers. His lips longed to taste the fine curve of her mouth, caress the tender corner between upper and lower lip, tease her tongue with his.

Lost in his thoughts Adam grabbed the hot handle of the skillet and quickly let it go. It clattered back to the stove loudly as he cursed, "Damn! Ouch, that's hot!"

Aubree jumped beside him, startled, almost tossing rice all over the kitchen. "Are you okay?" she asked anxiously.

"Yes!" He waved his hand and ran some cold water from the faucet to cool it down. "I think. I was lost in thought and grabbed that hot handle. Be careful. Don't pick the skillet up without a potholder."

The rest of dinner was silent. They carried their plates to the dining room table, amber light casting a warm glow on the gleaming wooden surface, seating themselves opposite one another at the table that could comfortably seat six.

"This is really good," she commented, discovering the chicken stir fry was flavorful and the rice was cooked perfectly.

"Thanks," he responded, and another awkward silence fell.

"Is it all right if I use the bathtub?" she asked as she carried her dirty dish to the sink. "After I clean this up. You cooked; I'll clean."

"I appreciate that. I'll go check on our patient and feel free to use the tub, shower—make yourself at home."

"I wish I could," she said wistfully, looking around the spacious kitchen. "What a wonderful home."

He had only had occasion to use the safe house on a couple of previous occasions and had never really appreciated all the home had to offer. Now he looked at it speculatively. "Yes. It is a nice home. My mom would have loved this kitchen."

She smiled at the tender tone of his voice when he spoke of his mom. "I think any woman would," she began to fill the sink with hot water, adding dish detergent and settling the few dirty dishes in the suds.

He was surprised that the simple domestic chore was striking him as exceedingly sensual. Flustered, he turned to check the soup left to keep warm on the stove so his hands wouldn't be tempted to cover Aubree's in the warm water, to carefully lather and caress those long elegant fingers.

"I need to check on Chip." His voice came out sounding gruff. Without another word he strode across the kitchen and eased Chip's door open enough to slip through, carefully easing it shut behind himself.

Aubree sensed his change in mood and sighed, wondering what was bothering him, why he was so brusque with her when she'd just felt like the ice between them had thawed a little. She finished cleaning the dishes and when he had not returned from Chip's room when she was finished, decided she would go ahead and retire. That bathtub was calling her, and she was not willing to resist.

Adam leaned against the wall behind Chip's door and took a deep breath. He ran a shaky hand over his shortened hair and rubbed his temples. He had to get control of his desire. Every time he looked at Aubree it seemed to spark another response in him. He'd never reacted to a woman this way and wasn't sure how to deal with it.

"Natalie," he whispered her name aloud to see how it felt on his tongue. He liked the play of consonants and vowels and repeated it again, "Natalie."

"What are you mumbling?"

He jerked his head up to find Chip gazing at him with a bemused expression on his face.

"Boy, you've got it bad," he drawled and smiled. "Can't say I blame you.

She's sure pretty."

"Ah," Adam waved his hand dismissively and moved away from the wall. "How're you feeling? Want to let me check those bandages?"

"Feel like I've been hit by something really big. Morphine's got me pretty woozy right now. Not feeling much pain. Let's just leave things alone, if you don't mind." He glanced down at his right shoulder. "I don't see any blood, do you?"

Adam peered at the bandaging and said, "Yeah. I don't see any either."

"Then we're good." Chip closed his eyes; the little bit of conversation having drained him of energy.

"I heated some soup for you. Will you try to eat some?" Adam asked.

"Yeah. Sure." Chip didn't open his eyes and Adam went back to the kitchen to get the soup. He noticed that everything else had been put up and at the other end of the dim living area the door to the bedroom was closed, a ribbon of light at the bottom. He could hear water running through the plumbing and imagined her preparing the bathtub for her bath. That was a dangerous line of thought and he quickly snuffed it, focusing instead on the task at hand.

Aubree turned off the faucet and slipped into the gently steaming hot water. She had never been much a bather, always preferring to take a hot shower, the water briskly cleaning her. Now, she luxuriated in the enveloping warmth, leaning her head back against the wall and closing her eyes in pleasure. She felt the tension easing from her muscles and was glad to just relax.

Tomorrow she would begin her new life in Wegah. She hoped the beginnings were not an omen of the future. The amusement park she had hid in had been incredibly creepy. The old rides, rusting and rotting, being overwhelmed by nature, had made her melancholy. She missed her dad and her brother. She even missed her mother and their stupid arguments. Now she was surrounded by strangers, one of which had been shot. The distance she had traveled and the vast country they had covered, not a living soul encountered between the walls of each hub, terrified her with the unknown secrets hidden just beyond sight. She felt incredibly small and very alone.

A tear slipped from under her lid, traveling down the smooth expanse of her cheek to drop into the water of the bath. She felt immensely weary. The hot water had drained her of her remaining energy reserves. She couldn't believe that it had been only yesterday morning that she'd left Midah.

She considered her situation now. Hiding in a house outside the protection of hub walls with two strange men. One was wounded and the other—well, the other was certainly unsettling. She thought she should feel fear at being here but oddly, knowing Adam was just beyond the outer door of the bedroom, made her feel safe. She took comfort in knowing he was watching over them. She ignored the small voice in the back of her mind that suggested how much safer would she feel if he were next to her?

She pushed the thought aside and rose from the tub. She dried herself quickly, slipping into the t-shirt she slept in. She wasn't sure what to do with the damp towel and washcloth. Maybe she should ask Adam.

She went to the door leading to the living room and stood uncertainly. She felt foolish asking such a stupid question. Surely it could wait until morning. Why bother him with such trivial details tonight? She knew he was exhausted and worried about his friend. She wasn't exactly keen on him seeing her in just her night shirt, either. She laid her hand on the door, wishing she could have one more opportunity to speak with him before retiring, and then turned off the light, moving carefully across the dark room and sliding between the cool sheets of the large bed. She was asleep within five minutes.

Adam stood in the dark living room. He could hear Aubree moving about in the room beyond and then silence settled, the house was still. The ribbon of light shone at the bottom of the door and he thought he saw a shadow. He envisioned her standing there, just beyond the thin wood of the intervening door. He raised his hand and lightly touched the door where he imagined her face would be, those hypnotic eyes casting their spell on him.

He stood there a moment, indecisive. Should he wish her a good night? Ask if she needed anything? A voice in his mind was quick to reply not to be foolish. If she did, she would have asked. If exchanging pleasantries were important, she would have done so before going to the bath. As he stood, he saw the ribbon of light wink out, vanish as swift as the moment of opportunity slipped away.

His hand dropped back to his side. He could hear the rustle of bedding and knew that she was in the bed. He would not torture himself with thoughts of that. Turning, he crossed to the remaining room just past Chip's, the narrow bed looking very empty even if it was small. He struggled to not think of Aubree in the other room, but crystal green eyes haunted his sleep that night.

CHAPTER TWELVE

"I just received a message from our team in Wegah. There's been another incident. This time a man was injured." Ben was pacing in his office.

Frank's face on the monitor scowled. "What happened?"

Ben shook his head. "I've suspected for a while now that we have a leak somewhere in Security. I let the word get out that the candidate replacement list for James was being sent via secure convoy."

"I've already got James' recommendations." Frank interjected, the scowl deepening.

Ben nodded. "I know. I thought I might be able to locate the source. I'm afraid all I managed to do was get a good man hurt."

"Will he recover?"

Ben sat back down behind his desk, rubbing a hand across his face, "Yeah. He took two bullets trying to protect that bogus list, one in the leg and another in his shoulder. The leg will recover fine, but the shoulder wound was almost fatal. Missed his lung by an inch. He could have gone into respiratory failure, collapsed lung—no way he could have gotten help quick enough. Pure luck that he pulled through. Luck and our Wegah man was quick thinking."

"Oh? Who's that?"

Ben smiled, "Adam. Remember Adam Miller? The one setting up the surveillance network. He made the run and got suspicious when the convoy was late getting to the meet point. Broke protocol leaving and thank God he did."

"Fortunate. I thought he was busy on the project. Why's he running convoy?"

"Some mandatory training scheduled that day for the Wegah convoy team. They normally don't run convoys on Friday's and had scheduled an all-day session. Local management decided to use Adam as a fill in."

Frank leaned back in his chair, shaking his head, "I don't like it, Ben. That was a hell of a risk to take."

"I wouldn't have done it if I'd known someone would get hurt," Ben replied bitterly.

"I know that. That wasn't directed at you. You still think we have a leak?"

"I know we do. It's the only way they could have known there'd be a convoy. I just can't trace it back to the source. It's got to be in Security, though. No one outside of Security knew about this."

"Have you considered we should be the cat instead of the mouse?"

"What do you mean?"

"Well, it seems we're playing a cat and mouse game with the Outsiders. I think they're better organized than we've given them credit for. If they're spying on us from inside, we need to find a way to do the same."

"I wish it were that simple, Frank."

"I don't see how it could be simpler. You just need to find the right man for the job. And make sure only you know about it."

Ben smiled, "Yep. Easy."

Frank chuckled. "Maybe I oversimplify. Anyway, I've been thinking about that a great deal for another reason. This incident just confirms for me that we've got to prioritize this. I've been thinking it's time we try to negotiate with these people." He turned in his chair and gazed out his window. "Things haven't turned out the way the original Council intended. The whole idea of work centers made sense when it was used for disciplinary reasons. We couldn't have prisons and jails in the hubs, and isolating the bad elements was a wise choice. Unfortunately, the concept has been abused. Good people are being sent to the centers."

"Any time you tie an incentive to something like that, someone is going to abuse it," Ben rejoined, rancor in his tone.

Frank sighed heavily, "Don't I know it. For God's sake, Ben, these people we keep calling Outsiders aren't outsiders. They're Americans, damn it! We always knew there were a lot of people that chose not to move to a hub. By completely excluding them and isolating them we've created this situation. How do we fix it now?"

Ben heard the frustration in Frank's voice. "I don't know, Frank. I think you're on the right track, though. If we could find a way to work with them."

"That, and the work center incentives have to stop. I'll be addressing that."

"That's long overdue," Ben couldn't resist saying.

Frank looked at him sharply. "I never supported incentives related to the work centers, Ben, and you know it! It never would have happened if we hadn't had that shortage a few years back. Even then it wasn't handled correctly. It was supposed to be an incentive for any volunteers. Not for forced assignments. Those incentives were supposed to be short term, not an indefinite benefit."

Ben shrugged, "Like I said, any time you tie an incentive to negative behavior, your incenting the negative. I never saw positive results from a negative motivator."

"True. It wasn't supposed to be a negative. If you'll recall we had the idea at the time that it might be good to open the hubs and give folks an option. Start decentralizing."

Ben shrugged, "That may be, Frank. I'm not questioning the good intentions. There are plenty of bad people that will find a way to take advantage of good intentions."

Frank gave Ben another sharp look and then sighed heavily, nodding, "You're referring to JB, Judy and Kate, I assume."

"They seem to be benefiting the most from these incentives right now."

"Yes, well, there will be no more RIFs in those hubs without my direct knowledge."

Ben nodded, "All right. I'll make sure my teams in those hubs keep me informed as well. If I hear of any activities, I'll let you know."

Frank nodded and glanced down at a piece of paper on his desk, "I'll be reaching out first to each of the work center directors. They'll be informed that any incentive offered for head count will result in severe disciplinary action. I'd like you to schedule an inspection of each work center. I want to know what the conditions are like. I'm hearing rumors I don't like of unacceptable conditions. I want a list of all personnel currently assigned to a work center."

"Human Resources should already have that," Ben offered.

"Should being the operative word. Lawrence informed me last week that HR had a bug in their database and somehow that file was corrupted. Seems mighty convenient to me."

"Hmmm. This is the first I've heard of this."

"It wasn't a security problem, no reason you should hear about it."

"Sounds to me like you think it is a security problem."

Frank shrugged. "I have my suspicions. Lawrence has IT looking into it, see if there's any trace of tampering or possible release of a virus. It's a long shot and I doubt they'll find anything."

"You think JB's behind it."

Frank laughed. "No trail will lead to her door. No, she's too smart for that. But, yes, I think she's the mastermind."

"When did IT get engaged?" Ben reached for a pen.

Frank held up his hand. "Let me run with this, Ben. You've got enough on your plate and I need you focused on finding that leak and securing our convoys. We need that surveillance system yesterday."

Ben laid the pen down, "All right, but if IT does come up with something, I'd like to know."

"You'll be the first. You'll send me the work center inspection schedule?"

"Before the end of the day."

"No one was supposed to get hurt!" Erick lashed out angrily at Jerry.

Jerry nodded; his expression grim. "One of the team panicked. When the driver got out, he thought he was reaching for a weapon."

"It was six to one! No one would draw down under those odds! I've been through the training same as you. He would have surrendered, was probably trying to!"

"Well that doesn't help us now, does it? What's done is done."

"Do you know if he was killed?"

Jerry shook his head. "We don't know yet but I'm trying to get answers. We've got some folks in Wegah, but none in Security. They're keeping a lid on it. All I've been able to find out is that someone was brought in injured the morning after the incident. Whoever it is they're keeping them in a secure location. I'll take that as a good sign we didn't kill anyone."

"I hope it was worth it," Erick grumbled.

"That's the hell of it. It was a bust." Jerry stood up abruptly and strode over to the kitchen area. "Want some coffee?"

"Yeah, whatever. What do you mean a bust?"

Jerry filled the coffee maker with water and loaded the grounds in the basket before replying, "I mean there was no list. It was a setup."

Erick sat stunned. "They know about us?"

Jerry shrugged. "No, I don't think so. If they did, they'd already be here. But I suspect it was a ploy to uncover us."

"If there was no list, what exactly did we get?"

Jerry laughed, "It was a list, of sorts. A list of locations where we can turn ourselves over to the authorities. It was addressed to the head of the rebellion and was signed by none other than Ben Larocque."

Erick studied Jerry for a moment before he quietly asked, "And who is that, Jerry? Who is the head?"

Jerry returned Erick's gaze. "There's no single person. We've got some communities, mostly those nearer the work centers. Those more isolated don't want to get involved. They've gone this long on their own and they're fine with things the way they are."

"So, who makes decisions?"

"Each community makes their own decisions independently. We only handle communications and the occasional runner like Sam through here."

"And that absolves you of responsibility?"

"I didn't say it did, Erick." Jerry's tone was brittle. "Make no mistake, people are going to get hurt in the fight ahead. I'm sorry someone got injured on this operation. I truly am. But a lot of innocent people are being hurt by the one's your defending."

"I'm not defending them," Erick's voice conveyed his frustration. "Just how much do you think Larocque knows?"

"I think he was fishing. I think he suspects a leak, and this was his first attempt to find it."

"Can he trace it back to us?"

Jerry shrugged again. "He'll know the communication came through here. It doesn't isolate us. We're only one link in the chain, but I'd rather we didn't have a spotlight turned on us. I've got the satellites back on their original programming, but it would be too easy for someone to trace our interference with their alignment."

"Did you see the email we just got from Frank?" Judy Rice's voice was frosty, and her blue eyes glittered angrily at Janet Byron through the monitor.

JB leaned forward, "I saw it."

"Kate's about to panic because of it. I just got off the phone with her. The email came in while we were talking."

"Kate is always about to panic," JB replied drily.

Judy laughed. "Yes. Well, I'm sure she'll be giving you a ring."

"Why? The message is clear. There will be no more incentives in return for headcount sent to work centers. Why does this create a panic for Kate?"

"It's not the incentive so much as the need to report RIF activity."

"Kate depends too much on RIFs."

Judy gave a half shrug. "I'd say we've all benefited from our ability to manage our own hubs."

JB studied Judy intently. "Are you suggesting, Judy, that I've abused the RIF program?"

"Not at all," Judy replied smoothly. "I'm merely observing that Frank Baba's intrusion is not necessarily welcome."

JB raised her eyebrows and smiled back at Judy.

Judy was unnerved by the lack of response and hastily glanced away. "Any word on the Nocitra replacement?"

JB's smile deepened, "Actually, yes. It appears we'll have a—hmmm, shall we say, a supportive voice in the Northeast."

Judy grinned back at her. "That's great news. Now if we could just lock down Midah."

JB frowned. "That's turning out to be a bit harder than I anticipated. With Diego coming around we'll have a solid fifty percent. Unfortunately, Baba still holds majority. We need Midah."

Judy nodded. "Lawrence has been extremely careful and none of my folks have been able to sniff out information. He's talking directly with Baba."

"Yes." JB turned her gaze to somewhere off screen, her face thoughtful. "What we need is someone in Security…"

Judy waited silently, scanning the latest batch of incoming emails, until JB finally said, "Well, I guess that about covers it. All RIF activity is on hold. Unless it's a clear case of a crime committed and then we let Security deal with it. In the meantime, if you talk to Kate, tell her to settle down. I'd prefer she not call me today. I've got back to back appointments."

Judy nodded, "I'll let her know."

"And I've got some ideas about Baba. For now, we just sit tight. Got it?"

"Done. I'll keep ears open on Midah. I hear anything, you hear it five minutes later."

JB smiled. "I can always count on you, Judy."

CHAPTER THIRTEEN

"How's that new manager from Midah doing? What's her name? Deckman. Something Deckman."

"Natalie," Adam offered. "Mind if I have another?" He gestured at the plate of jelly-filled donuts in the center of the conference table, taking one when the man he sat across from nodded assent.

"Yeah, yeah. Natalie Deckman. That's it. She settling in?"

Adam shrugged and nodded, "Seems to be. She's interviewing the candidates for her new team today. Should have everything set up within the month."

"Good. Good to hear. Anything on that incident last week? We get anything on surveillance?"

"No. None of the satellites were looking the right way. Which in itself is interesting."

"How's that?"

"I've started thinking we might have a leak. It was all just a bit too convenient."

Adam's director, Brent Gear, or Bent Gear as others were fond of calling him, was in his early forties and was best described as average. His weight, his height, everything about him was average. Except his intelligence. He was extremely sharp, and Adam was not fooled by the lazy droop of his eyelids as he doodled on the pad in front of him. Brent was never still. He gave a slight nod and said, "Go on."

"Well, for one thing it wasn't a normal day for us to be running a convoy. We always use Monday through Thursday for out outside meets. Fridays we focus on the hub. We never run on weekends. And it was the week before our hub hosts the Super Bowl. The chances of us running an off-schedule convoy were pretty slim."

Brent nodded in agreement. "So, they had to know we'd be there.

Could've been someone in Midah, Midweh or Wegah. What else?"

"I think they knew it was one man. I don't know if they knew about Natalie. They knew I was solo. There was only one car, that I know of, with two men that I could see covering me. There may have been another car, but I don't think so. A normal convoy has a lot more men and vehicles than this one did. Chip only saw the two cars, front and back. We know there was one overhead. That would mean they were well-informed on the size of the convoy."

Brent was nodding as Adam talked and set his pencil aside, linking his hands on the table before him as he leaned back in the padded chair. "Anything else?"

Adam shrugged. "This is pretty far out there but someone could have manipulated the satellites. If I could be so bold, I would suggest we check the satellite programming. Make sure we always have coverage and run a debugger. See if it's been with tampered with."

Brent flipped the top page on the pad, covered with doodles, and made a note. "Good idea. I'll get Communications to handle that. Meanwhile, how's your project coming along?"

"Good. I finished the last of my required training this week. Next week I'll be working with Natalie on the new team. Hers, and also mine. I plan on going out with the convoy team next week to run some new cabling and set up some additional cameras along Route 6. I'll need a crew from Infrastructure and a cable truck to assist with that."

"Got it. I'll give them a head's up before the day's over. Expect to hear from someone Monday to arrange what you need. Material and personnel."

"I've got a requisition list started."

"Good work, Adam. I like how you're settling in. Keep it up. And if you have any more suspicions, I'd like to know about them."

Adam rose, knowing he was dismissed. "Thanks. I appreciate the feedback and I'll let you know if I think of anything else."

As Adam reached for the door, Brent added, "Oh, one more thing. I'd like you to keep an eye on Natalie. She's an unknown factor and could have been the leak. Then again, maybe not. What do you think?"

Adam considered this and shook his head. "I don't think so, but I'll keep an eye on her." He thought to himself that he didn't need much encouragement in that regard. In fact, he needed to think of her a little less.

"Great. Got plans for the Super Bowl?"

"No. Not really. Probably watch the game at home."

"Why don't you take Miss Deckman out? I've got a couple of tickets here to O'Neill's. Private club room, party. Not the sort of thing my wife is very interested in. She's planning to host something at the house anyway. Interested?" He retrieved a slim leather portfolio lying on the surface of the desk, pulling out two ticket stubs and extending them to Adam.

"Hey, that'd be great! Thanks!" Adam accepted the tickets and made his exit. It would be fun to spend the evening with Natalie doing something other than work.

He found her at her desk in the mostly empty section of the floor where ultimately their joint teams would operate from. "How'd the interviewing go?" he asked as he dropped into the chair behind his own desk, directly across the aisle. He tried not to notice the shapely curve of her leg when she swiveled in the seat to look at him.

"Fair. There were a couple of good ones I've already notified HR that I want to move forward with. So, who'd you end up meeting with? Brent Gear or Bent Gear?"

Her smile was the one he privately thought of as wicked and he felt his pulse jump. The past week had shown him many of her moods and he hadn't found one yet that didn't excite him. "Brent, I'm happy to report. And please be careful saying that."

She raised her eyebrows and looked around the empty cubicles that surrounded them. "Sure. I'll do that."

"Anyway, turns out he had a couple of tickets to a private party at O'Neill's for the Super Bowl this Sunday. Want to join me?"

She felt a warm glow. Over the past week, spending her working days with him had only fueled her interest in him. So far, other than the candidates she'd interviewed from HR, she'd not had time to interact with many other people in the hub. She'd spent a good bit of the first week finishing up her required training, dividing her time between that and, with his help identifying the scope of work and size of team needed to perform it. They had worked well together, and she wanted to spend time with him on a more personal level. "I would enjoy that," she told him now, swiveling back to her monitor so he would not see just how pleased she was with the offer, feeling the warmth in her cheeks.

Shortly after she had accepted his invitation, Adam absented himself, leaving on the promise, "I'll be by to pick you up Sunday at five. There's a pregame dinner that starts at six. Should give us plenty of time to get there. I planned on droning it, if that's okay."

The thought of riding in a drone with him, the close quarters requiring passengers to sit close, was far better than the idea of sitting in a car, where his attention would be on driving. "I don't mind at all. Means we'll both be able to have a good time and not worry about getting home."

He grinned and saluted her with a phantom glass. "My thoughts exactly. All right, I'll see you Sunday."

After he left, she sat musing for a bit. Had the invite been merely one co-worker asking another? Did he feel pity that she was here all alone and didn't know anyone? She had learned in the past week that he had a sensitive side and he tended to treat her with gentle respect.

She missed her friends, wishing she could tell them about Adam, get their advice. She missed Sacha most of all. She thought Sacha would have liked him, might even have approved. She smiled at the thought of her friend and then pushed the melancholy that came with the memory aside. She didn't want to be sad when the future was looking so bright.

By the time Sunday afternoon arrived, she was a bundle of nerves. She had changed her outfit three times since two that afternoon when she'd first started getting ready. Her bed was littered with a rainbow of discarded clothing.

Her new apartment in Wegah was more spacious than the one she'd left in Midah. She enjoyed the increased size of her living space. She had a large bedroom and closet with a bath that had a separate tub and shower. It wasn't nearly as nice as the bathroom in the safe house had been, but it was larger than any she'd had before.

She stood in front of the full-length mirror hanging on the back of the closet door critically studying her image. She'd chosen a black hip length sweater with a smattering of rhinestones around the modest scoop neckline. A large pink flamingo done in flashy sequins climbed up the left side. A pair of lacy black leggings, black riding boots with boot cuffs in creamy ivory lace, completed the ensemble. Her long hair floated in waves past her shoulders. It would have to do. She wasn't changing again, she thought, pulling open the closet door to have one last look. She was just reaching for a white and purple sweater when a knock came at the door. "Well, guess we're ready," she whispered.

"Hi!" she said brightly, opening the door and hoping to mask the nerves she was besieged with.

"Hello," Adam replied, eyes expressing his admiration as he awkwardly held out a bundle of flowers. The bouquet held six red and six blue roses with sprays of silver and white frosted ferns. The foil wrapping was also done in an abstract pattern of red and blue. "I wasn't sure if you were a Chief or Cowboy fan."

"They're gorgeous!" she exclaimed, adding, "And I'm neither. I was raised a Redskin fan and I don't think I'll be changing just because my address did." She smiled and accepted the bouquet, moving into the kitchen to find something to put them in. "Come on in," she said as she moved away.

Adam admired her as she turned and went into the large galley style kitchen that was central to the layout of the apartment.

"I'm not sure I have anything to put these in," Aubree continued, trying to fill what felt like an awkward silence. "And I really appreciate you getting them. I suppose for tonight I'm a Chief's fan."

"Good to know you'd choose the home team," he offered teasingly.

"Well, being a 'Skin's fan, I'd be hard pressed to cheer for the Cowboys."

She found a plastic pitcher she normally made cold tea in and filled it with water, watching him through the opening between the kitchen and living area as he stood at her large window that overlooked a pretty park. He was wearing a well-worn Chiefs jacket. She noticed that on the back it said Kansas City Chiefs. "You've had that jacket a long time," she commented. "It's been a while since they were known as the Kansas City Chiefs."

He turned, glad for an opportunity to gaze into those wonderful eyes. He looked down at the jacket, the white leather arms worn in the elbows, the red leather front and back darkened to burgundy with age and use. "I went to college here before it was Wegah, when it was still Kansas City. Got it back then when I was senior. I only wear it now for special occasions." He gave her a smile that made her knees a little weak.

A stillness settled as she placed the flowers in the pitcher, arranging them and carrying them to her small dining table in the nook off the kitchen. "And this, then, is a special occasion?" she asked casually. Turning, she found him watching her intently.

"Oh, it's a very special occasion," he said softly as her eyes met his.

She blushed. "Is this a date, then?" she asked, turning to fiddle some more with the flower arrangement to avoid looking at him.

He crossed the room in a few strides, closing the distance to stand at her side. Gently he lifted her chin and turned her face to meet his gaze. "I'd like to call it one, if I may?" He gestured at the flower arrangement. "I believe is was once customary for the suitor to bring flowers?"

"Oh! A suitor now, are you?" she asked with a light laugh, stepping away to place a little distance between them in the close quarters of the dining nook.

He merely smiled and swept his arm towards the door. "Your chariot awaits."

The drone ride was everything she had thought it would be. It was an older model drone and only carried two passengers, the seats close together. As the drone lifted into the air it wobbled slightly and he laid his arm across the back of the seat, holding her shoulder reassuringly. "It's old but safe. It'll steady as soon as the automatic compensators adjust for our weight dispersion."

She nodded and swallowed. "We had a lot of these in Midah. I'm used to it."

His leg was pressed tightly against hers and she could feel the warmth he radiated. She settled more comfortably against him while he pointed out some of the highlights of Wegah along the way, the stadium glowing brightly on the edge of the hub. He had programmed their route to follow the Missouri river and it was enchanting to see the early evening lights reflected in the waters of the swift moving river, the large skyscrapers in the old downtown district, now Sectors Nine and Seven, sparkling like miniature stars.

O'Neill's was a large metal structure that looked like it had once been a warehouse and she felt like they got there far too quickly. They had to hover for a few minutes waiting for a clear landing site and the drone dipped erratically trying to hold itself in place. She felt her stomach spin and gripped the handrail tightly.

He laughed, "Relax! We'll be down in just a minute."

She also laughed in response, "That's my main concern." She shot him a grin to show she wasn't afraid. "It was always like this going to a 'Skin's game. I'd usually have the drone set me down a few blocks before the stadium and walk the rest of the way."

"Tender tummy?" he asked, cocking an eyebrow at her curiously.

She laughed again. "Not really. I just prefer my first beer to give me that feeling."

That made him laugh and the drone rocked precariously when he leaned back. She gasped at the sudden move and his arm tightened around her shoulders. She turned to let him know she was okay and suddenly they were face to face.

The kiss was fleeting, lips barely caressing. She felt every nerve tingle to life. She took a breath and was about to speak when the drone settled to the ground.

It was still early, and a long line was forming at the doors into the club. He strode confidently down the line of waiting fans, her hand grasped tightly as he pulled her along. She felt embarrassed hearing the grumbles and thought how humiliating it was going to be to have to walk all the way back to the end. They'd be even further back than if they'd just gotten in line in the first place like everyone else, she thought indignantly.

Instead, he handed the door attendant the two tickets and the door was instantly opened, a lovely young woman in a tight-fitting sequined body suit in the colors of the Chiefs smiling graciously and asking them to "Please follow me," as she led the way into the brightly lit tavern area. The cavernous space was mostly empty with servers frantically bustling about, checking tables. Tiers of glasses and buckets of ice sat waiting. The aroma of fried food carried out of the kitchen along with the smell of chargrilled steaks. Her stomach growled in anticipation.

Large television screens dominated all four walls, using the high ceiling of the old warehouse to maximum effect. No matter where you were in the bar, you'd have a view of the game.

They were led rapidly through the main bar area and through another door on the opposite end into a smaller, more intimate area. Two large-screen televisions opposed one another on opposite ends of the long room. Tastefully set tables with center candles were scattered well apart, plush carpet under foot, padded leather chairs arranged in groupings. A long bar with low lighting extended the length of the wall opposite the entrance, the long mirror behind giving an illusion of space. The maître d' checked the tickets and led them to a table for two on the right-hand side of the long room.

It was filling quickly and what had seemed spacious when they first arrived, quickly became crowded as the dinner was served and kick-off time approached. There were ten large speakers placed around the room and normal conversation quickly became difficult as the overall volume increased with the size of the crowd.

She caught the excitement as the two opposing teams took the field and everyone rose for the playing of the National Anthem. Then the game began, and she and Adam were intent, cheering along with the other Chiefs fans on the good plays, groaning on the bad and booing the referees with gusto for any call in the other teams' favor.

Adam kept stealing glances at Aubree, enchanted with her beauty. The more he was with her. The more beautiful she became. His fingers longed to touch the silky auburn tresses falling in waves around her shoulders. She had kept it pulled back at work and this was the first he'd seen her wear it down. It gleamed richly in the amber light and somehow made her eyes glow even greener, helped them sparkle even brighter. The kiss he'd stolen on the drone had only left him hungering for more. When the two-minute warning for the second quarter sounded he realized ruefully he didn't recall many of the plays from the first half he'd been so aware of her beside him at the table. As the first half ended with the Chiefs ahead of the Cowboys by three points, she turned a dazzling smile on him.

"Good game, isn't it? Thank you so much for bringing me! Beats sitting alone in the apartment watching."

The lights in the bar came up to full light, brightening the room, and the sound was turned down as a good many of the patrons chose to attend the halftime party in the main bar where a live band was performing.

"Do you want to go out and watch?" he offered.

She shook her head. "If you don't mind, I'd just as soon stay here. It's nice getting a break from all the noise for a minute."

He grinned. "Good. I was enjoying it, too."

"I'm glad it's a close game," she said. "It's never much fun when it's a blowout."

He nodded and glanced at the television screen. "Oh, hey—let me catch this quick." The screen showed the famous white sandy beaches of Hawaii, surf crashing and volcanoes smoking in the distance. "They're going to announce the winners."

She glanced at him curiously and then back at the screen. The volume was down so they couldn't hear what was being said but a list of names began to scroll up the screen.

Abruptly he tensed, leaning forward in his chair, arms gripping the armrests tightly. She heard him whisper, "Really?"

She glanced at the screen and the scrolling names, the image of the surf in the background. She looked back at him and met his gaze. "My mom," was all he said in response.

As she absorbed this news his cellphone rang. Glancing at the screen he turned back to her, "I'm sorry, Natalie. It's my mom. I'll only be a moment." Turning, he rose and left the table, saying, "Hey, Mom, I saw the announcement!"

He was back five minutes later, grinning. "That's amazing!" he said as he resumed his seat beside her, shaking his head. "My mom won the Hawaiian Retirement! She got the call during the second quarter, but they asked her to hold off calling anyone until the official announcement came at half time. She is so excited!"

Aubree smiled, trying to appear as happy for him as she could, and hide her reservations. She remembered overhearing a conversation once back in Midah about the Hawaiian Retirement and it wasn't something good. She was trying now to remember where she had been and what it was exactly that she'd heard.

"Speaking of Mom," he continued, looking a bit embarrassed, "I'd like you to meet her. Seems it'll need to be soon, now." He gave her another grin.

"I'd like that," she replied, reaching over and laying her hand over his. "I'd like that a lot."

CHAPTER FOURTEEN

Adam laid a heart-shaped white satin box wrapped with a red velvet ribbon on Aubree's desk. Surprised, she sat back, noting the grins being hidden by their new team members as they all tried to look like they weren't watching. She looked up at him questioningly.

With a small bow he dramatically pulled his hand from behind his back and laid a single white rose on top of the box and then he held out a card. "Natalie, will you be my Valentine?"

She felt the blush suffusing her cheeks mixed with the stir of unease she had begun feeling when he used her fictitious name. "I'd be honored," she murmured, accepting the card. They had been seeing each other steadily since the Super Bowl and she'd even been to meet his mother the past weekend.

Megan had been very gracious if preoccupied. Her small room had been crowded with the three adults and she had been nervously going through her belongings again to make sure she had everything packed. She would be leaving the next day.

"Oh, Adam," she had sighed, her eyes glittering with unshed tears. "I'm so excited, but I am going to miss you so very much."

Aubree had been sitting in the only other chair at the small round table and Adam had knelt at Megan's feet, clasping her hands tightly in his.

"I'll miss you, too, Mom." He'd brushed the now falling tears tenderly from her cheek with his thumb. "Don't cry. This should be a happy time." He'd offered one of his brilliant smiles as an example.

"Oh, my dear boy, your father would be so proud of you." She'd run a trembling hand through his hair and Aubree had looked away, wishing she could give them privacy in this intimate moment. "I think he would have liked Natalie very much. I know I do, and he always approved of my opinion."

Aubree had looked at Megan and found her offering a brave smile, hands now clasping Adam's tightly again. "Thank you, Mrs. Miller. I wish I could have met him."

Megan had smiled and looked back at Adam. "Oh, but you have. You're a lot like him, Adam. And he was a good man." She had looked back at Aubree, "I miss him every day." Then she had released Adam's hands and clapped hers briskly. "Now! Where is that list? I need to check it one more time." Like a small butterfly that can only sit on the flower for a brief instant, she was up and moving around the small apartment again.

It had been hard for Aubree, knowing that the woman she presented herself as, Natalie Deckman, was not who she was. It had felt wrong, especially knowing she may never meet this woman again and she was so clearly very important to Adam. Yet, Aubree justified, she was still basically herself. It was only the name and a fictitious background. It didn't change who she was.

As she broke the seal on the envelope she recalled, too, that she had wanted to follow up on the Hawaiian Retirement Program. She still thought there was something about it that Adam needed to know.

Her grim thoughts fled as she read the card enclosed in the envelope. A shadow couple, walking hand in hand, on a moonlit beach with gentle waves lapping at their feet, tender words flowing over them. Inside, below more endearments, a simple handwritten question: Spend the weekend with me, please? She felt a flutter in her stomach and her hand trembled slightly as she lowered the card to her desk. She reached for the rose to give her hands something to do. Its scent was exquisite.

"Red is more traditional."

"Excuse me?" She was startled out of her thoughts and looked at him quizzically.

He nodded at the rose, sitting down on the edge of the desk and leaning towards her. "A box of chocolate and a red rose is traditional on Valentine's Day. I thought the white was far more beautiful and your beauty deserved a rose to match."

Aubree heard her team lead in the next cubicle discreetly cough and her face flamed once again.

"So? What's the answer?" He smiled at her tenderly, leaning closer.

She met his gaze steadily. A weekend with him. Just the two of them. She could feel her physical response, excitement, fear; her heart hammered loudly in her ears and she was sure they could all hear it.

"I think I'd like that very much." She was relieved to hear her voice sounding normal if a bit breathless.

He grinned broadly and stood up. "Date! Tomorrow night."

She nodded and replied, "Now let's get some work done," being sure her voice carried to the nearby cubicles. She couldn't help but hear the titters of laughter in response. Smiling, she turned to check her email.

"Where are we going?" Aubree asked, eyeing the bundles wrapped on the back seat to see if she could spot any clues. Not seeing anything helpful she turned back.

Adam grinned. "Guess."

"That's unfair. I'm at a disadvantage."

"How's that?" he asked innocently.

"I don't know Wegah. It would be a little hard to guess, don't you think?" she replied a little smugly.

He grinned, "But you don't need to know Wegah. You've been where we're going once before."

She looked at him quizzically, "O'Neill's?"

He laughed and shook his head. "Guess number one is a strike."

"If you want to count that as a guess," she replied, her smile contradicting the sharp tone.

"And before you say it, it's not my mom's place either. I think there's a new resident, anyway."

That made her laugh. "Then I'm all out of guesses. We haven't been all that many places."

He glanced over at her; his expression serious. "I want to see every place with you."

The simple statement was filled with his sincerity and she felt herself flush. "That's very sweet," she murmured.

He reached over and caught her left hand in his, his thumb gently caressing the back of her hand and along her fingers. "I mean it," he added, lifting her hand and brushing a light kiss across the knuckles before releasing it back into her lap.

She felt her heart race and a tingle ran along her spine, nerves electric with sensation. They were nearing the walls encircling the hub where she had first entered Wegah on that traumatic morning almost a month ago and the memory reminded her of their night in the safe house. She glanced at him in surprise now. "The safe house?"

He grinned. "The one and only. I guess you did get it in three."

She grinned back, but then quickly grew somber. "Is it safe?"

His grin got broader in response. "It would be why we call it a safe house."

"I meant being outside of the hub. Alone."

He looked at her again before answering softly, "That's the idea."

She blushed again and looked out at the darkened landscape, the early winter night settling over the empty land beyond the walls, knowing the gates were now locked behind them until six o'clock the following morning. There would be no going back. Her pulse quickened at the thought of the long night ahead.

They arrived at the safe house twenty minutes later and she sat in the car while he turned on the lights and did a quick security check. She was beginning to fidget in the dark car when he finally returned, turning on the overhead and momentarily blinding her. "Everything okay?" she asked, a bit concerned at the time he had taken to return to the garage.

He smiled mysteriously, "More than okay. Come on in, make yourself at home."

She retrieved her overnight bag from the backseat. He had suggested she pack casual for the weekend and she had spare jeans and some long-sleeved shirts, a favorite sweater and a special outfit she thought she might find handy. Her bathrobe had been stuffed under the handles as an afterthought, no room to fit it in the full bag. Her bathroom essentials were in another small bag which she picked up from the back floorboard.

"Here, let me," he offered, coming around the back of the car and taking her overnight bag. "I'll just set your things in the big bedroom you used last time. There's cold cider in the fridge or wine on the counter. Help yourself."

She chose the cider and wandered into the living area. The gas fire was lit in the fireplace and she stood in front of it, hypnotized by the dancing flames. She sensed him at her side and spoke quietly, "Beautiful, isn't it?"

The silence extended and she turned to face him. He was gazing at her intently and when her eyes met his he spoke, "You have no idea."

She knew it was more than the heat of the fire making her skin feel warm. She gazed up into his eyes, gray in the firelight. His lips curved in a sensual smile as he looped his arms around her waist, pulling her against him. She felt an urge to brush back the dark drift of hair that fell across his forehead as he looked down at her and she allowed her hand to follow the thought. The strands were silky under her touch and she ran her fingers through his hair and down his neck to rest on his shoulder, her other arm circling his waist.

"Natalie, you are the most beautiful woman I've ever met," he told her earnestly. "And I don't just mean your looks. No complaints there," and she felt him shrug under her hand, "None at all. But it's who you are, too. You're a beautiful person."

She felt herself blushing deeply and lowered her head, leaning into his chest. "You make me feel like I am," she told him.

His arms tightened around her and she felt the rumble of his laughter in his broad chest. "See what I mean?" He leaned back to peer down at her and she looked up at him. "You don't even know how beautiful you are. Now, do you like your steak rare, medium or well-done?"

The simple question at first confused her and she frowned, desire surging through her, electrifying her nerves. "Hunh?"

He grinned, the dimples deepening, and she thought about kissing the corner of his mouth. "Steak. How do you like it?" he asked.

"Oh. Rare. Actually medium-rare. I don't want it bloody, but I like the center red."

He nodded and released her. "Make yourself comfortable. I'll throw the steaks on, salad's ready and I'll pop the potatoes in the microwave. We'll eat in about fifteen minutes?"

"Can I help? Is there something I can do?" she asked anxiously, wanting to be of assistance.

"Nope. Tonight, I've got it. Tomorrow night, we'll fix it together. Deal?"

She smiled and settled into the comfortable couch facing the fireplace, cider in hand. "Can't beat that deal. I've got clean up."

He served them steaks with baked potatoes and a salad with glasses of a fine vintage merlot under the dimmed chandelier in the dining room. He had the table set for two at one end, only the one pendant chandelier glowing weakly, shadows encroaching. She was enchanted.

"I have a surprise for you after dinner," he announced, sipping from the glass of wine.

"As if all of this weren't surprise enough already," she replied, smiling and tilting her glass towards him. "Thank you for a fabulous dinner."

"It was a little selfish of me," he responded. "I enjoy a good steak. In fact, I'd have to say this is my favorite meal."

She nodded appreciatively. "It's in my top list."

"What else makes the list?"

"Hmmm," she mused for a moment, sipping the wine. "This is really good," she offered, setting her glass on the table and cutting into the steak. "I would add shrimp brochette."

"What's that?"

"You've never had it?" she inquired, surprised.

"Never heard of it," he said.

"Oh, it's delicious. Shrimp wrapped in bacon and broiled. Yum! Maybe I can make it for you some time."

He smiled, "I'd enjoy that. Anything with bacon must be good. What else is on the list?"

"Oh, a lot of things. I'm a bit of a foodie," she admitted with a smile.

He laughed, "How about bubble baths?"

"Those are very high on the list," she nodded emphatically.

"Excellent. Eat up. Your bubble bath awaits."

"What? But I'll clean the kitchen first…" she swept a hand at the dirty dishes on the table while he shook his head in reply.

"Not a chance," he said. "What did you think I was doing when I made you wait so long in the car? My Valentine does not work on her special day. Since we couldn't properly celebrate yesterday, we'll have to make today her day."

She felt such a surge of emotion that it almost overwhelmed her. He poured her another glass of wine and started clearing the table.

"Now," he finally announced, the table cleared, "Why don't you sit in the living room while I finish getting your bath ready?"

As she settled once again into the comfortable cushions of the couch, she could hear the water running in the bathroom adjoining the master bedroom. She felt warm and the flames once again began to hypnotize her. She set the glass of wine on the coffee table in front of her and allowed herself to close her eyes.

She wasn't sure how long she might have dozed when Adam's light touch on her shoulder woke her. "Your bath is ready, Sleeping Beauty," he said tenderly.

He had transformed the large bathroom. Candles glowed along the wide ledge surrounding two sides of the large tub. The sauna was running, and bubbles formed a deep layer above the steaming water. Roses petals were scattered across the bubbles.

She set the glass of wine on the ledge and quickly disrobed, sinking into the hot water and feeling her muscles relax. The bubbles were lightly scented, and she inhaled the pleasant aromas of lavender and rose.

Having cleaned the dinner dishes, Adam nervously paced the living room, his own glass of wine now emptied and sitting on the coffee table. Had he bored her so terribly that she fell asleep? Or was she just that relaxed with him? He wanted tonight to be special for her, for them. He wanted this to be a memory they could build a future together on.

He must have been waiting about thirty minutes when a slight sound made him turn towards the bedroom door. Aubree stood framed in the partially opened door, the flickering glow of candles backlighting her from the room beyond. Her auburn tresses were dark as they lay still damp around her shoulders. She wore a white terry cloth bathrobe belted at her waist. Her green eyes gazed coolly at him across the room.

"The bath was delightful."

Her voice was husky, and he felt a physical stir in response.

She moved across the room, her empty wine glass dangling in one hand, the heart-shaped white box of chocolates he had given her in the other. She held the box out enticingly, "A chocolate?"

He smiled and crossed to retrieve a piece but before he could she selected one and raised it to his lips, setting the box on the table.

Slowly, he accepted the delicacy, savoring the sweetness of the chocolate.

She reached for his wine glass. "Would you like some more?" she asked.

"No." He took the glasses from her hands, setting them back on the table. Turning, he framed her face is his hands, tilting her head back to so he could look at her. "No, Natalie, you're all the wine I need." He lowered his head and kissed her deeply.

She felt her knees weaken and she leaned into him, drinking in the kiss, returning it passionately.

Groaning, he pulled away. "God, I want you so badly, Natalie!"

His voice was thick with desire and she felt her own body surge with response. She grabbed his hand and pulled him down on the plush white rug on the floor between the coffee table and the hearth. They knelt, facing each other, and he pulled her into his lap, cradling her in his arms, kissing her deeply, pushing the bathrobe off her shoulder.

He pulled back and looked down at her. Under the bathrobe she wore a lacy white negligee, the fire flickering across the golden color of her skin. His hands ran over the smoothness, caressing the curve of her buttock and stroking the firmly muscled length of her leg.

She felt as though she were on fire and leaned away from his embrace, shrugging out of the heavy bathrobe, letting it pool across his lap. His hand caught her breast and she caught her breath, leaning back across his arm as his mouth teased her nipple through the sheer material. Her hands caught in his hair, pulling him against her.

Carefully he laid her back, stretching out beside her. She looked up into his eyes, changing from blue to gray in the altering light from the flames, and she felt a rush of joy and desire. Her leg twined around his as her arms pulled him close.

"You are far too overdressed," she murmured in his ear.

He pulled back and rose, standing at her feet and began shedding his clothes. She shivered with pleasure when he stood naked at her feet, muscles creating shadows in the dancing light. He knelt again beside her and her hands wandered across the broad span of his chest, marveling at the muscles so firm beneath her fingers, the skin so soft. His stomach was a tightly muscled expanse and her fingers followed down to his manhood, grasping him and he groaned again.

"Now, Natalie. I have to have you now."

He pushed her back gently and his hands tenderly traveled down her body, exploring her breasts and her waist, the tender valley between her legs. She felt his light touch like a feather and a tremor moved along her nerve endings, her muscles quivering in anticipation. He felt her tremble and it pushed his ardor even higher.

He moved over her, and her legs twined tightly around his waist, drawing him to meet her, her hands clasping his shoulders tightly.

"Oh, Adam," she murmured, pulling his head down to kiss him.

As their lips met, he thrust, and their bodies joined. He held still and gazed into her eyes, enchanted again by her beauty, feeling her subtle movements.

"Shhh," he laid his finger across her lips, kissing her throat and her ear, lips brushing tenderly. "Be still. Move slow." Fingers brushing the hair back from her temples, his other hand cupping her rear.

She moved against him, urgent to achieve greater heights. "I want you, Adam."

Her voice was low and dusky in his ear, thick with longing, her breath tickling the hairs on his neck, a shiver ran through him. Slowly, he began to move, and she moved with him. Their pace increased, pressure mounting.

"Natalie!" he cried as he achieved climax.

"Oh, Adam," she moaned, shuddering, as she reached her pinnacle a mere second later.

The next two days passed too quickly for Aubree. Every moment with Adam was another discovery of how generous and gracious he was. Adam delighted in unearthing Aubree's sensuous side and they thrilled at their compatibility.

"I know relationships aren't really encouraged in the hub," Adam began tentatively Sunday morning as they were cleaning the house and packing to head back to the hub.

Aubree paused, hands submerged in sudsy dishwater and looked at him loading a cooler with items that needed to be cycled out. A team would stop by and restock the pantry later that week.

He added a chunk of cheddar cheese and straightened up to face her. "I want to be with you, Natalie. Every chance I have." He spoke earnestly, his eyes pleading with her. "We only have so many minutes to live. Any that aren't with you are a wasted opportunity."

She flushed with pleasure and reached for a towel to dry her hands. "Adam, it seems like we just met." She faltered, wanting to find the right words to explain how confused she felt.

He shrugged and put his hands on his hips. "So? Is there a rule on how long you need to know someone before you know how you feel about them?"

"Well, no. That's not what I mean. I'm trying to say, you don't really know me, yet."

He smiled and crossed the kitchen to stand beside her. "What about you, after this weekend, don't I know?" He kissed her on the lips slowly, his tongue gently caressing her lips before he moved to her throat. He kissed her where her shoulder and neck met and she shivered with delight, instantly melting against him, giggling as it tickled. "Like I know that spot," he murmured, and his hands began to move lower.

"Stop!" she cried, laughing, and pulled away. "Okay. So you know me! There is no doubt whatsoever that you are thoroughly knowledgeable on how to tickle me, Adam Miller!"

He laughed and chased after her, catching her easily and leaning her back against the counter, bracing his hands on either side of her. "I've got you now," he whispered.

She grew still and looked at him. "Yes, Adam, you do."

He understood she was referring to far more than their immediate situation and he tenderly kissed her again before stepping back, once more serious. "I meant what I said. I'd like to spend more time with you."

She nodded slowly, her eyes never leaving his. "I would like that, too, Adam. But let's take it slow, okay?" Inside she was a snarl of nerves. She wanted very much to extend their relationship. How could she do that when he didn't even know her real name?

"We'll go at whatever pace you set, Natalie." His words were tender and sincere, and the name struck a chill through her.

CHAPTER FIFTEEN

Janet Byron finished mixing her cocktail. "Are you sure you won't have one?" she asked her guest, sprawled comfortably in a chair in her living room overlooking the Missouri River. JB occupied the penthouse suite at the top of the tallest building in Sector Eight.

"No, Aunt Janet, I think I'll pass. I had a couple on the flight from Midah and I feel tired enough."

JB nodded approvingly and took the other chair, setting her glass on the table between them. "I'm glad you were able to stop by. I gather you'll be staying a few days?"

Drew waved his hand expansively. "I have a week before I need to be in Soweh."

"You're welcome to stay as long as you like. I'm sure you'll be anxious to arrive a few days early and settle in. You'll let me know your plans?"

It did not escape Drew that while it was posed as a question it was clearly an imperative. "Of course."

JB smiled and sipped her cocktail. "How was Midah?"

"Boring. I was ready for a change."

"Good. I'm glad to hear that. There's a new team forming in Soweh. A pet project of Baba's and Larocque's. I managed to ensure you'll be part of it."

"I appreciate you looking out for me. I did have some unfinished business in Midah."

"Oh?" She leaned her chin on a finely manicured hand, forefinger resting along the side of her face as she leaned towards Drew in her chair, tucking her legs under her. "And what exactly is this unfinished business? You know we try not to leave loose ends."

Drew smiled back at the wicked tone in his Aunt's voice. "A family motto, almost."

She smiled in response and tossed back the rest of her cocktail. "Continue," she said, setting the glass back on the coaster.

He laughed and shook his head. "It's no matter, really. Just a little bit of personal business. A case of a missing person, shall we say? It's not a big deal. May I get some ice water?"

"Help yourself," she waved towards the mini bar on the wall of the large living area. "Suit yourself. Meanwhile, aren't you at all interested in this project?"

Her voice was silky smooth, and he recognized the signal that it was time to get down to business. He filled a glass with ice and then with cold water from the dispenser. He took his time and when the glass was full, he took a deep swallow. Let her wait a moment, he thought to himself as he refilled the depleted glass. Then he returned to his chair with lifted eyebrows, saying as he settled back, "I am most curious. I'm anxious to hear the details."

It was a small gesture of defiance, but it was not lost on JB. She smiled, her ice blue eyes narrowing, enhancing the crow's feet at the corners. This one will take some watching, she thought to herself. Best to keep him on a short leash. "It seems Baba is interested in infiltrating the Outsiders. Do you know Mitch Lasater? Ever hear that name?"

He thought for a moment, frowning, "I have heard that name. When I was in the military…" She waited patiently while he considered. "Ah," he finally declared, smiling faintly, "He was in some sort of elite ops team in the Navy, stationed out of Packy—when it was still San Francisco."

"Yes," she drawled smoothly, "That would be the same man. He's not much older than you."

The barb stung, as it was intended to. The implication was clear. You aren't in the same class. For a moment his true hatred of this woman flared but he choked it back quickly. He knew she had an uncanny sense and he couldn't risk exposing himself. He drank more water and smiled as he set the class on the coaster. "He was already a lieutenant, I seem to recall, when I was coming out of boot camp. Anyway, what about him?"

Her eyes narrowed a fraction and he wondered if he'd pushed her too far. Instead, she returned his smile before continuing, "I understand he's to be the leader of this new team. You'll be working for him."

"With, Aunt Janet. I'll be working with him." He spoke quietly, voice firm.

Her smile deepened. "That's why I enjoy working with you, Drew. You are so very astute."

He nodded at her in pleasure and acknowledgement of the compliment. "Thank you," he said softly.

She nodded pertly and continued, "That's correct. You'll be working with him, for me. I'll expect you to be my ears and eyes, Drew. I think you know I'll go far on this Council." Her eyes glittered as she studied him.

He nodded and smirked, "I have no doubt."

"I need someone I can…" she paused, her fingers lightly tapping against her lips as she stared off thoughtfully. "Someone I can depend on to take care of, shall we say, delicate situations?" she finished, turning her eyes on him, pinning him with a direct stare. "I'm thinking that someone could be you, Drew."

He studied her face and could only detect sincerity. "I have no doubt about that, either. If you need something," he paused, holding her gaze intently, "Anything. Well, I'm sure I could be useful."

She returned his gaze keenly and then smiled, "Well, I'm glad that's settled. I could use a freshened drink. You still good with that water?" She rose and moved gracefully to the bar, mixing a fresh drink.

"Yes. Thank you," he replied. He didn't think it was a good idea to have clouded faculties when dealing with this woman.

"So," she said, sinking back into the chair, "Tell me about this unfinished personal business."

He contemplated silently, fingers drumming soundlessly on the arms of the chair. Finally, he spoke, "It's just a rather odd situation, really, mind you." His tone was nonchalant, and he gave a half shrug. "There was a girl I was interested in. I believe it was mutual." He waved a hand dismissively as if that were to be expected while JB smiled and nodded encouragingly. "Anyway, she disappeared a short time ago. Just vanished." He snapped his fingers.

"That is interesting," she mused. "People don't typically vanish without a cause. Security was keeping an eye on her, I assume?"

"Oh, no," he chuckled. "No. In fact, her father is no less than the Vice President of Human Resources. Mike Holten."

"Oh, really?" she purred, eyebrows arched, eyes drilling into him.

He nodded, "Yep. Would make her the great niece of Lawrence Johnson."

"You don't say?"

Drew grinned at his Aunt's avid interest. "Her mother, Sheri Holten, is Johnson's niece."

"Well that certainly is interesting, I would have to agree. You say she just disappeared?"

He nodded. "Around the middle of January, I guess. No trace. I checked all the normal transportation databases and there was no record."

"Could she be holed up at Dad's?"

He frowned and shook his head. "I don't think so. You'd have to know Aubree. She wouldn't choose to live under the same roof with her mother if hers was on fire."

She laughed and toasted him, drinking deeply from her cocktail. "I, too, find it odd that the great-niece of Lawrence Johnson would vanish without a trace. It rouses my curiosity." She smiled wickedly at Drew; eyes gleaming coldly. "I may do some snooping of my own."

Drew smiled back at her. "I was hoping you might."

Drew folded the last shirt and laid it on top of the other clothes in the flight bag. His cellphone lying on the bed beside the bag lit up and an image of his Aunt appeared on the screen. He picked the phone up, moving to look out the window at the hub sprawling out below him. "Yes, Aunt Janet?"

"Ah, I caught you in time, then? You haven't left yet, have you?"

He glanced at the clock on the nightstand. "No. I have several hours before I need to be at the airport."

"Excellent," her voice purred in his ear. "I wanted to remind you, eyes and ears."

He frowned impatiently. "As we agreed."

"You'll use the secure line I gave you. Never call me on any number but that one. And one more thing, Drew."

"What's that?"

"I'd like you to keep an eye on Mr. Baba. Learn his daily habits. Find any vulnerabilities." Her voice was low, and he felt a shiver crawl up his back.

"I'll do that."

"I also wanted to let you know I have word on our little birdie."

"Oh?"

"Yes. The one that flew the coop. I found her nest."

"That was quick."

She laughed, "I find most things are, dear nephew. It's quite ironic, actually."

"In what way?"

"Miss Aubree Holten currently resides in Western Gateway Hub, posing as a Miss Natalie Deckman. I thought you might find that to be interesting."

He stood frozen, staring out at the buildings in the distance. Aubree was in one of them. He opened his mouth to speak but found he couldn't, his throat thickened, and he coughed.

"What was that?" she asked.

He cleared his throat. "Excuse me. I coughed. That is interesting. Do you know where I might locate her?"

"As a matter of fact, I do."

Aubree carried her cafeteria tray across the compound lawn to the small park she and Adam had gotten into the custom of using to share lunch. He was out with a crew hooking up the new surveillance system at the meet point in Des Moines. She had caught his excitement the past week. Tomorrow the new system would go online and be fully functional.

It meant, however, that she was alone today. She had spotted their group sitting at a cluster of tables in the outer courtyard and they had waved her over to join them, but she had declined with a polite shake of her head and a nod towards the park.

One thing she and Adam agreed on was not socializing with your employees. An occasional happy hour was okay but better to not make it a habit and become buddies. It could cause a lot of disruption in a team if the leader was seen to favor anyone and Aubree didn't want to sow those seeds.

She set her tray on the concrete table where she typically sat with Adam, grateful for a moment of silence. Birds were busy in the trees and Aubree welcomed this harbinger of spring. She was tired of winter and ready to welcome a new season.

The silence was broken by a voice that sent a shiver of fear coursing through her, freezing her blood and filling her with dread.

"Well, Natalie, are you enjoying your lunch? May I join you?"

Her stomach was a frozen block of ice and she couldn't move, muscles paralyzed. Drew slid onto the bench seat across from her, folding his hands calmly on the table in front of him.

Carefully, she laid the BLT she had been about to take a bite from back on her plate, pushing it away from her, dropping her hands in her lap, fighting an urge to jump up and run. "Drew. I wasn't expecting to see you."

"No, I would guess you weren't." His smile was lethal. "I can't help but wonder why you felt it so necessary to…" he waved a hand in the air, "Disappear the way you did. Do you have something to hide, I wonder?"

The ice in Aubree's stomach melted and she had an urgent need to go to the bathroom. Her nerves felt jittery and she knew her hands were shaking. "How did you find me?"

Another smirking sneer, "Did you really think it would be so hard?"

She had no answer. Perhaps they had been naïve. They had thought they were doing everything right.

"Aubree, I will always find you. But please do us both a favor and don't run again."

All she could do was stare. It occurred to her that this was how the mouse felt when the cat finally trapped it and there was no escape. Her heart was hammering frantically in her chest, the impulse to run almost overwhelming her. She could feel her pulse pounding in her temples and she tried to focus on relaxing. Of all days for Adam to not be here. Or, maybe that was a blessing. How would she explain? Her eyes searched Drew's face desperately.

"I'm sorry," he continued acidly, "I should have called you Natalie. I'll be sure to be more careful in the future."

"What are you doing here, Drew?" she hoped he wouldn't detect the terror she was hearing in her voice.

"Oh, just dropped by to visit over lunch." His smile was predatory. "I can't hang around, as much as I'd like to. But I will be checking in with you."

She remained silent, studying him now that her initial fear was beginning to subside.

"You never did tell me why you ran away in the first place? Hiding something, perhaps?"

"Hardly," her voice was filled with the loathing she felt. "I decided to pursue an upward career move." She gave a nonchalant shrug. "Did you think it had something to do with you?" She could tell her barb had scored a sting.

"I am far too intelligent to assume anything with you, Natalie." He gave her another smile and then stood up. "Well, I really do need to run now but it's been great seeing you. I look forward to a longer visit real soon. Remember, don't run."

In silence she watched him walk away, the after effects of adrenalin leaving her weak and trembling.

"Corinne, I am so glad I was able to reach you," Aubree breathed in relief.

"Aubree! How are you? We miss you! Everyone sends their love."

"Thanks, Corinne. I miss everyone, too. I'm good. Homesick at times but otherwise liking it here."

"Good! Good to hear."

"I did have a bit of a surprise today."

"Oh? What was that?"

"Drew. Drew appeared at lunch."

"No!"

"Oh, most definitely yes."

"I heard he got reassigned. Don't tell me he's in Wegah!"

"It would appear that way. I didn't ask him."

"Oh, Aubree. All this for nothing!"

Aubree mused for a moment. "I wouldn't say that. I've met someone, Corinne."

"I heard about that, too." Corinne's voice was cool.

It was Aubree's turn to be surprised. "Oh?"

"There's someone I want you to meet. A group, actually. They're reluctant though because you spend all your time with some guy from Security."

"Adam." Aubree was angered that Corinne would give her such little credit. "And do you, or they, think I would jeopardize something so important?"

"No, Aubree, no one thinks that. I know you and I told them. But they don't know you. Just how serious are things with this Adam?"

Aubree turned in the small cubicle she was using in the free area of the office building, a place with communication hook-ups where people could attend to private business when necessary away from the eyes and ears of other associates. She was using the secured line they had agreed should be safe. "Pretty serious, Corinne. I like him a lot."

"Hmmm. What do you think about him? I mean, as relates to what we do?"

"He's a by-the-book type of man. I don't know, Corinne. I mean, I think if he knew the truth about some things, he'd be willing to think about it. He doesn't strike me as the sort to jump to conclusions and I don't think he's a stick in the mud type. It's too soon, though. Not something I want to discuss with him."

"No, I don't think you should. What about Drew?"

"Now that's a much bigger problem. He knows I'm going by Natalie. He called me that."

"Wow. He's got to know someone that knows someone."

"I'd appreciate you sharing anything you might hear. And in the meantime, I wanted to ask you something."

"Sure."

"What do you know about the Hawaiian Retirement Lottery?"

There was silence for so long that Aubree was about to ask the question again when Corinne finally replied, "Healthcare Act 3136."

"What's that?"

"Why do you ask, Aubree?"

"Adam's mother won. She was one of the winners during the Super Bowl."

"Oh, Aubree. Oh, dear. I am so sorry."

Aubree felt the first tendrils of cold wrap around her intestines and begin to curl in her stomach. "Why? Why do you say that, Corinne?" Her voice was low, a whisper.

"Healthcare Act 3136 is the assisted passing act."

Aubree's mind didn't want to accept what the words clearly told her. "No. His mom's in Hawaii, right?"

Corinne's voice was soft and gentle. "No, honey. His mom has passed."

CHAPTER SIXTEEN

"How was your day, beautiful?" Adam asked, planting a kiss on Aubree's forehead as he gave her a quick embrace in front of the Chinese restaurant in Sector Seven they had discovered they both enjoyed.

"Good," she murmured, pulling him down for a better kiss. She was filled with anxiety and she hoped she was able to hide it. It was difficult mustering an appetite. She neatly deflected the conversation back to him by saying, "Tell me about yours."

He grinned, "I'll wait until we're seated. After you, my dear." With a flourish he held the door open for her.

The smells of fried food made her stomach uneasy and she sank into the booth the attendant led them to, folding her hands in her lap and leaning forward towards Adam with a smile, "So, go on."

He grew somber and gazed down at the tabletop for a moment, clearly searching for words. Finally, clearing his throat, he started, "Well, it comes with some bad news, I'm afraid." He lifted his blue eyes to meet hers and she saw there was very little gray tonight, they were as blue as fresh blueberries.

"Oh? You don't seem too upset so I can't imagine it's all that bad."

He smiled again. "No, but it means a temporary separation." His hands crossed to grasp hers tightly, so tight she winced from the pressure. "Sorry," he grinned and eased his hold a bit. "The installation in Des Moines went perfect. Not a hitch. Everything came up online just as I'd planned."

"That's great news, Adam!" She was genuinely happy for him and squeezed his hands in response.

"Yeah, except they want me to catch a flight to Romoh tomorrow morning."

"Oh," she felt her heart sink. She hadn't been sure how to tell him about Drew and now it seemed it wouldn't matter.

"It's only for a little while. I'm not being relocated," he explained, his thumbs tenderly caressing her hands, so small in his.

"You're leaving so soon?"

He nodded, unable to hide his excitement, "I'm going to get to meet Ben Larocque!"

"That's fantastic, Adam! I'm so happy for you."

He grinned and his enthusiasm was infectious. She felt some of the ice that had chilled her all day beginning to thaw in the warmth of his presence. "I just wish I could tell Mom!"

She felt the ice reform, the chill shooting through her as fast as the headache you get from drinking something cold too quick. It was a wonder he couldn't feel the difference as her fingers froze in his. She couldn't tell him now. Not now when he was so happy. Her tongue was glued to the roof of her mouth.

"I've got to spend some time this evening finalizing the hub plan. That's what the meeting in Romoh is all about. Larocque wants to know the plan and timeline," he continued enthusiastically.

"Do we even need these?" he nodded towards the menu placards and she shook her head. "What're you having this evening?" he continued, not noticing her silence.

"I think I'll start with egg drop soup," she thought she'd be able to eat that easily enough.

"Great idea. I'll have the same. And some egg rolls. And maybe some pot stickers?"

She nodded, "Really, that will make a meal for me."

He paused and studied her. "Are you feeling okay?"

"Wonderful! I guess your news stunned me, is all."

He again grasped her hand in his and grinned. "I'll only be gone ten days. I guess Ben's got some other aspect of the project he wants to review with me."

She nodded and was relieved from further conversation by the waiter who arrived to take their order. Adam ordered for them both, adding an order of fried rice and orange chicken, knowing it was her favorite.

"I guess I'll run by the apartment after we eat. I'll need to pack. And like I said, I need to pull up the project plan and review it. I can drop by and see you after, if you want?" His blue eyes met hers and he gave her a suggestive smile.

She reached over and laid her hand on his, "I was hoping you'd ask."

The rest of dinner passed quickly, and she was able to let him fill the silence as he talked excitedly about the upcoming meeting in Romoh and wondered what Ben Larocque would be like. He couldn't believe he was getting to meet the President of Security. It could be a big break for him.

When he left her at the door of her apartment, promising to be back in a couple of hours, she felt like she was going to be sick from the nervous tension. She wasn't sure if she should tell him what she knew about his mom or wait. She tried to think what she would want, and she decided she'd want to know.

It was almost ten o'clock before she heard the knock at the door. For a moment before she answered, she wondered wildly if it might be Drew. Heart pounding, she opened it and Adam came through, sweeping her into a tight embrace and kissing her deeply.

She returned his kiss, relaxing into the strength of his arms, enjoying the feel of the hard length of him pressing against her.

"Get all your packing done?" she asked breathlessly as they pulled apart.

"All ready to go. You have my entire focus." His smile was tender as he followed her to the couch in the living room.

"We need to talk, Adam."

"Why so serious?" he asked, settling into the couch beside her.

"It's about your mom."

"What about Mom? I've been starting to worry. It's almost six weeks now since she left and it's not like her to not call. Did she call today?" His tone was puzzled as he looked at her quizzically.

"No," she said quietly, folding and unfolding her fingers nervously in her lap. "Adam, she's not going to call."

A silence settled in the apartment and he looked at her tensely. "I don't think I understand you, Natalie."

The name stung and so did his tone of voice. She stiffened a little in response. "I did some checking on the Hawaiian Retirement Program."

He didn't say anything, eyes gray and stormy watching her closely.

She swallowed and went on. "It's a program under Healthcare Act 3136. Passed in 2027."

"That doesn't mean anything to me," his tone was wooden. He stood up, walking over to the window and keeping his back to her, hands laced behind.

She stared at the tense muscles across his shoulders. "I didn't know about it either until I did some research. It was a vaguely written bill at the time it was put to vote. They termed it as assisted passing. It was a measure to allow corporations to make the necessary decision to end suffering or when productiveness had ceased. It was part of a larger bill and my guess is most people didn't know what they were voting on."

He finally turned to face her. "I still don't understand what you're talking about, Natalie. What's this got to do with my mom?"

"Adam, think about it. Assisted passing. Your mother has passed on, Adam. I'm sorry, but she's not alive anymore."

"Bullshit!" he exploded, and she drew back in surprise. "That is complete bullshit, Natalie. You expect me to believe that all those people that have won the retirement were instead killed? What utter nonsense. Who told you this?"

Her eyes pleaded with him, "Adam, it's true! You have to believe me!"

"Well, I don't!" he almost shouted.

"Please, Adam. Lower your voice. Someone will notify Security."

That made him laugh. "Pretty good. But true. My apologies," his voice was dripping now with sarcasm. "I didn't mean to raise my voice."

"Adam, please. Sit down."

"No. If it's all the same with you, I think I'd prefer to go home. I've got an early flight to catch."

"Adam, please. Don't go like this," her voice was pleading, and she rose from the couch and walked towards him.

Brusquely he pushed past her and headed for the door. "I need some time right now, Natalie. I need some space. Maybe I'll call."

Then he was gone, and she stood in the middle of her living room feeling like everything was beginning to collapse, and never as homesick as she suddenly felt.

Adam stared glumly out the window of the small airplane as it headed west, chasing the night. He wished he could sleep but it eluded him now as it had the entire night. He'd stayed up until almost one reading about the healthcare act Natalie had mentioned.

The facts were plain. There had indeed been an act that allowed the corporations the power to terminate the elderly when they reached a nonproductive age. The language was not so clear, not so stark, but when you cut through all the legalize that was what it came down to. The act had passed with more than seventy percent support. The fact that it had been bundled in with a referendum that legalized recreational marijuana at the former federal level probably had a lot to do with it.

Finding the information about the healthcare act hadn't taken as much time as researching the little available on the Hawaiian Retirement Program. There was very little information. It had first appeared in 2030 as part of the Super Bowl halftime show. There were lists of winners but nothing about its inception. He could find no link between the program and the healthcare act.

He'd spent the last couple of hours doing some research on previous winners from the lists published. All were listed as deceased. He hadn't made it through the entire list, but he'd gone through a good sampling. Two from the previous year that he'd checked were passed away already. He had grown too tired to keep looking. What he had been able to learn in each instance was that the cause of death was always listed simply as natural.

He wondered how Natalie had made a connection between the program and the act. He'd been too angry at the time, too absorbed in his own disbelief, to want to know how she came by her information.

He longed to call her. Had wanted to when he first read about the healthcare act passing. By then it had been almost midnight and too late to call. He imagined her sleeping alone in her bed and he was angered all over again. Only this time the anger was self-directed. She had been right about the act. Might she not also have been right about the program?

The flight from Wegah to Romoh was short and it seemed the little plane was starting its descent shortly after achieving altitude. He watched the flat terrain of the plains east of Romoh slip beneath the wings of the plane, the Rockies towering in the distance, their heads dark under forbidding clouds.

The pilot landed the plane smoothly on the runway and they taxied to the gate. He wasn't certain what to expect. He had the address for the Security main headquarters, and he assumed he was to take a drone. As he came out of the secure area, however, he spotted a tall, lean man holding a placard that said Adam Miller. Adam approached, grinning, and extended his hand. "Hi! I'm Adam Miller."

The other man assessed him with dark brown eyes set in a finely chiseled face. "Pleasure to meet you, Adam. I'm Ben." The man grasped Adam's hand in a firm grip. "Hope you don't mind me picking you up, but I was making the run out to our Wegah meet point and thought you might want to tag along."

Adam was momentarily speechless and at a loss. He never expected that someone as important as Ben Larocque would personally pick him up at the airport. He covered his discomposure, quickly responding, "That would be a great start."

Ben cocked his head at the duffel bag Adam carried in his right hand. "Any other luggage?"

"No, sir. I tend to travel light."

Ben grinned in response and turned on his heel towards the parking area beyond the large terminal, most of it gloomy and powered down to conserve energy, only a few gates operating.

Ben didn't talk as they made their way out to the large parking area and a small cluster of vehicles parked near the terminal entrance. He thumbed a remote and Adam saw the lights on a large black Hummer flick on and off. He followed Ben to the large vehicle, throwing his duffel in the passenger side back seat before pulling himself up into the passenger side.

Ben settled into the driver's seat, the console almost wrapping around him like a fighter jet cockpit. He thumbed the keyless start and the motor rumbled to life, thrumming through the floorboard and up through the soles of his boots.

Ben maneuvered the large vehicle out onto the freeway that connected the remote airport with Romoh. The walls of the Rocky Mountain Hub were much closer into the city and the airport itself was outside of the walls. Rolling hills, eerily devoid of trees spread out around them. The Rocky Mountains loomed off to Adam's right as Ben headed south.

"Tell me what you know about the Romoh to Wegah meet point." Ben's voice was low, his tone a moderate alto, pleasantly pitched. His complexion was olive tinged and his hair black. Thin, aristocratically arched eyebrows defined almond shaped eyes split by a hawk like nose above thin lips. His brown eyes were on the road, right hand nonchalantly gripping the top of the steering wheel, left resting on the side of the door.

"It's at the old TA Truck Stop on Route 70 in Limon." Adam spotted an old road sign and added, "We're about an hour and fifteen minutes away."

Ben chuckled, "Very good. You were surprised when I met you back there."

Adam tried to suppress his surprise again but was unable to completely hide a slight flinch and he saw Ben smile.

"You'll learn that I'm very much involved, Mr. Miller. Hands on, I suppose some would say. I don't consider myself a micro-manager," he glanced at Adam. "Some people are bothered by that. What's your take?"

The man's bluntness and quickness increased Adam's admiration of him. "I like a manager that stays involved. You're right, you know."

"Oh?" Ben asked.

"There is a difference between a micro-manager and an involved one. Just like there's a difference between a manager and a leader."

"Oh, very nicely put," Ben replied, real admiration in his tone. "I, too, have done a little homework ahead of our meeting and I appreciate that you did the same."

Adam shifted a little in his seat, pleased with the recognition and warming to this charismatic man. "Thank you."

Ben nodded. "I like what you've done at the Wegah meet points. We've got excellent coverage for a large area and we can control it all from the security headquarters location in Wegah. I hear it works perfectly and is already up and running."

"Yes. Kudos to the Infrastructure team. They strung a lot of cable."

Ben's smile deepened, "Another motto of mine own. Credit where credit is due."

Adam smiled in response. "Perhaps we attended the same school?" he ventured playfully.

Ben laughed outright. "Perhaps! I went to Cornell."

"No. Missouri State."

Ben's tone grew more serious. "I knew that, of course. I've studied your background, as well, Adam."

Adam grew somber, watching as they approached the intersection with Route 70 where they would head east, away from Romoh.

"You wouldn't be here if I hadn't already reviewed and approved." The statement was offered in the pleasantly toned yet firm voice. The quality of that voice made Adam suddenly understand what the phrase steel in a velvet glove meant. Ben's voice was steel cloaked in velvet.

"I appreciate that," Adam strove to maintain a firm tone to match, wanting very much to impress this man.

"I have another program I'm getting off the ground. Something that Frank Baba and I want very much to succeed. I think I'm going to need your program looped in to make it work."

Adam's interest was sparked, and he turned alertly towards Ben. "I'm all ears."

Ben smiled. "Not quite so fast. We'll discuss it in great detail over the next week. I've got a man coming in from Soweh I want you to meet. He'll get here day after tomorrow. Between now and then I'll have you fully briefed on the partner project."

For the first time in hours Adam felt a return of his optimism. Here was an opportunity to work side by side with one of the ten most powerful men in the nation. Even as he turned his attention back to Ben, green eyes watched alertly in his mind and Adam forcefully pushed the thought of them away.

"Oh, Daddy! It's so good to hear your voice!"

"Aubree! What are you doing calling like this? What time is it?" Mike Holten's voice was filled with alarm.

Aubree laughed, "I guess it doesn't matter, now, Daddy. I saw Drew today."

"You what!"

"Yep. Right here in Wegah. So, I don't guess it matters if we maintain a cover."

"Are you okay? Tell me what happened."

"I'm fine. He startled me. I was eating lunch and he just suddenly showed up. Sat down and called me Natalie. Asked me why I ran."

"And you said?"

"I told him I was pursuing an upward career move. That doesn't explain the name, but I didn't need to. He left after telling me he'd be back."

"Well, maybe it's time you came home."

Aubree paused. She had known her father was liable to suggest it and she'd been tempted. Returning to Midah now that Drew was gone meant life could be pleasant again and she'd have the company of her friends. But she wouldn't have Adam. She did important work in Midah and she would be satisfied returning to continue her efforts helping OUR, but she expected to have the same opportunity here once she was more accepted by the local group. It was normal that they'd be reluctant to accept her when there was so much at stake. "No, Daddy. I've thought about that, but I think I want to stay."

"Oh!" Mike had not expected this response; he had thought Aubree would want to come back.

"I'm enjoying the work. And," she paused, uncertain how to continue,

"Well, I've met someone."

He father was silent for a long moment. "I see," he finally said, his tone neutral. "Tell me about him."

"It's Adam."

"The one you're working with? The one in charge of the program?"

"That's him."

"He's in Security, right?"

"Right. In fact, he's on his way to Romoh right now to meet Ben Larocque."

"Wow. Already moving in big circles, I see. You won't mind if I do a little background check on Mr. Miller, do you?"

She chuckled, "I was hoping you would."

"Pretty serious, you say?"

Aubree hesitated, "I think so. But what is that, Daddy? What is serious these days? Corporations don't want you getting married. Kids are raised in school institutions starting at four. I mean, I'm confused, really. It doesn't seem like I can follow the model you and Mom set."

It was Mike's turn to hesitate, "It hasn't turned out the way it was supposed to."

"What do you mean?" she asked. She hadn't really expected her father to answer her question and she paused now to see what he would offer.

"The original members of the council. Well, not all of them. Everyone tends to think Lawrence was the brainchild, but it wasn't. It was William Adamson. Lawrence and I had long conversations when your mom and I were first married. I knew a lot about William's vision. But greed is a powerful driver, Aubree. I know you've heard the phrase about power corrupting and absolute corruption. It was too tempting for some folks. The power got to them. The hubs aren't conforming to the original intent."

"What does that have to do with relationships?" She was honestly lost.

Mike laughed. "Well, divorce is messy and costly. Corporations found that performance suffered. It was much cheaper to discourage marriage. It wasn't hard to do, actually. Marriage as an institution was already on shaky ground. It just needed someone to pull the plug, is all. No, the collapse of the family as a functioning unit was never by intent. It was a convenience."

"Hmmm," she mused, "I guess I never really thought about it. When I was little and got sick, Mom staying with me. Or that time she got really sick with the flu and you had to stay home and take care of both of us."

"Right. If one member of the family got ill the corporation lost one or even two functioning employees. Unproductive." Mike's tone was dry.

"Wow. And kids. It doesn't seem right, raising them in dormitories."

"Have you discussed all this with Adam? Any idea what his position is?"

"Not really," she replied pensively. "I think family is important to him though."

She told him about the incident with Megan and her argument with Adam.

"That's a hard one, Aubree. I hate to tell you, but Corinne was right. If Megan Miller won the Hawaiian Retirement, she was selected for assisted passing. It was familiar to you because Lawrence and I discussed the healthcare act over dinner. Both of us were strongly opposed to it. Corporations should never have that control. You haven't talked to him since the argument, then?"

"No. He had a flight early this morning to Romoh. I could call his cell. I don't know. I don't know what I'd say."

Mike was silent for a moment. "You may be right. Give him some time. He may come around on his own. If he was as close as you say, then this was quite a blow to him. I'm guessing you haven't told him about Drew."

"No." Aubree's voice reflected how miserable she felt.

"Or who you really are?" Mike's voice was soft.

"No. Oh, Daddy, I've really messed things up!"

CHAPTER SEVENTEEN

"Good evening and greetings from Southwestern Hub!" The camera centered on Edward Sanner superimposed over a view of the Las Vegas strip. "I'm here on special assignment and will be bringing you a live update from an exclusive interview with Frank Baba. As always, count on True News to bring you the most accurate information, news you can depend on. Before our feature story, let's check in with Erica. Erica? How are things in the Rocky Mountain Hub this evening?"

The camera feed changed, and Erica Campbell's flawless features filled the center of the screen, a closeup of the Rocky Mountains etched starkly against a stunning sunset, sun reflecting redly on the underside of puffy white clouds.

"Good evening, Edward and America! It's a beautiful spring evening here in the Rocky Mountain Hub. Our leading story today is the meeting between Russian emissary, Sergei Sokolov, and Lawrence Johnson, who met today in Moscow."

The screen changed to show two men crossing an elaborately decorated room to shake hands. "The meeting was primarily focused on the current global issue of food shortages," Erica's voice continued smoothly. "At one time, the United States led the world in agricultural production, next to Russia, and it represented approximately five and half percent of our gross national product. Since the Cataclysm of 2019 that figure has dropped to three percent and the rest of the world is feeling the pain, not just Americans."

The screen changed to an aerial view of a vast wildly overgrown field that seemed to go on for mile after mile. At the farther edge of the horizon a distant line of mountains was just barely visible. "A large reason for this drop in GDP is because most of our population now resides inside a corporately sponsored hub. At one time our population was widely dispersed in the more rural regions and produce was the main source of income for these country people." The screen now showed an image of a farmer driving a tractor in some field, rows of corn surrounding him.

This image changed to a massive field with neatly ordered rows of some green crop. "Corporations have assumed the management of food production, but crops were damaged heavily in recent years with numerous natural disasters ranging from hurricanes to tornadoes. The mild winter of a few years ago resulted in the largest infestation of grasshoppers seen in almost three decades. Crops were wiped out seemingly overnight. Typically, the United States is able to stockpile about two years' worth of product but that has been eliminated with recent losses." A large empty warehouse filled the screen, a single forklift sitting forlornly in the vast empty space.

The camera on Erica resumed feed and she smiled. "Join us this evening on Channel 2103 as Shannon Wayne talks with Dan Norris from the Environmental Resource Group where he unveils an exciting new project that could change the future of agriculture and save a starving world!"

The camera image cut then to a commercial. The commercial featured a portly man dressed in white overcoat, white net covering what must surely be white hair, kindly smile on his face as he stirred a huge pot of something. Midwestern Hub cheese! A tagline cheerfully read. Handmade the artisan way using recipes and cows from Wisconsin! Available through your local Supply Chain. Try some today!

Edward Sanner's eerily bright blue eyes met the camera squarely as he announced, "This evening, we're thrilled to be the only news organization that brings you access to our leaders as we met today in an exclusive one-on-one interview with Speaker for the Council, Frank Baba, here in his office in Southwestern Hub. We took the opportunity to question Speaker Baba on some of the key concerns facing our nation today."

The image changed to one of Edward Sanner sitting chummily across from Frank Baba in Baba's large office, view of the Strip spreading away from his elevated perch above the city. "Top in world issue's today, Speaker Baba, seems to be a serious shortage of food. We've heard rumors of starvation in some countries and our own production levels are down. Rumor also has it that our own stockpile has been severely depleted."

"One at a time," Frank said, a charming smile as he held up one hand in mock defense. "Let me tackle those separately. It's true there is a current shortage of food and some countries are really struggling. Southeast Asia was hit with one of the worst monsoon seasons on record and rice production was hurt severely. As you know the world relies heavily on the rice produced in this region of the world. On the heels of this disaster we suffered a drought in Russia that lowered the output of wheat. Two very critical crops. A summit held in Hyderabad uncovered a source of relief in Australia and New Zealand where a surplus of both rice and wheat were stored."

"That was fortuitous!"

"Indeed," Frank continued drily. "As for the United States production level, our Environmental Resource Group has been working hard to find alternatives to extend our growing season in parts of the country and ways to protect the crop while it's vulnerable."

"We're pleased that we'll be airing a segment this very evening where Dan Norris will unveil the project they claim will solve many of our agricultural problems, from weather to pests!" Edward interjected smoothly.

Frank grinned, "That's right! After a lot of trial and error the team has delivered on a solution and we can't wait to implement it. We've got a top team now setting up the foundations to initiate the project at ground level. In fact, we've already had a groundbreaking ceremony at the first site sponsored outside of the Southeastern Hub. Our initial projections indicate this one location could increase our GDP by as much as half a percent within eighteen months."

"Impressive!" Edward paused, reviewing his notes. It was his characteristic delay before dropping his bombshell question designed to unseat his subject. "Besides this leap the Energy Group has achieved, we hear that you have other plans in motion. Plans that include the non-hub population?" his smile was challenging.

If he had hoped to catch Frank Baba by surprise, he hid his disappointment when Frank chuckled and replied, "Glad you took the conversation in that direction, Edward. As a matter of fact, I do. As you know we've learned there are people living outside of the hubs. We don't know how many, and we don't know where. I believe engaging with them and reestablishing lines of communication may lead to a solution that would benefit everyone."

Edward Sanner was for perhaps the first time in his recorded television history struck speechless. He had not expected Frank Baba to openly admit he was attempting to work with the Outsiders. Now, he stammered in response, "That's quite surprising, Mr. Speaker. We've always held that these were generally violent and aggressive people with little desire to work with us. What leads you to believe the situation has altered?"

Baba laughed outright, "Pure fiction! Why do we believe them to be violent people? Where is the evidence of that?" His tone was now challenging, and his humor had disappeared. "It is my hope that I will find a way to establish contact with our disenfranchised citizens that live beyond the protection of corporate hubs."

The screen shifted back to a view of Edward Sanner sitting at his console in the Southwestern Hub newsroom. "For more, tune into Channel 2313 tonight where my full interview with Frank Baba will be aired in a ninety-minute special starting at eight eastern. Now, here's Barb with national weather."

"The big news today, Edward, is a late winter blizzard raging across the Midwest today. It looks like we're going to get lucky as none of the hubs are in the path of this one, and that's a real good thing because it's a bad one. Heavy snow is falling and will continue to fall through tonight in the Dakotas and western Minnesota. The snow will taper off tonight and Minnesota may see some freezing rain continuing into tomorrow morning. The Western Gateway and Midwestern Hubs can expect high winds and low temps coming their way as this one blows itself out in the plains. Midwestern may experience some snow if the storm picks up any lake effect as it moves into the Great Lakes region. Elsewhere in the country, spring is progressing on pace with especially warm weather right now in the lower western part of the country. It should be pretty warm where you are, Edward." She gave him a knowing smile.

Edward Sanner smiled back and nodded, "It is very hot here in Southwestern—and not just the temperature outside, Barb." He grinned suggestively and Barb's laugh carried across the soundtrack. He composed himself and nodded somberly at the camera. "That concludes the global and national segments of today's broadcast. Various news broadcasts can be located in the 2000 series of channels and our website is always up to date with the True News you need to know. Switching you now to your local broadcast, have a good evening."

A new pair of news anchors appeared on the screen. On the left was a middle aged woman with long brown hair wearing thickly rimmed brown glasses through which over large blue eyes peered and seated at her side was a man, also middle aged, with light brown hair that was already well-receded on his sloping forehead, a handlebar mustache framing pursed lips.

"Good evening, this is Erin Young reporting live with Jamie Williams from Southwestern Hub. In local news a woman was badly injured in a fire in her apartment in Sector Seven early this morning. Local fire crews quickly got the blaze under control before it could spread to other units in the building. The fire originated in the kitchen area of the unit and is being investigated as to cause. The woman was treated for smoke inhalation and burns to her hands and arms which local health authorities said were the worst burns you can sustain. They hope the woman will regain use of her hands, but numerous surgeries will be needed. A fund has been set up for the victim and you can locate details on our website."

"Thank you, Erin." Jamie's voice was surprisingly high-pitched, almost girlish. "I'll be sure to check that out and remember, folks, it's easy to set up a VIP through your manager. A Victim Investment Plan allows you to contribute credits on a steady withdrawal, ensuring availability when victims need it most, right after an emergency. You can even specify where you want your credits applied, right down to a specific sector level. Ask your manager for details today. Now, we'll see what's going on in sports with Lori Beattie."

A heavyset woman with a squarish face, iron gray hair bobbed in a short mannish cut, was centered on the screen wearing a white button up shirt, sleeves rolled up, under a red quilted vest. "Thanks, Jamie. In tonight's news we honor the passing of a local sports legend. Josh Derse, former coach for high school football here in Soweh, passed away in his home at the age of sixty-five. Former students and coworkers remember Derse as a hard but fair coach, quick to recognize and promote talent. Derse had been ill with a pulmonary disease and is believed to have passed from complications related to his illness. The family asks that donations be directed to the Youth Athletic Program in his honor."

"Sad news, indeed, Lori." The screen shifted back to Jamie. "We'll break for a local word from one of our sponsors."

The screen burst suddenly with images of sensational events around the world: towering buildings engulfed in flames, a plane crash wreckage strewn across a field, a ship surrounded by a slick of oil and then black. Over the black screen, in bold white, blazed Media Resource Group. An attractive young woman dressed in a taupe suite that fit her like a glove walked into the dark screen. "Hello. I'm Karen from MRG. Our commitment, and our motto, is only True News will ever be relayed from our news teams. If you heard it here, you can count on it. Our website is always accurate within minutes as our nationwide team verifies and publishes all the relevant news that you need to know. Don't limit yourself to your daily news requirement. There's so much to know, and not enough time. As a wise man once said, we're never done learning. Sign up for a customized news feed delivered to your inbox daily at our website, courtesy of MRG." She smiled seductively and disappeared.

Jamie was back and saying in his irritating voice, "Leisure and hospitality services under the Facilities Resource Group has partnered with Infrastructure to offer a Hike or Bike Program that will launch the first of May. IRG has developed numerous trails in local area parks and there will be group activities to hike and bike the trails with a contest for most miles logged at the end of the official program in June. Contact your area FRG office for applications and program rules. Sounds like a fun way to explore the hub and get some exercise, Michael!"

"It sure does, Jamie. I plan on signing up right away! Good evening, folks. Michael Casey here with tonight's weather forecast. Today's high was seventy-two and we expect lows in the lower sixties tonight. A good night to open those windows! Hard to believe there's a blizzard going on somewhere to our northeast. Tomorrow will be a bit cooler as we have some cloud cover moving in and temps will drop about twenty degrees by Wednesday. It won't stick around, though, as we climb back up to eighty by Friday! It'll be a sunny and beautiful spring weekend, so get out and check out those parks!"

"Thanks, Michael." The screen cut to Erin. "We'll wrap tonight's news with a story of true heroism. Jim Plant, a gutter cleaner with the Infrastructure team based in Sector Five was on his way to work, passing the local Preschool Dormitory, when something caught his eye. He saw a small form hanging from one of the second-floor windows. Jim instantly ran over and encouraged the youngster to let go, catching him safely when he did."

The screen showed a bashful young man, hair cut in a ragged fashion, dressed in stained coveralls, holding a young child in his arms. The young man appeared afraid he'd hurt the child and held him awkwardly away from his body. The small boy gazed up with wide eyes.

"The boy, a four-year-old lodged at the dormitory, apparently lost his balance while looking out the window and tipped out. School authorities are investigating why he was able to open the window. Meanwhile, the director for the Educational Resource Group has awarded Jim one thousand credits for his heroism in saving the little boy." Erin smiled a saccharine smile and paused before adding, "That will end tonight's broadcast. Have a wonderful night!"

CHAPTER EIGHTEEN

"You've gone too far, Frank!" JB's tone was furious.

Frank sighed heavily and leaned back in his chair, studying the distraught image on his screen. "And exactly how have I done so, JB?" his voice was controlled, calm.

JB strove to match his control but her voice trembled from the strain and the extent of her anger. "You had no right to initiate a program involving Outsiders."

"I have not initiated any program with any Outsiders, Janet," Frank spoke her given name deliberately and slowly. "I have announced an intention to make the effort. There is a very big difference."

"Not in my opinion, there isn't. And not in the opinion of a few others on the Council. You should step down as Speaker. You're out of line and have overstepped your limits," JB's tone was crisp now, words coming staccato.

"I don't think so. If you feel so strongly, convene a Council meeting to discuss it. Or collect the necessary votes and signatures from your peers to force my resignation."

"You know that would never happen," JB snapped waspishly.

Frank smiled in return, "No, I doubt it would."

"You should have brought your idea to us before you acted on it. Next, you'll be suggesting people leave the hubs."

Frank laughed and leaned forward, "Funny you should mention that." His laughter died and his tone became serious, "I have considered it."

"That's insane!" JB burst out. "This country isn't ready for that, Frank. We worked too hard to salvage things to have it all spin out of control now, just when we're about to step back on the world stage. Just about to resume our proper place of power in the world."

"And that's what it comes down to, isn't it, JB?" Frank's tone was soft, the look in his eyes steel. "Power."

She froze, her eyes narrowing into slits as she glared at him across the miles. "I object to that, Frank. I am trying to put what's best for this nation first." Her tone was frosty, and her blue eyes glittered angrily. "You've forgotten what it was like in the twenties. Riots, people starving in rural areas as everything began to break down. Banking went first. No money. That led to riots. Mass suicides as companies failed and retirement savings vanished. A government sworn to protect us, failed because of one man. One inept man led to our downfall. We can't allow that to happen again."

"And we won't allow it. The Council is the right idea, but it was executed wrongly. You say you're thinking about the best interests of the nation. But no, JB, you aren't. It's time this Council started thinking about everyone in this nation. It's time we started thinking about solutions that include a valuable resource. One of the best resources this nation ever had and has always relied on. Its people."

"What? Some ignorant country bumpkins? I don't see how they could be of any practical use."

Frank shook his head sadly, "No, you wouldn't. A narrow mind is not capable of seeing beyond known horizons. You don't really believe the way your running your hub is the way it was intended? Sending people to work farms and fattening your accounts? Ruining lives to settle your personal vendettas? Oh, I've heard what happens to people that cross you, JB. I've got people in your hub. A whole staff don't forget. Those people outside the hubs are the survivors. You don't think we can't learn from them? Your shortsighted as well as narrow minded."

JB stiffened further as her rage mounted higher. "I run an efficient hub. We have zero crime and zero tolerance if there ever is any. Residents are offered an extensive variety of entertainment with minimal interference. My people are happy and provided for. You won't find anyone suffering hardships here."

"There're a few in Tulsa that might disagree," Frank said softly.

JB colored at the reference to the work center nearest Wegah where she'd sent many of her hub reductions. "Naturally you'd take the word of a dissident and troublemaker. No one is sent to work centers without cause."

Frank couldn't suppress a laugh, "Who's cause, JB? Theirs? Or yours?"

She returned his laugh with an acid smile but was unable to hide the flush that crept into her cheeks. "We've wandered from the main point. You go too far, and I will be discussing this with the other members of the Council."

"You do that, JB. In fact, I'll have it added to our next agenda."

She terminated the call and rose from her desk in aggravated frustration. The man was infuriating. Accusing her of lusting after power. It was those same country bumpkins that came running to the corporations for help in the first place, looking for a bail-out. Well, they got it. They had housing, food, medical and could even afford entertainment. Life wasn't so bad for them. In fact, it was quite pleasant for the majority and wasn't it the majority that ruled?

She pressed the intercom button on her desk phone. "Kirby, please hold all calls. I want no interruptions of any kind until you hear otherwise."

"Yes, ma'am," came Kirby's crisp and immediate response. JB smiled, knowing nothing on earth could move Kirby to pick up that phone or allow that door to be in any way touched for as long as JB wanted. She dismissed the thought from mind and quickly dialed a number.

"Drew," she purred into the phone. "Are you getting settled?" She tapped manicured nail against her upper teeth as she listened.

"Good. Spare me the details. Have you had much progress on my other little task? Learning any interesting habits?"

Silence while a frown descended. "I had a very specific request of you, Drew. I don't want to hear about meetings and all-day sessions. You waste my time with useless details yet don't have the detail I specifically requested. I'm most disappointed."

The silence on her end grew longer and slowly a smile formed. "Very well. Keep me informed on that progress and, Drew," she paused before finishing, "Have the detail I asked for the next time we talk, will you?"

Aubree straightened the clock on her living room wall shelf and surveyed the room again. Nervously, she glanced back at the clock and her stomach did a slow roll. Adam should be here soon. He'd said he would be there at around one thirty that afternoon. It was Saturday and she had been at loose ends all morning.

He'd called late the previous evening, just as she had decided to turn in. "Natalie? It's me, Adam."

As if anyone else's voice could cause her heart rate to speed up like his did.

"Yes, hello." What a lame response, she'd thought at the time, but had been too surprised by the call to muster a better reply.

"I'm going to be in Wegah this weekend. I was wondering if we could talk."

"Talk? Sure. I'd like that."

He'd told her he'd be by at around one thirty and that had been it. She'd spent the night tossing and turning, unable to achieve a deep sleep. At some point in the night she even lay wondering if he was already back but knew that wasn't possible. The gates closed and flights didn't come in after dark.

When the knock finally came, she was surprised how calm she felt. She smoothed the olive-green blouse she was wearing over white slacks and opened the door, her eyes locking with his.

"Hi." If her voice was a little breathless, the short word covered it.

He nodded, a questioning smile beginning to form on his lips. "How are you?" he asked.

She gave a small shrug. "Okay." Gesturing, she opened the door wider, "Come on in. Can I offer you something to drink?"

"Thanks." He stepped through, wandering into the living area as she closed the door behind him. "An ice water would be fine."

She went into the kitchen and got him a glass. When she returned, he was standing at the window, his back to her.

"I'm not sure where to start," he said to his reflection in the window.

She studied the taut muscles in his back as he stood with his hands clasped behind him, looking out at the little park below her building. She set his glass on a coaster on the coffee table and sat down at the other end. "Where would you like to start?"

He turned and looked at her. "I've missed you, Natalie."

She winced at his use of the name. Quickly, so that he wouldn't misunderstand, she said, "I've missed you, too." She hesitated and then added, "I have so much to tell you."

He stood a bit longer, just drinking in the sight of her sitting there. Her auburn hair fell in glossy waves against the darker color of her blouse. Her green eyes somehow seemed even greener. Perhaps because of the color of the blouse.

"I want to apologize," he told her, crossing and sitting at the other end of the couch, picking up the glass of water.

"Apologize for what?" she asked.

"For losing my temper the last time we talked. For leaving here angry." He drank from the glass, carefully setting it back on the coaster. "And for not calling sooner."

She looked down at her hands and nodded, "I accept. Your apology." She hesitated again. "And I'm sorry if I hurt you."

They were both silent. Finally, he stirred a little uncomfortably and said, "I did research the act you mentioned, and I know you were right. I couldn't find a link to the program, but I couldn't disprove it either," he paused, feeling her eyes on him. "I'm curious how you found out about it."

"My former boss," she said softly. "I talked to her. I told her about your mom. She was the one who told me."

He looked over at her. She was sitting stiffly in her own corner, fingers nervously interlocking, relaxing, interlocking, fidgeting in her lap and then interlocking again. He reached over and grasped her left hand in his right, fingers warmly clasping hers, thumb tenderly caressing.

"I think she's right," he said carefully and pulled a letter out of his back pocket. He gave her fingers another squeeze before he released her hand and withdrew the letter from the envelope. "This was delivered to me in Romoh three days after I got there."

He held the single sheet of paper out to her and she unfolded it.

Dear Mr. Miller,

We regret to inform you that your mother passed away yesterday. Her passing was peaceful, and she went in her sleep. During her short stay here at the Hawaiian Senior Retirement hub in Honolulu she endeared herself to many of the staff and fellow retirees. She was active and engaged in the many activities we have available. We will all miss her deeply and send our condolences to you in this time of sorrow.

It is not practicable to return her remains to the mainland, so we have taken all necessary care for her interment. A small ceremony will be held. Her personal effects will be sent to your known residence.

Many condolences,
Jennifer Holzinger
Managing Director

"Oh, Adam," she said, folding the paper and handing it back. "I am so sorry."

He nodded, "In all of my research I haven't found one lottery winner that is still alive, Natalie."

She swallowed, "Adam, I have to tell you something. My name isn't Natalie." She watched him carefully as she spoke the words and saw him tense alertly, turning to her.

"Then who are you?" he asked, voice toneless, eyes void of expression.

"My name is Aubree Holten," she paused but the name meant nothing to him, she saw no spark of recognition. "My father is Mike Holten." Again, no reaction. "He's VP of HR in Midah."

He gave a minute shrug, "All of which means nothing to me. Why would you lie? Why have you been deceiving me?" Agitated anew he rose from the couch and stalked back over to the window.

She sighed, "I didn't want to lie to you. From the very first. I had no choice."

"We always have a choice, Nata..." he paused, biting the word off angrily before continuing, "I'm sorry. What was it? Aubree? We always have a choice, Aubree."

"Yes, Adam, we do!" It was her turn to be angered. How dare he judge her when he didn't know? "I had a choice to make long before I ever met you." She stood up and walked to the center of the room. "It just so happens that choice led to meeting you! And I don't regret that! I regret the lies! I regret having to deceive you! But I don't regret that it happened!" The words came out explosively, her anger and frustration pouring out of her.

He was taken aback by the flood of words. Having turned to face her midway through the tirade he stood now, hands dangling helplessly at his side while a part of him longed to reach out, grasp her, pull her close to him. Instead, he spoke coldly, "And just what choice was it that you had to make, Aubree?" The name was said bitingly.

She felt a stab of pain at the bitterness in his voice. "There was a man. In Midah. He was with Security." She said the last almost accusingly. "My father couldn't protect me, and he had made his intentions clear. That I wasn't interested or willing, didn't seem to matter."

"And you say he's with Security?" Adam's voice showed his doubt at the veracity of this statement.

"He is. His name's Drew Shipley. Andrew Shipley. He was assigned to our sector in Midah."

"Why didn't your father just report him? Why didn't you?"

"Report him for what, Adam?" Her tone was laced heavily with her frustration. "No crime was committed. He expressed an interest. That's not a crime. My father tried but hit a dead end. Drew was off limits. My father thinks he must be well connected."

"So, what? You ran?" He was confounded. "Seems a bit drastic."

"What was my other choice? Stay and eventually fall victim? What protection did I have from someone in Security? This job opening was available, and I saw an opportunity."

He shook his head, gazing at her in wonder, before dropping his head into his hands and running his hands back through his hair. "I can't admit I understand, I don't. I don't know why you couldn't tell me."

"I couldn't tell anyone, Adam! I wanted to. We figured by changing my name, Drew wouldn't be able to track me down. Moving with the convoy meant there was no record of my trip. No trail for him to follow. Then, once I was here and knew you, I couldn't tell you then, either. It wasn't that I didn't trust you, I was under strict orders not to tell and I didn't want to burden you with my problems."

He laughed shortly, "Good try. Too good." He shook his head again and drank off the last of the water. "Mind if I get more?"

"No. Go ahead." She waited until he returned and settled back on the couch before she continued. "Anyway, it was all a wasted effort. Drew found me."

He looked at her in surprise. "When was this?"

"The day before you left," she told him bleakly.

He sat silently for a minute, thinking, then said, "Oh, God. You mean the day we had our argument?"

She nodded miserably, "Yes. I was going to tell you everything that night. I guess I really messed it up, didn't I?" Large tears welled on the bottom lids of her eyes, ready to spill over. She dashed them away angrily. "I was going to tell you about your mom, me, Drew, everything. Only I never got past your mom. And I'm so sorry!" The last came out as a wail as she succumbed to the sobs that were trying to tear her apart.

He slid down the couch and put his arms around her. "Shh, shh now. It's okay. It's going to be okay." He kissed the top of her head, smoothing the silky strands as he cradled her tightly against him, feeling the sobs shaking her.

She raised a tear streaked face to gaze up at him, green eyes brilliant with still unshed tears. "I missed you, Adam, so terribly. I told my father about you. He wanted me to come home."

His arm tightened around her shoulder at the thought of her leaving. He desperately wanted her to stay, yet he wanted to be sure it was what she wanted also. "It's not your fault about my mom, Aubree." He tried the name out, liked it. He smiled a little and said, "I sort of liked the name Natalie. Aubree will take a little getting used to."

She gave a tremulous smile in response, "I promise I will never lie to you about anything else ever again," she said solemnly.

He reached up, taking her chin in his hand and holding her face gently, his eyes searching. Finally, he smiled and planted a tender kiss at the corner of her mouth, "I believe you, Aubree."

She took a deep breath then, "Adam, I told you I told my dad about you."

He nodded and smiled encouragingly.

"Well, he told me for a fact the Hawaiian Retirement Program is part of the assisted passing act. I thought it was familiar because I heard him and Lawrence discussing it at dinner one night. I was too young and didn't really pay attention."

He nodded, "I'd rather know the truth. That letter was a little too," he paused, searching for the right word, "Too convenient. No details as to cause. She was in perfect health. People don't just pass in their sleep for no reason. I plan on getting some answers."

"If there's anything I can do I'd like to help."

He nodded his thanks, "By the way, you mentioned something about Drew finding you?"

She grimaced and then told him about their lunch encounter. "It was creepy. I haven't seen him since but I'm very careful. I've been spending a lot of time here at home."

"Probably a good idea. I'm going to see what I can find out about him. I've got access to things in Security most people don't. And I'm in pretty good with Ben now. How long do you plan on maintaining the false identity?"

"That's a little tricky. I'm going to talk to Dad about it. Get his advice. I don't like being someone I'm not, but it raises too many questions now to just announce I'm someone else. Like I said, a real mess I've made."

He laughed, "I think we'll manage our way through it, Natalie." He said the name teasingly and she laughed with him. "In the meantime, just be careful like you've been doing. I'll call you when I track him down. Now, how does dinner this evening sound?"

"Only if it includes dessert."

Adam strode into Ben's office at a little after seven. He'd gotten there as quickly as he could when his flight arrived, leaving out of Wegah at five thirty that morning.

"Adam!" Ben exclaimed, glancing up from his monitor. "Just the person I was hoping to see this morning." He waved his hand at the chair across from him. "Bring that around here. Something I want to show you."

"Not until I get some answers."

Ben sat back, startled, eyebrows rising, "Okay. If it's within my ability to answer, I'll be glad to."

"I got this last week." Adam slapped the letter about Megan down in front of Ben. He sat while Ben read the letter.

"I'm very sorry for your loss, Adam," Ben's tone was sincere. He folded the letter and handed it back to Adam. "Would you like some time off? Get away for a bit?"

"No. What I really want is the truth, Ben. My mother won the Hawaiian Retirement Lottery this year. I saw it during the halftime show like the rest of America did. Like we do every year."

Ben winced, "I see." His gaze broke from Adam's, his eyes straying over the few items on his desk.

Adam studied him, his heart sinking as the reality settled in. "How'd they do it, Ben?" His voice was a whisper, tortured, "How do they assist them? Why do they sell us dreams? I bought my mother extra lottery tickets this year! She wanted to win so bad, so I thought, why not? What's the harm in a few extra tickets? I killed her, Ben!"

Ben's eyes rose, startled, to meet Adam's, "No, Adam. No, you didn't. Don't even think it. Look, it's true. I won't lie to you. There is no retirement in Hawaii. No hub in Honolulu with gray hairs kicking it up on the beach. I wish there were. There ought to be. At least, that's what Frank and I and quite a few others on the Council think."

"People need to know the truth, Ben! My God, I bought those tickets!"

Ben sighed and leaned forward over his hands, face and voice earnest, "I am truly sorry, Adam. I assure you that Frank Baba, Lawrence Johnson and myself do not agree with this heinous practice. Lawrence was vehemently opposed to the assisted passing act. He predicted it would be abused. Originally, it was for those individuals that were suffering. Alzheimer's, Parkinson's, a whole host. It seemed humane."

Adam was horrified, "Humane to kill people? No matter how it's done or in the name of mercy. Death is pretty damn final."

Ben sighed heavily. "I agree with you. One of the Presidents, I won't say

165

who--he's not in office any more anyway—decided his senior population was over budget and he had insufficient housing. This happened a while back, understand? Well, this President cooked up the Hawaiian Retirement scheme. It was only supposed to be offered in the one hub, the one time. Well, you see how that worked out. Lawrence tried to stop that, too, but was unsuccessful. It was supposed to offset and stop some of the then rampant RIF activity."

Adam sat shaking his head, staring at Ben, baffled, "How do you men sleep at night? This is terrible, Ben."

"Don't I know it, and sleep comes hard, Adam. I wish I could say I slept like a baby, but I don't sleep so well." He glanced at Adam and met the stony gaze. "What choice do I have? What choice does Frank have? People in the hubs depend on the corporations and their leaders for their very livelihoods. We can't have open war and dissent in the Council. We're trying to reestablish a foothold on the world stage. To undo the wrongs of the past." He laughed harshly and stood up, pacing over to look out at the distant mountain peaks. "We can never undo the wrongs. We can only move forward. And we are. Slowly. Frank's plan is to de-centralize. Oh, the hubs will still be around but Frank wants to open them."

He turned and looked at Adam for a long moment. "What I'm telling you is not for general consumption. Is that understood?"

Adam nodded and watched while Ben resumed his seat. "It's a long-term plan but Frank is dedicated to carrying it out. I'm committed to helping him. So was Lawrence, but now he's retiring. It may be a short set back as we'll have to assess his replacement. Lawrence is handpicking, but all the other Presidents were handpicked as well. Handpicking doesn't stop greed once someone gets a taste of power."

"I wouldn't know, sir," Adam's tone was dry.

Ben allowed himself a brief smile, "No, you wouldn't. Another reason we need to shake things up. We have strayed quite far from the original constitution. Not that they teach that in school anymore. With legal volumes occupying entire libraries, and still we have not mined all the aspects of our complicated law, why teach the laymen the fundamentals? It only causes confusion." Ben's tone was sneering, and he looked off into the distance past Adam.

He seemed to shake himself and leaned forward over his folded hands, eyes engaging Adam's earnestly. "And this is what happens when one man," he paused, "Or ten, hold ultimate power. This is what happens when corporations control education and media. Your very knowledge is controlled. We have to stop it, Adam, and I believe you're the right man to join our team."

"I'd like to help, Ben. I really would. I'm not sure what I can do, but count me in."

Ben nodded, "Excellent. There's someone I want you to meet. Means you'll need to go to the Southwestern hub. I was hoping this Wednesday. That is, if you're up to it. My offer of some time off is sincere. I can appreciate how you're feeling right now. I lost my mother a few years back. It still hurts to think of." He was gazing at the backs of his hands, splayed on the blotter before him, a sad and yearning expression on his face.

For perhaps the first time Adam really felt a connection with Ben Larocque. He'd thought over the past week that they had much in common, thought along similar patterns, but he'd still been very much in awe of Ben the man. Now he saw him as any other man. A man that could still grieve for his dead mother many years after her passing. This was a man Adam felt he could trust and believe in.

"I appreciate the offer, but I think I'd rather keep busy. In fact, some travel and digging into some work is exactly what I need."

Ben's smile was tinged with sadness. "Yes. I understand that, too. Few things can offer the solace a job well done provides. All right. I'll let our man know it's a go. His name is Mitch Lasater. He'll meet you himself at the airport. I'll let him explain his project. I'm looking for you to loop in."

Adam cocked his head quizzically and replied hesitantly, "Okay. Any clues?"

"I'd rather you confer with Mitch after you hear what his project is all about. The key is communication. I will need a way to communicate with Mitch and the network you're setting up could be a key component to that plan."

"Fair enough. I assume Mitch knows about me and my project?"

"Absolutely. He's already got some ideas and that's why I want you to talk to him first. And, Adam, one more thing..."

"Yes?"

"This office only."

"Sir?"

"Only this office knows about you meeting Mitch. I want it kept that way. I don't mean this building, this floor. I mean, this office. Beyond those doors, not a word."

"Understood, Ben."

"That includes Aubree Holten, Adam," Ben's gaze was direct.

Adam felt himself flush. Ben had done a lot of homework. Adam reflected to himself wryly that Ben had probably known the truth about Natalie, Aubree, before Adam himself had been told.

"Not a word beyond that door. About meeting Mitch." Adam's gaze was as direct as Ben's.

Ben smiled. "Good deal. You'll be taking a, ah," Ben paused, searching and then smiling, "A class trip, shall we call it? A class trip with Mitch and you'll be gone a few days. I'll see you here in Romoh when you get back."

CHAPTER NINETEEN

Drew studied his face in the clear spot he had wiped in the steamy mirror, critically surveying the handsome features. He filled his palm with lather and was about to apply it when the slim black phone that never rang lit up, displaying Janet Byron's face.

He grimaced. Bitch! He was still angry at how she had treated him the last time they'd talked. Like he was her lackey, her dog. Here, boy! Fetch! Fetch this, bitch! For a moment he considered ignoring her but was already rinsing off his hand and reaching with the other for the phone before the thought was even consciously formed. He still needed the old bag.

"Yeah?" he barked, opening the connection.

Steel blue eyes peered at him sharply, assessing, "I interrupt something?"

"A shave. You just missed joining me in the shower."

"How entertaining," she smiled a waspish smile, "You'll recall the subject of our last discussion?"

"How could I forget?" he couldn't resist snapping back.

She frowned, "Don't get snippy with me. Have you had any luck?"

He shrugged, reaching again for the can of lather. Why should she interrupt his shave? "Not much. He does have one weakness that I've discovered so far."

"Oh? What would that be?" She reminded him of a cat, a big predatory cat.

"He prefers to drive himself around in an older model Corvette. One of the late nineties models."

"How interesting. It would be a shame if something were to happen, wouldn't it?"

He switched from his review of his face in the mirror to his aunt's icy blue eyes on the small screen. "An accident, you mean? With him in it?"

"I would never suggest such a thing, Drew. But it would be a shame, wouldn't it?"

Adam studied Mitch Lasater and decided instantly that he liked him. The man stood at an equal height to Adam. His muddy brown eyes assessed Adam intelligently, alertly. His face was hardened, and lines were etched deeply around his eyes and mouth. Dark hair was cut short in an almost crew cut hugging his scalp. His handshake was what Adam expected, firm and brief. Pump and release. "Nice ta meet'cha. I'm Mitch." His drawl was Southern lazy, vowels rolling, and consonants swallowed. His smile matched, dimples deepening still more.

"Pleasure's mine," Adam returned, falling into step as Mitch promptly turned and led him out of the terminal onto the tarmac and parking area beyond. Arizona heat rose from the cracked pavement even though it was still early spring.

"You gotta cell phone? Stupid question, I know you do. I suspect you may have more than one. No matter. I don't care how important you think they are. You get them and turn them off. Now." His voice was no nonsense and he paused in his stride to face Adam who pulled up quickly beside him.

"Okay. Sure." Adam complied. He carried two phones, one of which had been given him by Ben himself. He'd never had reason to carry more than one before. He hesitated before turning that one off as well, looking at Mitch with a smile and cocked eyebrows. "All right, Chief. We all set now?"

Mitch smiled broadly in response. "Cool. We're cool. Follow me. When we get in the Hummer those two logs go in the glove box and they do not come out until we are back at this terminal. Am I clear?"

"Ten four." Adam grinned.

Mitch returned it and they arrived at the big dark green Hummer he was referring to. Adam swung up into the passenger seat, placing both cell phones in the glove box in front of him. Mitch settled behind the driver's seat and reaching over locked the glove box before inserting the key in the ignition. "Just a precaution," he quipped as he fired up the engine.

Adam wasn't really surprised when Mitch headed out into the desert to the south away from the hub. As if picking up on his thoughts, Mitch said, "We'll be meeting up with my team and spending the night at a former town called Searchlight." He grinned at Adam, "We thought the name was appropriate to the mission."

Adam laughed and looked out at the bleak desert scenery rolling past. Everything was shades of gold, yellow and tan, the afternoon sunlight harsh and he was glad for his sunglasses. The sun glared off every surface and heat shimmered in the distance above the hardpan. "And what is the searchlight seeking?"

Mitch grinned again, "Citizens, naturally."

They were coming into an area where jagged peaks climbed into the sky to their right, the highway winding along between tall walls decorated with symbols of the old west: oil wells, cows and, of course, cowboys on horseback. "Those are the McCullough Hills. Colorado River is off in those mountains to our left. Searchlight isn't far from Lake Mohave. Maybe we'll take a stroll over there this evening. I thought we might sit and palaver first for a bit."

Adam's eyes ached to see some green, but none was to be seen other than the old faded signs mostly fallen along the roadside. "You mentioned we'll be meeting your team. How big is your team?"

"Small group. To start anyway. There are nine of us including myself. Each is skilled in an area that with our combined efforts should give us the knowledge to succeed out here," he waved vaguely at the harsh desert around them.

"Hard to believe anything could live out here," Adam commented.

Mitch laughed, "It's not easy! But it can be done. There are a lot of little towns scattered out here. Each one offers shelter and that's the first requirement. So, we've got that covered. Eventually, we'll find other people and hopefully we'll build a network. Establish a relationship. That's the goal."

"That's not what they say in the Media. The Media reports we're trying to infiltrate. That's a slightly different concept. A bit more aggressive. Relationship implies positive and friendly. Not the tone from Media at all."

"Of course, it isn't!" Mitch hooted. "There are some, not all, but a lot of upper level management that prefers the hubber to be afraid of what's outside those walls. Who do you think owns Media?"

Adam shrugged, "I'm in favor of anything with positive goals. I don't like the idea of going out and strong-arming people just living their own lives."

"Exactly. That's why it's so important my team succeeds. We've got to establish that first contact in a positive way. Otherwise, it won't be handled right."

The rest of the drive passed pleasantly and with each passing mile Adam felt more comfortable with Mitch. They were close in age and discovered that Mitch had attended a rival college a few years ahead of Drew. They spent a good deal of the time reminiscing about old football matches between the two teams.

Searchlight ended up being a dry and dusty spot in a long narrow valley between two mountain ranges. Adam's eyes were tired of the endless tans and whites and browns. Mitch pulled into the parking lot of a stone-faced building, roof a rusty red. The huge sign on the verge of the road, massive in proportion to the building, declared this was Terrible's Road House Searchlight. Any color the sign ever had had long since been bleached by the sun and the relentlessly blowing wind, scouring the surface with tiny particles of sand.

Adam noted five other vehicles in the parking area. Two were four-wheel drive pickups, there was a boxy Jeep and two dirt bikes leaning on their kickstands.

"Let's go meet the gang," Mitch said cheerfully, heading for the double glass doors at the end of the structure tucked into a small alcove.

The inside was dim and felt cool compared to the air outdoor. A black doorway led into a back room beyond. Seven people were lounging around a big table in the shadowy room.

"Heya, Mitch!" a broad chested man, shirt tight against bunched muscles, boomed in a deep voice, grinning when he saw Mitch and then nodding genially at Adam.

"Hey, Gambie," Mitch responded, looking around the circle and frowning, "Where's Drew?"

Several exchanged glances, all looked puzzled and a couple shrugged.

"Dunno," a swarthy man with thick black hair and thunderous eyebrows said in a surprisingly soft voice.

The only woman in the circle, an attractive blonde with well-toned muscles in a tank top said, "I saw him just before I left the hub. Said something about an aunt." She shrugged tanned shoulders.

"Well, we won't wait on him. If he's not here at twenty-two hundred we roll without." He half turned towards Adam, "Team, this is Adam. He'll be along for the ride this time. Go easy on him," he grinned, and the tension eased as a few of the people laughed or chuckled, Adam along with them.

Adam grabbed a chair and pulled it over between the man Mitch had called Gambie and the swarthy man with the soft voice.

Mitch took a seat and laid a map in the center of the table. He laid his index finger next to a dot and said, "This is our destination. Lake Havasu City. We'll be two and a half hours from the Southwest Hub. It probably isn't far enough but it's a good place to start. We'll be setting up a base camp there and the plan is that most of you won't see the hub again for a very long time. I'll be taking Adam here back Friday morning. That should give him time to do what he needs."

Mitch looked over at Adam, "We need a way to communicate back to Southwest and to Baba. Now, it's got to be very secure, very mobile. Lake Havasu City looks to be a good site. We've got water from the Colorado River and we ought to be able to make it habitable for a while. We've got to think longer term, though, and that will mean being able to communicate even if we have to move. No fixed communications."

Adam was nodding, understanding the challenge.

"All of us in this room know Security has access and monitors every form of communication they know about. We know there are computers that monitor every communication as it happens watching for specific key words or phrases and highlighting them for additional review. We have to stay outside of those listeners."

Adam shook his head, "That's a tough one. To be mobile, you need to be wireless. All the bands are watched."

"All?"

Adam cocked his head, looking at Mitch alertly.

Mitch rose and walked over to what once must have been a serving counter. An oversized paperback book sat on the dusty surface. Picking it up he tossed it to Adam, who caught it awkwardly as it sailed across the room. Glancing at it he saw it was a college manual on radio frequencies and transmission wavelengths.

"I think you'll learn otherwise," he nodded at one of the men sitting opposite Adam. "This here is Frank. Frank's specialty in Security is communications. He'll be spending some time with you over the next couple of days."

Adam smiled at Frank, "Look forward to it."

"All right," Mitch clapped his hands. "Let's get some grub on. We've got time to catch a few winks before we head out at ten." He explained to Adam, "We'll travel at night, just like we suspect people outside the hub do. If we keep our vehicle's headlights on low beam it's not enough illumination for a satellite to pick up on. Tiffany and Michael run lead on the bikes, checking road conditions and any blockage we might need to skirt around. They get a thirty-minute head start. We've got short band radios to keep in touch. We'll reach Lake Havasu City around midnight. Plenty of time to check it out, pick a place we can use. Questions?"

Ben's email began blowing up with incoming urgent messages, his instant messaging program lit up like a Christmas tree as he started getting a massive volume of pings that he couldn't possibly hope to respond to, at the same time his cell phone lit up and Frank's anxious face appeared on the screen.

"Frank? What's going on? My computer just went crazy."

"I imagine it did," Frank said drily. "Considering there was just an attempt on my life. I'm sure that's what it was."

"What?" Ben was shocked. "Tell me what happened."

"I had scheduled the 'Vette for a tune up. It was overdue for an oil change. I had a technician from Supply pick it up to drive it to the shop. It blew up when he turned the ignition. Or I assume that's when it blew up. That parts a guess. Maybe he put it in drive. Who knows? We'll find out, of course. Your team here is already working the scene."

"Damn. Right there at your office?"

Frank nodded grimly, "It was in the lot where I always park it."

"Damn it, Frank, I always said it wasn't a good idea to drive that car."

That pulled a smile out of Frank, "Yeah, but not for those reasons."

Ben smiled too, "You're going to have to take some extra precautions, Frank. Lay low. Let my team provide some extra coverage and security for you. I'll talk to Charles. We'll get a detail assigned to you. And no personal vehicles for a while, okay?"

"Sure. Look, it bothers me like hell about this guy from Supply. I want to see if he's got any family."

"Sure. Easy enough for my guys to trace back. I'll have that for you within the next hour. I feel bad, too, Frank, but I'm really glad it wasn't you in that car."

"Yeah, me too, Ben. It was a last-minute request, the oil change. I was thinking of maybe taking it out for a drive this weekend. Knew it had been a while and thought I'd better get it done. No one would have had advance notice. I had just made the arrangements."

Ben considered this. "So, it really was an attempt on you. Not a warning."

"That's my guess. We'll find some rigging somewhere on the car. I don't doubt that. I also don't doubt we won't be able to trace it back to its source."

"Don't be so certain of that, Frank. You'd be surprised what a forensics team can uncover. I'll be discussing that with Charles, too. He'll have a crack team on it, I'm sure, but we'll make sure he's got access to the best diagnostic equipment in the country."

"All of which takes time. Something we have precious little of, at the moment."

"We have all we need, Frank. This doesn't change anything."

Drew straddled the hot Harley on the shoulder of Interstate 40 a little east of Holbrook, Arizona. The map spread out on the gas tank showed the Petrified Forest was just ahead. There'd be a building there he could use. He squinted into the sun rising to the east as he folded the map and put it back in his pocket.

He'd stuck around long enough the previous day to see the explosion. He'd waited on the roof of a building about a mile away. The sound of sirens had been sweet as he'd wheeled the Harley out of the garage bay he'd left it in. He got outside the hub using a little-known gate unmanned, and at the moment, unmonitored thanks to a little tinkering he'd done. There was a gas station not far from the gate and he could hide there until dusk. It helped that any available Security personnel were most likely converging on the distant scene.

At ten that night, lights on low beam, Drew had headed south on Route 93 to Kingman. At around midnight, he had chuckled knowing Mitch and the team were just on the other side of those mountains to his right. He'd told that bitch Tiffany that he needed to go to Wegah, his aunt needed him. Tiffany had rebuffed his initial overtures, but it seemed she was that way with everyone. He assumed she was a dike though she'd been a bit chummy with one of the men, Michael. It didn't matter. She didn't hold a candle to Aubree and Drew smiled as he considered his destination.

Travelling only at night would slow him down a little but he should be in Wegah the day after next. Their reunion would be so sweet. He smiled to himself, pulling into the visitor welcome center for the Petrified Forest.

CHAPTER TWENTY

"Honey, there's no reason you need to stay in Wegah to do this job, is there?" Mike Holten's tone was comfortingly reasonable and Aubree was relieved just hearing him.

"If it weren't for Adam, I'd agree with you."

"Why does Adam have to be Wegah? I thought his project would eventually cover every hub. In fact, it seems logical to me that the two of you might spend time at each hub. In any event, leave Wegah and become Aubree Holten again. It's the simplest way."

"Until someone from Wegah sees me and remembers me as Natalie."

"What are the odds of that?"

"I'd like to discuss it with Adam."

"Of course. I wouldn't make any major decision without consulting with your mom first."

"Ugh!" Aubree grimaced comically and Mike laughed.

Just then the door to the small cubicle she was using for her private conversation rattled and an imperious rap came on the glass to the left of the knob.

Not masking her irritation at this interruption, she said, "One moment, Dad." Turning, she opened the door.

There, official badge displayed in one hand, a curious crowd gathered behind him, stood Drew. "Aubree Holten, also known as Natalie Deckman, you are under arrest for suspicious and covert activities suspected to be of a seditious nature. You will be taken into custody and conveyed to our Midah facility for questioning. You have the right to remain silent…"

She collapsed backwards, feeling the hard edge of the desk surface against the backs of her thighs. Off behind her, she heard her father frantically calling, "Aubree! Aubree! Listen to me! Aubree!"

Quickly she turned, grasping the phone before Drew could stop her,

"Dad! Get hold of Adam! He's in Romoh!"

Drew was squeezing into the confined space behind her, arm reaching over and closing over hers, applying pressure. It hurt too badly to hold the phone and her fingers relaxed, the phone slipping out and bouncing on the hard surface of the desk. She saw the screen crack, her father's face oddly distorted.

Then Drew had her arm behind her back, pulling it up between her shoulder blades and she gasped at the pain, bending over to relieve it.

"Stop!" She cried.

He grasped her other arm, slipping on hand cuffs before allowing her arm to fall to her side and then cuffing it in the other wristlet.

She could only look stunned at the amazed faces of her coworkers and employees as Drew spun her out of the enclosed cubicle.

"Make way. Let me through," Drew called, pushing Aubree along in front of him. She could hear the quiet rustle and whispers as the crowd closed behind them.

Adam was reluctant to say goodbye to the seven people he'd met a brief two days previous. The time they'd spent in Lake Havasu City had been enjoyable and he would miss their camaraderie.

Tiffany and Michael were clearly a couple and the rest of the group was very respectful of it. For their part, they didn't flaunt it.

Gambie, Jim Gamboa, was the genial giant of the group. His size, however, was not his main skill. He was a medical practitioner and a skilled botanist.

Wayne Bickel was the swarthy one that Adam had sat beside at that first meeting. He tended to be quiet and rarely engaged in much conversation, preferring to spend his free time whittling away at small bits of wood. Adam had seen some of his carvings and they were fabulously detailed miniaturizations, one of a lion and the other a bird of some sort. His specialty was geography. He knew where water was likely to be found.

William was the electrician and he spent some time the last afternoon with Frank and Adam talking about electrical requirements for the mobile communications Adam and Frank thought they'd need. He was intelligent and quick to grasp new concepts. Adam was impressed with his ability to predict possible outcomes and avert potential problems.

Allan Fagley was the last member and seemed to be a small engine wizard. Actually, any engine, not just small.

Frank Selwold, the so-called communications expert, was no less than a genius. He told Adam about an entire spectrum once used by the government that no one had bothered to maintain when the government shutdown occurred, private industry preferring to stay on their traditional platforms.

Those first two days most of the members were busy conducting a house by house search of the immediate area. Over time they would cover every building in the small city. One of the first things the team did was take a group hike to the London Bridge. The bridge had been relocated from London back in 1967. They walked across the broad paved surface marveling at the centuries of people, both great and miniscule, that had traversed before them.

Tiffany swore she got a chill at one point as they crossed. "You know," she told them as they reached the far end connecting the mainland with an island of sorts in Lake Havasu, "They used to impale heads of people they'd killed on pikes at the end of the bridge. To let people know what they did to traitors and thieves and the like. You didn't want to be an enemy of the state. I've heard the bridge is haunted."

"They had their bridge, we have work centers," someone muttered in response.

Someone else coughed as if to cover the awkward moment.

Adam considered how different he felt here, in this city under open skies, horizons bounded by mountains to east and west instead of by walls. The river fed in from the north creating the pooling lake. It was a small lake at less than twenty thousand acres and the deepest spot was ninety feet with an average of thirty-five. A little breeze ruffled the steel blue surface, reflecting the underside of clouds.

It had been a new experience for Adam and for the rest of the team as well. He had even overheard some conversation about it.

"Odd knowing there's no camera on you," Michael had commented as they had stood outside of a former bank they had just checked. The building had been empty, even of furniture. Bare plaster, carpet so dusty the color was no longer determinable, depressions filled with gray puffs showing where the legs of desks had once pressed deep into the pile were all that remained.

It was an odd feeling. Odd and yet liberating. Adam felt a yearning he'd never experienced before. A freedom. Now, returning to Southwestern Hub with Mitch he felt a touch of depression. The thought of returning to life in the hub was oppressive.

They had left Lake Havasu City in the pre-dawn dark at three that morning. The sun was just now touching the eastern horizon a tender shade of golden blue as Mitch maneuvered into a spot back at the airport terminal.

"That's your ride," he nodded at the slate blue Hyundai Palisade in the spot beside Adam. "The team liked you. Hell, so did I," he grinned and threw a handshake at Adam which he returned with a matched enthusiasm.

"I think I'm jealous of you guys," Adam laughed, yet his eyes betrayed his sincerity. "You take it easy out there. I won't wish you luck. You don't and won't need it. Maybe keep a ghost watch on London Bridge."

Mitch laughed, "Yeah, we'll do that. Hard to see ghosts when you've got a panorama of stars to look at like you see there. Anyway, I've got some things to do in the hub today before I slip out before lock down. I'll have Frank move forward with setting up comm on that spectrum we talked about. You'll see to it you've got something with ears to hear."

"On it," Adam said, swinging open his door and jumping to the ground.

"Oh, hey! Hold up!" Mitch leaned over and unlocked the glove box and tossed the two cell phones to Adam. "You can have those back now!"

Adam gave him a salute as Mitch put the Hummer in reverse and was soon gone from sight. Slipping behind the wheel of the Palisade, Adam thumbed on the two phones. His main device began buzzing immediately.

Hoping it was Aubree, he checked and saw he'd missed two calls from an unknown number. The area code wasn't immediately familiar to him. He saw in the lower right of his device screen a flashing alert for urgent voice mail. Checking, he saw there were two messages. The first message caught him by surprise.

"Adam Miller? This is Michael Holten, Vice President of Human Resources in MidAtlantic. I need to speak with you immediately. Please return my call."

Adam sat stunned. Why would Aubree's father be calling him? The second message had been left ten minutes after the first.

"Adam, this is Mike Holten again. Look, I'm not sure where you are right now, but Aubree needs you. Drew Shipley has arrested her. I've talked with Security here and they can't find anything on an arrest warrant. They don't know anything. I need your help. She needs your help. Please call me."

Adam went back to the missed call log and hit redial on the number.

Mike Holten answered on the second ring, "Hello?"

"Mr. Holten?"

"Yes. Who's this?"

"Adam. Adam Miller returning your call. What's this about an arrest?"

"Adam! Where are you? It's been four hours since Drew arrested Aubree. Wegah surveillance confirmed he left the city headed towards Midweh."

"I'm in Rocky Mountain Hub, Mr. Holten."

"Damn!" Mike swore softly. "And call me Mike, please. Sorry to meet you under these circumstances. Aubree speaks very highly of you. Seems you've won her over."

Adam paused, not wanting to think where Aubree was right now. "Thank you. I think pretty highly of her. I'm heading for Wegah as soon as I can. I should be able to get a flight out of here this afternoon. I have to see Ben Larocque first."

"Good. Maybe he can help you. I'm doing what I can here but I'm not Security. With no record of an arrest I just keep hitting stone walls. I can't even get the Security Vice President in Wegah to return my calls."

"I'll find her, Mr. Holten. I promise."

When Adam arrived at the Security Headquarters building in Romoh, he walked into a beehive of activity. Normally the office was calm, voices hushed and muted, carpeting softening the sounds of employees as they moved around. Today, there were people rushing about with papers grasped in their hands, apparently on important missions. Clusters stood about, voices low, but Adam caught the excited pitch all the same, speakers gesticulating ardently. He had to dodge around a couple in the corridor leading to Ben's office.

Ben's administrative assistant, J.D. Hamner, glanced up as Ben approached his desk. "Hey, Adam. How's it going? Go on in. Ben said to let you through as soon as you got here."

"Adam!" Ben cried, glancing up from his monitor as Adam entered the office. "Have a seat!" He waved expansively at the chairs across from him, eyes already glued back on his screen.

"Boy, have things blown up while you were gone! I trust things went well and that's moving forward. You'll let me know, of course, as you make progress and when I can expect to go from dark to light, so to speak. While you were gone there was an attempt on Baba."

Adam sat stiffly on one of the seats, sitting on the edge as if poised to stand at any moment.

"Our guys are working through the material from the site. Found a detonator. No surprise. Figured we would. Got a crew trying to trace the components. Oh, and I have a little bad news, too. Something I need to you to take care of."

He turned away from his monitor completely, facing Adam across the surface of his desk. "It seems you made a comment to Brent that he followed up on. You said something about you thought maybe the satellite program had been tampered with. Well, turns out it had been. Fortunately, the guy that traced it works here and brought the information to me. Brent doesn't know. Yet. I'll be obligated to tell him, of course. I figure I can buy us a little time, though. There's a remote site, up north of here in the Rockies. Someone there manipulated the bird. I've checked. We've got two men. One or both are working with the Outsiders. We've got to get to them before Brent does. Hell, I'll have to send the investigating team myself before I even let Brent know. Looks mighty suspicious if I don't. That's where you come in."

He finally paused in his tirade, eyes studying Adam's wooden expression. "I guess I could have started with hello?" he offered Adam a smile.

Adam shook his head. "Wow, Ben. I guess things have been busy. I could tell from all the commotion out there that something was up. Well, things have happened for me, too. That girl, Aubree Holten, has been arrested. Only there's no warrant for her arrest anywhere that I can find. A guy named Drew Shipley walked into her office this morning and said he was arresting her for seditious activity and taking her back to Midah. He was seen on camera leaving Wegah in a late model Continental. I don't know how I can help with this crew in the Rockies', but I've got to get back to Wegah.'"

Ben had frozen while Adam was speaking, "Did you say Drew Shipley?"

Adam nodded, "Yeah. He and Aubree have a history. I won't go into it now but he's the reason she's in Wegah posing as Natalie Deckman. He's up to no good and I'm afraid I'm already too late."

"But that's not possible, Adam. Drew Shipley was right there with you and Mitch and the team. Wasn't he?" Ben was perplexed.

"No." Adam suddenly made the connection. "Shit. Drew! There was a Drew that never showed up. Mitch didn't mention his last name and I didn't think it was remotely possible it could be the same guy."

"So, we don't know where Mr. Shipley was when the attack was made on Frank. Interesting. I'm going to ask for some information on him. I guess we are in a bind, aren't we?"

"I'm sure someone else can help with the remote team problem, Ben. I've got to get to Wegah."

"I understand, Adam. Well, I guess I don't really. I wish I did. I never let myself get close enough. I almost did once." Adam waited while Ben looked out at the distant mountains, a smile just touching the corners of his mouth. "Anyway," he finally said, "Go to Wegah. I understand. Then come back here. Bring her with you. I'll delay sending this along to Brent. I can say I'm doing some background checking of my own—which I intend on doing anyway. We'll address it when you get back."

Adam cleared his throat and shifted nervously. "That's just it, Ben. I don't know if I'll be coming back."

"What!" Ben was rocked and sat back suddenly in his chair, legs pushing him backward as his hands grasped the edge of his desk. "What do you mean, Adam? I need you to finish this surveillance installation and this communication with Mitch."

Adam chuckled, "Anyone can do that, Ben. The whole thing's on my computer. I've laid it all out. Someone just needs to implement it. I've done what you needed. I created the plan. As for Mitch, you don't need me. You've got someone far better in Frank Selwold. Man's a genius. I know computers but he knows communications. Besides, I still plan on working with Mitch and his team. Just not the way you thought, maybe."

"I don't understand, Adam. You're bright. I like you. Genuinely. I've enjoyed working with you this past week and having you around. I can promise you'll go far. I need men like you. You don't treat me like I'm different. You aren't afraid of me."

Adam smiled, "No, Ben, I'm not. Which is why I must be honest with you. I respect you and there's a part of me that wants nothing more than to be the man you just described. But that woman? Aubree? I'm in love with her. I want to spend my future with her."

Ben frowned, "Okay. So far so good. I'm failing to see an issue. There's no law against you and Aubree deciding to have a relationship. Arrangements can be made for housing."

Adam laughed, "It's not just housing, Ben! What about kids? We'll be expected to just hand them over to the Educational Resource Group when they're what? Four? Three or four? I don't think so. Frankly, Ben, the higher I seem to go through the Corporation, the grimmer it gets. Things like what happened to my mom. I don't think I can work for someone who can sanction that."

"Well, what do you think you'll do?" Ben wanted to be angry, restrained himself. He liked Adam too much and he couldn't refute the things Adam was saying.

"I want to try it out there. Outside the hub. I'm hoping Aubree will join me." Adam said it softly. Ben had the power to arrest him for just saying it.

Ben shook his head impatiently. "Go on, Adam. You're upset right now. Hell, you have a right to be. Don't decide right now. Find Aubree. Talk to her and then call me. Come back."

Drew was silent as he navigated the large black sedan through the gates of Wegah. Aubree sat huddled in the corner behind the driver's seat, rubbing her sore wrists. At least he had removed the cuffs after he'd shoved her in the back seat. She figured it was about ten in the morning and she tried to settle in for what she thought would be a long day of driving.

She was surprised when he took a familiar exit. Alertly she watched and her heart sank when the destination was beyond doubt. As he pulled the long car into the garage, sealing them in the interior darkness, she feared she might scream. Not here! Not here of all places.

She was flooded with memories of her weekend here with Adam. To have Drew destroy those pleasant associations would be more than she thought she might bear. She sat unmoving in the backseat as he went through the familiar routine of disabling the alarm and turning on the light. Even then she sat unmoving.

Brusquely he opened the back door, "Get out! Why are you just sitting there?"

She shook her head, "You said you were taking me to Midah. Why are we stopping here?"

He scowled, "We can't make Midweh before dusk. I don't know their safe house location, so we'll be staying here tonight."

Slowly, she got out of the car, keeping as much distance between them as possible. Even so, she was forced to brush against him as she slid along the quarter panel of the car as he loomed at the back door. He slammed it shut and turned towards the house. "Follow me," he ordered as he strode away.

Knowing she had little choice, she followed reluctantly. Tears blurred her eyes as she saw the familiar kitchen. Memories of fixing meals with Adam made her look quickly away only to find her gaze resting on the dark doorway into the master bedroom. She flushed as another set of memories threatened to overwhelm her.

"Why don't you have a seat there at the dining room table? I'll see what's available to drink"

Numbly, she moved over to the dining table, carefully choosing a seat that didn't have memories, a seat she had not used before. She was facing the kitchen and she watched as Drew pulled two sodas out and carried one over to her. He was just setting the can in front of her when his cell phone chirped.

Frowning, he turned away, pulling the device out of his jacket breast pocket, glancing at the screen. He cursed quietly, "Damnit!" Glancing back at Aubree, he commanded, "Sit there and drink that. Don't snoop around. There are alarms. I've got to take this." Then he went back out into the garage, closing the intervening door behind him.

Drew pressed the connect button on his phone as he pulled the door closed.

"Where the hell are you?" came his aunt's strident voice. "What's this nonsense about you arresting the Holten-Deckman girl?"

Drew swallowed hard. "I told you I had some unfinished business."

"I don't give a good God damned shit about your unfinished business, Drew! Especially not when it interferes with my own business. You get your ass back here now. I am not kidding you, Drew. I want you inside these walls before dusk and I need you to be visibly at my side when I attend an important meeting this evening. Am I making myself clear to you?"

"I'm just taking a short vacation, Aunt JB. I'll be back Monday morning."

"You will be back today. Was there something unclear about what I just said?" The words came out tautly and were delivered in a slow cadence, her rage seemed to radiate out of the phone at him. "You are about to seriously fuck up everything I've been working for. It was not easy to get you on that crew and it's not too late to fix the damage you've done. And all for nothing!"

"What do you mean, all for nothing?" he snarled back.

"Would you call it a success?" her tone was sharp and filled with sarcasm. "When an accident doesn't have the desired results, Drew, I don't consider it much of a success. If anything, you've only made it harder now to reach him."

Drew was stunned and rendered speechless. "I don't understand. I watched the explosion."

She paused, "You actually thought you succeeded, didn't you?"

"Of course, I did," he replied quickly.

She gave an ugly bark of laughter. "Oh, you ineffective idiot!" she snapped. "He wasn't driving, Drew. You got the wrong person."

"What?" he was dumbfounded.

"Well. Incompetent and, apparently, ignorant. No matter. I can fix things, but you've got to be here to make it work. You will be here. Today. At my office. By five. Clear?"

Drew wanted desperately to refuse her, realized he could not, "Okay. I'll be there."

She closed the connection without a further word.

Angrily, he went back into the house, glancing at the clock on the microwave. It was almost noon. He turned and looked hard at Aubree sitting still at the table. She refused to meet his eyes, keeping her own firmly fixed on the can she held clenched in both hands before her.

"I have to go back to Wegah," he announced flatly, and she finally raised her gaze to lock with his. "You will stay here," he spoke firmly, as if by a mere command he could make her obey. "You are still under arrest, Aubree. If you leave, I'll know. The minute a camera spots you, you'll be apprehended and returned to my custody. Spare us both the hassle."

She knew he spoke the truth. She could not return to Wegah. Facial recognition programs monitoring every person captured on every external camera throughout the hub enabled Security to identify and locate anyone anywhere within minutes. She would get no further than a few blocks from the gate before she'd be caught.

"I'll be back tomorrow," Drew promised.

CHAPTER TWENTY-ONE

Adam arrived at the Security Headquarters office in Wegah at fifteen minutes after four that Friday afternoon. The first thing he'd noticed on his arrival at the hub was the unusual activity and heavy presence of Security personnel visible in Sector Eight. The Headquarters office itself was buzzing as he stopped by the dispatch desk.

"What's all the fuss about?" he asked the desk clerk, a young man with owlish eyes.

"What? You don't know?" The owlish eyes grew even rounder. "There was a threat on Council Member Byron! VP called in all personnel. There's a meeting scheduled, followed by a press conference. I think the meeting's at six."

"Really," Adam said, disinterestedly. "I just got in from Romoh. First I'd heard."

"Oh. Something I can do for you?"

"No. Just wondered what was going on."

The little owl swiveled to peer at a cluster that was gathering in an office doorway across the large office space and Adam understood he had been dismissed. He had no interesting details to share.

As Adam approached his desk, he caught the furtive glances of their team members as he walked between their cubicles. None would look him in the eye, all suddenly very busy on their computers. Silence had settled over the section.

Adam sat at his computer. He quickly accessed the arrest warrant database and did a hub-wide search of arrest warrants for Aubree Holten aka Natalie Deckman. It would take the database a while to scan the records for all ten hubs and he leaned back watching the progress bar at the bottom of his screen. It seemed to inch along slowly. After an eternity the bar reached one hundred percent and the screen blinked. One line appeared at the top and he sighed in frustration. No search results found.

Determinedly, he started over reversing the names. Natalie Deckman aka Aubree Holten. Another wait. Same results.

"Damn!" he swore softly and saw his team lead's head turn slightly in his direction. Adam sat musing. He could think of no other options along that route.

Changing tactics, he exited the arrest database and went instead to the Security Employee Information Database, SEID, pronounced like said.

SEID: Welcome, Adam Miller. How are you today?

ADAM: I'm good, SEID. I need information.

SEID: Certainly. What name would you like me to retrieve?

ADAM: Drew Shipley. Andrew Shipley.

Adam leaned back expectantly, waiting for the employee data sheet that would tell him everything about Drew's background. Instead, he discovered SEID wasn't done.

SEID: Why do you require this information, Mr. Miller?

Adam didn't like SEID's change in tone. ADAM: You do not need to know that, SEID. Please provide requested information.

There was a pause which was extremely unusual for a machine and Adam began to feel uneasy.

SEID: I will provide what is available.

Usually the resulting employee data screen was broken into several sections. There would be the most current photo on file along with known location and contact information. Beside that would be a Sector section, the location and assignment detail. It would include reporting manager and department hierarchy. Another section would have key skills highlighted and a final one for resume, or history.

Adam had never seen the screen he saw now. The photo was blank with a large question mark superimposed. When he scrolled his cursor over it, script came up that advised "No picture available". He was not aware of a single other instance of a photo not being in the database. It simply wasn't possible. Everyone had a badge and every badge had a photo that Security itself had taken, including those for Security personnel.

All the other sections were similar. All data was blank. SEID had provided absolutely zero. He knew it was useless to try again. For whatever reason, Adam was blocked from Drew's records.

Frustrated, he pushed back from the terminal. There was nothing he could accomplish here and he was full of nervous energy. Then an idea occurred, and he called over to his lead, "Marlene, I'm heading over to convoy escort if anyone is looking for me."

She turned her head, eyes focused somewhere on the carpeting between their cubicles. Adam tried not to look at the yawning empty space where Aubree should be sitting.

"Sure," Marlene mumbled before quickly looking back at her keyboard.

Adam was at convoy just as they were getting ready to release the normal crew and the skeleton evening shift that monitored the surveillance system came in. Adam caught William Magee just as he was coming out the door. Glancing over his shoulder, Adam could see the work area inside was empty of anyone else on the team that he knew.

"Hey, Adam!" Magee exclaimed, instantly chummy.

"Magee," he replied cordially. Magee liked to talk. "I was wondering if I could take a look at some of surveillance tape."

"Working on the manhunt, hunh?" Magee asked conspiratorially, turning back to lead Adam into the office space. "Sure. Come on into the back-conference room. We've got a terminal set up there with access to the video logs. Been busy as hell all day with them boys from Internal Ops in and out."

"I'll bet," Adam murmured, hoping Magee would keep talking.

Magee was all too willing to comply. "You think the perp slipped out? Went through one of the meet points? I knew them guys would find a way to trace back that message JB got. Who was it?"

Adam smiled, "Now, if I did know that you know I couldn't possibly share that information."

"Oh, we're old pals, Adam. I know you aren't like some of those other guys. Get promoted and forget where you came from. No. You've done what you could to take care of your old team. I can see that."

Magee's obsequiousness was just short of nauseating and Adam had all the information he needed, anyway. "Well, it's getting late and I'm holding you up," he sat down at the terminal and turned half away from Magee. "It sure was good to see you. Appreciate you letting me in."

"Any time," Magee chirped happily and disappeared back down the now dimly lit hallway.

Adam did some quick calculations. He had the time when Drew exited Wegah with Aubree heading towards the Des Moines meet point. He reviewed the video logs for the time frame, letting the tape run forward on fast motion, but there was never any footage of a Lincoln Continental passing through the Des Moines surveillance net or any other vehicle.

He closed the video log and sat back, idly watching the media footage scrolling on the live feed of the home screen. He sat up alertly as the camera centered on Janet Byron, standing in front of a bank of microphones. The volume was muted but a teleprompter provided the script.

"I want to assure the residents of our Hub. I know rumors have abounded today. I've heard several of them myself," she smiled and chuckled. "Contrary to what the more dire ones would have you think, I'm alive and doing well." She held her arms up above her shoulders and did a little pirouette. Members of the media group could be heard chuckling with her. JB was all seriousness when she turned back to the camera.

Adam unmuted the speakers and turned up the computer volume.

"The part of the rumor that is true is that an attempt was threatened. Due to the quick action of our local Security Resource Group personnel the threat has been addressed. There is no reason for any of our citizens to be concerned. You are safe, as always, and are under no immediate danger. In fact, the threat has left the hub completely as my dear nephew Drew has confirmed for me."

She turned and held her left arm out to the man standing slightly behind her. "My nephew, Andrew Shipley, is with the Security Resource Group, and came immediately to my assistance when I received the threat. He has been by my side and was instrumental in tracing the source of the threat. I wished to offer him public recognition for his outstanding service on my behalf."

Polite applause could be heard offscreen as Adam sat transfixed staring. It wasn't possible. The man was supposedly with Aubree! If he was with JB, then where was Aubree?

Adam felt fear like he had never known. He jumped to his feet and quickly went into the main room, eyes scanning the empty space. At the live feed terminals two men sat, slumped in their seats, watching the feed on the screens.

As Adam watched idly over their shoulder, trying to decide what his next move should be, the terminal on the right suddenly blinked a flashing red icon in the bottom right. The operator clicked on it and read the small text displayed.

"Odd," he muttered.

"What's that?" his partner asked, leaning over to peer at the screen. "Hmm. That is odd. No one should be there. Let me check my logs."

Adam walked over, making them aware of his presence. Fortunately, he knew the man on the right that had received the alert.

"Hey, John. Whatcha' got?"

"Alarm at the safe house. Weird, too. It's the number four alarm."

"That's not possible," the man Adam didn't know responded.

"Well, you saw it same as I did. Number four alarm was activated."

"It's a glitch," the other guy announced. "That or the last person there didn't close it securely. Come on, we've got to keep an eye on that footage. They think the perp will try to move tonight."

John glanced up at Adam, "So, hey, Adam. Good to see you, man. What can I do you for?"

Adam cocked his head to one side, "You going to get someone to check that out?"

John shook his head. "Nah. Look, we've got our hands full. Orders from the top to keep an eye on both Des Moines and Salina. Our guy's gonna be passing through one of them some time tonight. Like Arnie here says, it's a glitch."

"Tell you what," Adam offered, "I'll make a run out there and check it."

"No way you'll make it back before lock down."

"I'll stay there and be here when they open the gates in the morning."

John laughed and shrugged, "Hell, makes no never mind to me. Knock yourself out."

Adam headed down to the basement, and smiled when he saw Roxy at the desk, very aggravated expression on her face.

"Hey, sugar," she said as Adam walked up, "I haven't seen you in a long time."

He smiled back at her, "It's been a while. Look, I know there's no official req but I need a set of wheels. Last minute emergency. We just got an alarm at the safe house and what with the manhunt and all they've got no one to check it out."

"Wow. They asked you?'"

"I volunteered."

She smiled, "I've got you covered. What do you need?"

"Four-wheel drive. Full gas tank."

"Thought you were going to the safe house?"

Adam shrugged, "Yeah, but I may need to go off road."

"How about the Dodge? Got a real nice four-wheel Hemi that's got a lift kit and purrs like a kitten."

Ten minutes later Adam was headed out of the underground parking bay in the king cab cherry red pickup truck. He would have preferred something a little less colorful but was glad to have the beefed-up off-road capabilities.

He just managed to get through the gates before they closed, and dusk was settling heavily. Adam had a hunch he knew something about that tripped alarm. The number four alarm was for the door that connected the garage to the utility room. Only someone already in the house could have activated that alarm.

Aubree sat for a long time after the ratcheting sound of the lowering garage door ceased. Shadows lengthened on the wall as she thought about what to do.

Rising, she quickly searched through the interior of the safe house, checking every room and every closet. She hoped she might find a phone in one of the rooms. There were outlets for them but no phones anywhere, and none stored conveniently on any shelves that she could spot.

Returning to the living room she stood undecided in the middle of the floor. One thing was certain, she was not going to be here when Drew came back. Were they even really headed to Midah?

She went again to the drapes that kept her hidden and peered out at the landscape. The house was on a very slight rise above a paved macadam circle. The expanse of lawn was not very large, and weeds had overcome what must once have been neatly tended lawns. Now, tender green grass shoots waved, and sturdy weeds thrust up, as a breeze came out of the southwest. A couple of mature trees stood at the furthest edge corner. Her eyes wandered up the limbs of the trees, new green leaves lightly waving in the late afternoon sun. She finally spotted what she had known must be there. A camera. Which meant they had the house under surveillance. She had no doubt other cameras covered all the other approaches to the building. She let the blackout curtain fall back into place and stepped back to the middle of the room. She could do nothing until dark.

But what to do then? She couldn't go back to Wegah. Even if she could cover the distance on her own, in the dark, on foot what would she do when she got there? She had no one to turn to. Adam was somewhere in the southwest of the country, in no position to render assistance. If she could reach a phone, reach her father, she might have some chance. He could quickly get her local protection while they sorted this out. She was, after all, innocent.

Then again, as Drew had said, she would be recognized instantly if she entered the hub. Cameras covered all public areas in the vast walled expanse. A simple command in a program and facial recognition would search for her. And it would not stop until it located her, or it was told to stop.

No, she couldn't risk going to Wegah.

What she needed was a vehicle. Maybe she could find her way to Midah. At the very least, she could reach Midweh where her father could get her help. Drew would have a vehicle when he returned. Somehow, she had to get that vehicle.

She scrounged around in the kitchen and prepared herself a small meal. She didn't know when she might get her next one. With that thought in mind, she made a bundle to take with her. Cans and boxes of easy consumables. Maybe not high in protein but better than nothing.

Occasionally she would wander to the living room window and peer out the side of the curtain, watching as shadows lengthened in the spring evening. Once, at the farthest edge of the house across the circle she saw two does creep out, their forms graceful as they cautiously proceeded into the lawn to eat the tender new growth of grass still struggling against the encroaching weeds. Aubree was frozen, transfixed by the sight of them. They grazed for a while and then a sound startled them. Their heads sprang up and she saw the long muscles of the lean haunches tense and bunch as the deer prepared to spring. Suddenly, the tails shot up flashing a fleecy white and the deer sprang from sight to her left. Aubree stayed for a while watching to see if she could spy what had startled them but could not spot anything. Eventually, sighing deeply, she let the curtain drop back into place.

It was late in the afternoon when she decided she should check out the garage. She would move the bundle of food and conceal it somewhere so she could slip it into the car. She opened the door between the utility space and the garage, using the light switches to turn on the overhead light.

She looked around; she would need a hiding place. As she had remembered, one wall was lined with gas cans and they would offer no cover. Across and under the two windows of the further wall were stacked more crates of canned items and water. She eyed the water and decided she would grab some if she could.

She turned her attention to the counter that stretched the length of the wall opposite the double garage door. The counter was a little above waist height, maybe about three and a half feet off the ground. Large doors hid the space beneath the counter. She opened them now, hoping she might find a suitable hiding place. She was disappointed. The cabinets held shelves that not even she could hope to squeeze into, and they had cans of paint, disinfectant, rags, more tools, grease, caulk and an assortment of nuts and bolts. She closed each, growing bleaker as she moved down the line.

Finally, she had reached the end and stood beside a large round trash bin. There was a gap between the counter and the wall, behind the trash can and Aubree eyed the space speculatively. It might work. Pulling the can out she was able to step into the space behind and by kneeling would be concealed from anyone in the garage unless they were to walk up to the trash can. She thought it was unlikely Drew would and satisfied with her plan returned to the house.

With nothing to do, she sat at the dining room table, trying to resist the urge to chew on her fingernails as time seemed to drag by. Dark settled and she became aware of the many sounds the older home made as the air outside cooled and it settled.

Unfamiliar with the noises, she grew uneasy. She wandered into the large master bedroom and contemplated sleep. Sitting on the side of the bed she remembered lying there just a few months ago in Adam's arms.

She had awakened that night, sometime in the very early hours of the morning. The room had still been dark, but a nightlight cast a warm amber glow over her shoulder. She had been lying facing Adam, their legs entwined, his arm over her waist, holding her lightly in his sleep. The light had been just enough for her to see his face as he slept, lips curved in a tender expression and she yearned to kiss them. Not wanting to wake him, she had instead studied his face, boyish in his repose.

She shook herself from the memory now, her hand smoothing the counterpane where they had lain. No, she wouldn't be able to sleep here alone.

Rising, she left the room. As she did, she had another inspiration. She went back and locked the door that connected the master bathroom with the bedroom. When Drew returned, she expected him to follow his normal routine. He would come in the house, disable the alarm and then, no doubt, search for her. The locked door would provide a delay. How long before he broke it down? Before he figured out, she wasn't there? Maybe no more than minutes. All the same, it bought her more and she needed it all.

She sat again, this time in the darkened living room, trying not to look at the dark maw of the fireplace across from her or the white rug at her feet. The sounds again began to encroach.

She would feel more secure with a weapon. On this impulse she remembered the wall of tools in the garage. Surely something there would be useful. It was now full dark outside and had been for almost an hour. She turned on the overhead, eyes squinting as they adjusted to the bright light.

She surveyed the wall. Any of the tools might be used as a weapon. If you were trained. She was not trained. She remembered all too well how easily Drew had overwhelmed her in her apartment in Midah and again in Wegah. She saw the warped image of her father in the cracked phone screen. She had been no match for Drew's superior strength.

With that thought in mind the wall of gleaming steel suddenly seemed far less impressive, the individual items less effective in her unskilled hands. She spotted a long thin blade, a narrow saw of some sort with a sharp point on its end. That ought to do quite well, she thought and began to reach for it.

She was just about to touch the wooden handle of the reciprocal saw when she heard the garage door opener above her click. She froze and then her heart slammed as the door began to ratchet up. Turning, she watched in horror as the door began to inch upward, as frozen as the does had been earlier. Just as quickly she recalled her hiding place and began to turn that way when the door froze. She did as well and was then plunged into darkness.

Adam pulled into the driveway at the safe house and studied the exterior of the building. He could see no light at any of the windows, but with the blackout curtains inside it was unlikely that he would even if she had the house ablaze.

He began to open the garage door and was stunned when the opening door revealed a ribbon of light. Quickly his hand moved to still the motor and stop the door from rising. Every instinct cautioned him not to reveal the safe house. The light of the garage door would be a beacon in the dark night. He pressed the button to turn off the light, his hand automatically moving to reengage the door. As was typical, the door lowered when he first pressed the button. Pressing a second time, he waited as the door rose.

Pulling the red pickup into the space, he lowered the door, waiting until it was completely down before proceeding with exiting the truck. He had not had his head lights on as he entered yet his eyes, accustomed to the dark as they were, had not seen anything as he pulled in. He slipped out now and eased the door of the truck so that it was not quite closed.

The lights had been on in the garage for a reason. He thought there was a good chance someone was hiding over by that garbage can he remembered in the corner. He began to ease himself along the front quarter panel of the truck towards the front end.

Aubree had not been able to close her hand on the saw when the garage was plunged into darkness. Her hand fell to the bench and the only thing her fingers could grasp were the cables to the car battery charger. Grasping them tightly in her hands she dropped to a crouch, unable to reach the shelter of the garbage can.

The truck stopped, hot grill inches from her head where she crouched beside the counter. She knelt, terrified the truck would crush her against the cabinet. Heart racing, she held her breath until the engine stopped, silence deafening as the engine ticked. Her ears detected the click of the driver's door opening and the sound of feet falling lightly to the concrete. She waited for him to go in the house. Silence roared and again she held her breath, body held motionless, calf muscles beginning to ache with the unnatural demand.

Adam eased his way around the front corner of the truck, pausing and staring as hard as he could at the corner where the trash can stood in deep shadow. It was too dark; he could see nothing. He took a cautious step forward and suddenly his leg was jabbed by something blunt. Two points were being thrust hard against each side of his calf. In surprise he kicked and shook his leg, hollering, "Hey!" and jumping back in surprise. "What the hell? Aubree is that you?"

Aubree sat motionless. Adam? She was confused. How was that possible? Cautiously, she stood, easing the sore muscles and whispered, "Adam?"

"Oh, God! Aubree! Just a minute!"

She heard him moving and was blinded as light flooded the garage. Then she heard him laugh. A deep laugh. In surprise she looked at him. He stood beside the door to the utility room pointing at the cables she held.

"Is that what you hit me with?" he finally managed to ask.

She nodded, face flaming.

"Did you think it would hurt me?" he asked and then went off on another peal of laughter. "I am so sorry," he managed to say as the laughter tapered to chuckles. "You are very brave, and I am incredibly proud of you, and I am so glad it was me in that truck. Come here!"

She raced to him, throwing her arms around his waist. "Oh, Adam! I was so scared!" She clung tightly to him, her body trembling with the after-effects of adrenalin. She pulled away, grasping his face in her hands. "How did you get here? Why? You're supposed to be in Romoh. I don't understand." Her eyes searched his and then she added, "I don't care! Kiss me!" pulling his face down to meet her lips, and he eagerly complied, crushing her against him.

"We have to leave," she told him urgently when they pulled apart. "Drew's coming back and I don't want to be anywhere near here when he does."

He held her away from him, grasping her arms, and looking at her intently.

"Did he hurt you?"

"No. No. He brought me here and then he got a call. Right after we got here. I don't know what was said. He went out in the garage. After that he came back in and said he had to leave. Said I was under house arrest and he'd be back tomorrow."

"And you were what? Going to electrocute him?" he tried to cut it off, but another snort of laughter escaped. "I love you," he added, kissing the tip of her nose.

"You caught me off guard!" she defended herself indignantly.

"I did indeed. Come in the house, beautiful. We'll leave. Don't worry. We need to talk first."

"Adam! I'm so glad you called. We have trouble. JB is trying to pin the threat against her and the attempt on Baba on you. She claims to have supporting evidence and, I must admit, circumstantially, it doesn't look good. We both know it's not true but it's my word against her evidence. We both know how that plays out. It's irrelevant that the same can be said of Drew Shipley. She's providing him an alibi. Which just confirms for me that she's the one really behind the attempt on Baba. When can I expect you to come in?"

Adam reached over and folded Aubree's hand in his. He smiled at her as he told Ben, "Ben, I thought I was pretty clear the last time I saw you."

"Things have changed since then. We need to clear your name. I can protect you here in Romoh. We'll work this out."

Adam shook his head even though Ben couldn't see him. "It doesn't matter, Ben. They need a scapegoat. I get that."

"But it won't end there, Adam. They'll come after you."

"Really? I doubt that. I'm not big enough in this power play. I'm just a convenient solution right now. No, I don't think so. But I do feel responsible for the person at the communication site that I exposed. I've discussed it with Aubree and we both agree we want to do the right thing. Can you give me the coordinates for the site? I'll go there myself. I'm hoping I can use them as an entry to a group on the outside."

Ben hesitated before replying. "I can probably hold off sending this report to Brent until the end of the week. With everything else going on it would be easy to say it got buried on my desk and slipped my mind. That give you enough time?"

Adam laughed, "I'm probably already halfway there. I'll be there tomorrow night. That's plenty of time."

"And Miss Holten? She's well?"

"Nice of you to ask," Adam said a little coldly. "She's fine. You could do me a favor."

"If it's in my power."

"Let her dad know she's okay."

There was silence on the phone for a long while and Adam almost said something when Ben finally answered, "Sure. I can do that, Adam. I wish you'd reconsider. There are those of us trying to do the right thing. We could use your help."

Adam's eyes searched Aubree's face and he shook his head. "No, Ben. I respect you tremendously. I enjoyed working with you and honestly, I'm really confused. I can't get my mind wrapped around how someone like yourself can be part of something like—I don't know, what is it called? How does a corporation come to have the power of life and death over the citizens of this nation and they, like blind sheep, allow it? Ignorance. And the way you corporate leaders have the media twist things, report half the truth or just the part that benefits you. You control everything."

He took a breath. Ben was silent, knowing he was not finished, allowing him time to collect his thoughts. Finally, he continued, "I do want to work with you, Ben. Just not there, in Romoh. Or from any hub. I want out. Aubree and I want a future together. Maybe a family. We couldn't have that in a hub. And this, this Corpocracy you've built--it's going to come down, Ben. As much as I respect you, we're on opposite sides now. I can't condone assisted passing. God only knows what else goes on that we don't know about. But I intend on uncovering it."

He stopped then, his eyes locked with Aubree's and she squeezed his hand tight, raising it to kiss his knuckles. He gently brushed the back of his hand along her smooth cheek, marveling again that she had chosen him.

"I hope you do, Adam. I really hope you do. I'll send those coordinates and you'll have the time I said you would. It should allow you a good head start. I'll hope to hear from you. You know where Mitch is."

"Yes, I do. I'll be in touch with him and you'll probably wish at some point that you didn't hear from me."

Adam turned the key over in the ignition and he and Aubree continued to head west in the dark night.

EPILOGUE

Adam stood now facing the rising sun, the small city of Eureka Springs spread out below him, the crumbling façade of the Jesus of the Ozarks spreading his arms above the distant tree line on the opposite mountain ridge. He gazed down at the beautiful form cradled in his arms. The amazing green eyes were open wide, surveying the scene and he wondered again at her perfection. He kissed the smooth forehead, covered in newborn downy hair. Those green eyes turned to survey his face and he swore a smile burbled on her cupid bow pink lips.

"My little two percenter," he whispered in her ear.

Beside him Aubree's silvery laugh floated on the breeze.

"Our little Laelynn," her voice was filled with the love of a new mother, the infant in his arms her center of existence now, as she should be.

He smiled tenderly and pulled Aubree close with his other arm. They stood on the fourth-floor balcony of the old Crescent Hotel. It had been built in 1886 and the locals liked to claim it was haunted. If it was, neither he nor Aubree had yet to see a ghost though there were times Laelynn's eyes tracked things his could not see. The cats that lived in the lobby often did the same.

"Tell me again what it stands for?" he asked, tucking the warm blanket closer around Laelynn.

"Flower of hope," Aubree supplied, bending and kissing the downy cheek. "I did some research on names. Laelynn is Canadian. My mother— and don't get me started about my mother—well, she's originally French Canadian. So, I don't know—it felt right. Doesn't it seem right to you?" She pulled out of his embrace and turned to admire father and daughter in the rising light of the sun, golden rays reflecting off Laelynn's wispy curls.

"Oh, Laelynn is perfect." He looked down at the subject of their attention and smiled so tenderly Aubree felt her heart ache in response "Oh, yes," he added, almost too soft for her to hear, "Laelynn is perfect."

Planting another tender kiss on Laelynn's forehead, he grew more serious. "I heard from Erick this morning."

"Oh? How's Sam doing?"

"They're good. Sam just got back from visiting Jerry. He's got a new partner."

"Hmm. Is that good or bad?"

"Remains to be seen. Jerry needs some time to feel him out."

"I'm glad Ben protected Jerry," Aubree said softly, remembering the night she and Adam had traveled west through the dark night, arriving at the remote communication site early in the morning.

Erick had been sleeping and Jerry had been distracted with a game of solitaire, not seeing the pickup when it passed the observation camera at the lower level.

When the knock came at the door, he was startled badly. His hands fumbled as he unlocked the door, opening it cautiously.

"Who's there?" he asked brusquely.

"My name's Adam Miller. I need to speak with you. I've got someone with me." Adam stepped aside so Jerry could see Aubree standing behind him. "Her name is Aubree Holten. Please, let us in," he showed his empty hands and Jerry opened the door wider for them.

"Sure," he muttered, "Come on in. You say your name is Adam?"

Adam nodded. It was springtime and the temperatures at the lower altitudes had been pleasant but this high up the air still had a bite. He rubbed his hands and gestured for Aubree to proceed in front of him.

Jerry went into the small kitchenette. "I'll make us a pot of coffee. Have a seat at the table there."

He and Aubree sat together, looking around the utilitarian space. "There's someone else here?" Adam asked.

Jerry nodded and gestured towards the back where a doorway led to a darkened hall. "There's a man sleeping back there." He turned as the pot began to brew and studied them, leaning against the counter. "Where are you from?"

"I used to be with Security," Adam told him. "I was in Wegah. Part of a project to set up a surveillance system." He waved his hand, "All of which doesn't matter except I may have made trouble for someone here."

Jerry raised his eyebrows, "And how might that be?"

Adam hesitated. What if the other man, the man sleeping, were the leak? What if this man wasn't the one? "Who controls the satellite program?" he asked carefully.

Jerry smiled, "That would usually be me. Erick's been learning it, but I mainly manage it. Why?"

Adam relaxed a little. It was still possible it was Erick, but more likely

Jerry was their man. "I suggested to my director that I thought someone had tampered with the satellite when the attack in Des Moines happened. I guess I was right."

Jerry studied him quietly for a moment. "Are you here to arrest me?" he asked softly, body tense, his eyes now moving to Aubree questioningly.

Adam laughed, "No. On the contrary. We need your help. I came to give you a head's up that you've been exposed. And I was," he hesitated and took Aubree's hand in his, "Well, we were hoping you could help us. We need to find someone on the outside to help us get away."

Jerry was silent, watching them. Wordlessly he turned and filled four cups of coffee. He carried two to the table, indicated bowls of sugar and powdered creamer, and said, "I'd better get Erick up. Why don't you fix your coffee the way you like it? I'll be right back."

He disappeared through the doorway into the back and they heard muted conversation. Jerry was back quickly and carried the other two cups to the table, keeping one for himself. The three sat silently until Erick came into the room, still buttoning up his shirt.

He squinted against the light, eyes adjusting to the brightness as he struggled to awaken. "Morning," he mumbled as he took the seat at the last cup. Only then did he really see Adam and he sat up in surprise, coming fully awake. "Adam! Man, what are you doing here? I haven't seen you in—how long has it been?"

Adam grinned, "Erick! I didn't know you were here! Hell, it's been a few years. I'd heard that you'd been RIF'd and I'd been meaning to find where you got assigned, but just never got the chance."

Erick leaned back in his chair, a bitter chuckle escaping, "That project they assigned me to with Communications didn't go so well. Seems they needed someone to blame and," he spread his hands out, "here I am!" Then he smiled warmly at Jerry, "But it's all been for the good. Other than the weather around here I've been happy. Now, what brings you here?"

Adam quickly caught Erick up on why he and Aubree had made the trip.

Jerry turned now to Adam when he was finished, "We can help you. I'll send a message right now to our contact. She might be here as quick as tonight. Probably tomorrow."

Adam nodded, "Good. You'll come with us, of course. I take it your both working for the outside now?"

Jerry crossed his arms and smiled, "Erick will go with you, I suspect. I think I'll stay here."

Adam frowned and Erick slapped his hand down, "Damnit, Jerry. You will not. You'll go with us. What choice do you have?"

Jerry shrugged, "Maybe I have a chance. If you go, well, I can claim innocence. Pin it all on you."

Erick shook his head, "They won't buy it. They probably have a history, can go back. They'll see you were doing it before I got here."

Jerry shrugged again, "That's the chance I'll take. We need this communication site. If we both go, we know it's a loss. If I stay, there's a chance, just a chance, that they'll buy my story."

Adam was nodding, "It's possible, yes. And you'll have the support of Ben Larocque. I'm sure of it." Quickly he told them what he knew about Ben and Frank.

Sam had arrived that same night. Adam and Aubree were ready, and Erick tried one more time to convince Jerry to join them, but he was resolute in his decision, urging them to go on and get out of there.

Adam had learned from the small outpost where Sam lived that there was a community known to be living in the Ozark Mountains. A small city known as Eureka Springs. Adam had been stunned. His parents had owned a lake home there when he was a teenager. He felt a yearning to see it again and Aubree quickly agreed.

They had parted company with Erick then, when he chose to stay with Sam. They had seen the welcoming glint in her eye and the shy smile she had tried to hide when Erick had told them that he thought he might stick around those parts a bit longer. What was the rush? He could always move on and catch up with them later.

It took them several weeks to cross the country from the Rocky Mountains near Denver, down through a corner of Kansas and then into Oklahoma before finally reaching their destination nestled in the Ozark mountains of northwest Arkansas.

They had traveled mostly at night, stopping and spending a week or two at the small towns they learned of as they traveled. They had been surprised at just how many communities there were, scattered in isolated pockets, escaping notice. Adam welcomed the chance to speak to them, thrilled to find democracy surviving in these enclaves. Slowly, he began to build a network.

Where Aubree had once viewed the vast empty distances with something very near fear, she now saw them as sketches of beauty no man could equal. The vast prairie they crossed filled her now with delight.

Sometime during the journey, she realized she was pregnant. She had missed her cycle for three months. The first time, she had thought it was only nerves. By the end of the third month, though, she was certain and had physical symptoms to support her theory.

Shyly, she had shared her concern with Adam. They had asked for, and gotten, a pregnancy test from the practicing physician for the small town they were in. He had gladly confirmed her suspicions. Adam had been delighted but a new concern now entered the picture. It was late October and Adam's urgency to reach Eureka Springs and get settled intensified.

They arrived in the middle of November and for Adam, it had been as if he were finally coming home. Aubree had been delighted with the small city nestled on the two opposing mountains, the numerous springs dotting both slopes while buildings made of large boulders, carved from the nearby mountains, stood weathered against the test of time.

The city was perfectly situated to elude the sharp eyes of the satellites above. Roads twisted around overhanging rock bluffs while trees towered and provided covering shelter spring through fall. No major interstate passed near and there was a local committee that made sure there were major obstructions at key locations to deter the inquisitive. Paths existed but could not possibly be traced.

The city residents were happy to keep a low profile and their motto seemed to be, leave them alone and they'll leave us alone. It had worked well enough all these years. Adam hoped that with time he could convince them of the importance of breaking down the hub walls. He sensed restlessness in the youth of the city and some of the elders were more inclined to consider change but it would be a long time coming to this small corner of the world. All of which made it an ideal place for him and Aubree to settle in.

"I worry, Adam," Aubree said now, laying her hand on his arm. "I worry what the world she's in might do to her. If the corporations got hold of her..."

"Shh," Adam said, shooting her a stern look. "Don't even say it. The old phrase? What was it? Visualize it and make it happen? Don't visualize it."

"This is a good place," Aubree said, feeling a warmth as she thought of the many wonderful people they'd met that lived in this old city, despite the hub threatening a mere six hours in either direction, north or south. Wegah or Gullub. That they managed to remain undetected was a blessing, but she knew it could end at any time. "We can give her a good life here," Aubree felt certain of it.

Adam took a deep breath of the late winter air; the chill was beginning to take effect and they would need to go in soon. In his arms Laelynn stirred, small hands waving in the air as if to embrace the beauty of the Ozark Mountains and the ancient city nestled in its heart.

He held her up and out, towards the rising sun and she giggled happily, chubby legs churning.

"Laelynn," Adam declared in a firm voice, "I promise you this. All you see, is yours to enjoy. No one to tell you how or where to live. I promise that we will restore the Democracy that once ruled this land. We will wrest it away from the corporations. We will tear down Corpocracy!"

ABOUT THE AUTHOR

Cheryl King is an author who lives in Eureka Springs, Arkansas. She is the author of *Rare Coins, A Collection of Short Stories.* Her story 'Red Sky at Dawn' from this collection was chosen for inclusion in the 2019 edition of eMerge Magazine, the online magazine of the Writers' Colony at Dairy Hollow in Eureka Springs.